38

What
Follows
After

Center Point
Large Print

Also by Dan Walsh and available from
Center Point Large Print:

The Deepest Waters
The Discovery

**This Large Print Book carries the
Seal of Approval of N.A.V.H.**

What
Follows
After

DAN
WALSH

CENTER POINT LARGE PRINT
THORNDIKE, MAINE

This Center Point Large Print edition is published
in the year 2014 by arrangement with Revell,
a division of Baker Publishing Group.

The text of this Large Print edition is unabridged.
In other aspects, this book may vary
from the original edition.
Printed in the United States of America
on permanent paper.
Set in 16-point Times New Roman type.

ISBN: 978-1-62899-105-5

Library of Congress Cataloging-in-Publication Data

Walsh, Dan, 1957–
What follows after / Dan Walsh. — Center Point Large Print edition.
pages ; cm
Summary: "Two brothers run away from their Florida home, head for
their aunt's house in Georgia, and refuse to come home until their
parents get back together. When things go terribly wrong, their parents
must come to grips with years of neglect and mistrust in order to
recover their beloved sons, their love for one another, and their
marriage"—Provided by publisher.
 ISBN 978-1-62899-105-5 (library binding : alk. paper)
 1. Large type books. I. Title.
PS3623.A446W47 2014b
813'.6—dc23
                                                2014007838

What
Follows
After

1

The Present

The young look forward, the old look back.

Someone way smarter than me said that. Guess I'm old then. If you saw me, you wouldn't need to be told. But the looking back part, been doing a lot of that lately. So much so, I've been driving Elaine nuts.

Funny how the memory works. You can think you forgot something, like it's gone for good. Then you hear a song from fifty years ago, and it unlocks a door. One you haven't opened for so long, you forgot it was even there. A flood of images and sounds—and all the emotions that go with them—come rushing in. It's great when it's a nice song and opens a nice door. Not so great when the room behind that door is stacked with boxes of pain.

The song itself was stupid, the lyrics, I mean. I didn't even like it back then. Seems like I would, coming from a beach town. Had a catchy tune, I'll say that. I was in the car when I heard it. Before that, I'd barely heard it over the last several decades. The few times I had, it triggered a replay from one of the worst moments of my life.

I'm talking about "Surfin' Safari" by the Beach

Boys. I'm not a superstitious man, don't believe in omens, but considering what I had come here to do, I've gotta say . . . I got a little spooked hearing it again. I reached over and shut the radio off. Of all the songs that could have played on the thirty-minute drive here (and I wasn't even listening to an oldies station). What did it mean? Was God trying to tell me something? Like maybe, turn this car around?

I was pretty shaken up when I heard it. Pulled the car over to the side of the road, thought about calling Elaine. But I already knew what she'd say. She thought I should let the lawyer and real estate agent deal with it. Get whatever we could and buy something else. Another property, something that had no attachment to the past. *"We can even find a place on a lake if you want."*

But the market was terrible now. We'd only get about half of what it was worth. But here's the funny thing . . . Elaine and I had just been talking a few weeks ago about how much we wished we could afford a little getaway place, somewhere on the water, because we both liked to fish. Or if the fish weren't biting, just to sit there. That was part of our retirement dream, a waterfront place. All sorts of possibilities for something like that here in Florida. But our pension fund got creamed a few years back. Like most folks, we've been digging out ever since. And like most baby boomers, we didn't have enough years left to close the gap. A getaway place was totally out of reach.

Then out of the blue, a registered letter came from some attorney in Louisiana saying I'd inherited a three-bedroom house right on the water, near this little town totally forgotten by time. *This* seemed more like the providence of God. The house was mortgage free; the taxes were even up to date. At first, I thought it had to be some kind of prank. But as soon as I saw the dead man's name on the letter, I knew it was real.

He'd written me a few years ago, promising one day I'd get just such a letter. It was the last time we had communicated. I didn't believe it, couldn't imagine how he could've held on to the property all these years, considering what had happened. So I just put the whole thing out of my mind.

But here it was, in my hands, big as life. Elaine and I owned a perfectly good waterfront home, all ready to go. So, should we use it or sell it? That's what I had driven here to find out. I put the car in drive and got back on the road, headed toward the place. I hadn't been here in fifty years, not since I was eleven, but I didn't need a map. The scene was burned into my mind.

Everything seemed the same. The little downtown area, if you could call it that, hadn't changed one bit. I could see every street, every building, every curve in the road, just the way it had been.

The question was, though, and this was how Elaine had put it to me: *"Can you spend time there without dredging up the past? Can you replace all the fear and pain with something positive? 'Cause that's what it'll take."*

I honestly didn't know. I suppose that's why I'd come. Brought my fishing pole with me, some clean linens and a pillow, a suitcase, my Bible, and a couple of good books. I aimed to give the place a fighting chance. That was the idea anyway. People nowadays call it "facing your demons," but I don't like the sound of that. I think demons are real, and I'm quite sure I don't have any living in me. All I'm facing is a ton of bad memories. If being here didn't put an end to them, we'd sell the place, buy something else.

Simple as that.

Turning down the last dirt road leading toward the water, I remembered having one of those "getting everything out" sessions with my father before he died. About what happened here. The talk had been his idea. During my teen years, he had told me bits and pieces of the story, hard as it was to hear, the stuff I'd have no way of knowing on my own. There was that other long talk a few months after Elaine and I had gotten married, one of those man-to-man things. Dad had wanted to make sure I knew all the life lessons he'd learned because of what happened in '62.

Years had passed, decades really, and the subject

never came up again. Until that final conversation just before he died.

I pulled into the long dirt driveway leading to the house. I could just see it through a stand of overgrown oleanders. Slowing to a stop, I thought, Dad was right. There were still a lot of things I hadn't understood about what had happened back then. That last conversation with my father was tough to sit through.

Dad hadn't started out as a good father, but he'd ended up one—so I listened. Hard as it was. And just like at the end of each conversation we had about that time in 1962, he said, "Sometimes, we only appreciate the things that matter most when they are taken away."

Life in America at that time was so different than how things are now. You had to live through it to appreciate how much. JFK and Jackie had ushered in a new day full of hope. People called it Camelot. The economy was booming. The world was at peace, had been for over ten years. People still owned radios, but everyone was in love with their new TVs. It was the era of *I Love Lucy* and *Leave It to Beaver*. Life was simple. Things made sense. Families were happy.

At least they looked happy. When they weren't happy, everyone understood you were supposed to pretend.

One particular week in 1962 the world almost ended, and that's not an exaggeration. Everyone who lived back then knew it was true. Historians would later say things were even worse than President Kennedy and the politicians had let on. In some ways, even worse than they realized. If God had looked the other way for a single moment, we'd all be dead. Every single one of us.

Of course, the world didn't end back then.

But for our family, one part sure did.

2

I got out of the car but decided for the time being to leave my things. Thought it might be wise to take a quick once-around before I settled in. As I walked toward the house still painted that odd shade of green, I glanced to my right and left, trying to catch a glimpse of the neighbors. I was alone. Wasn't even sure anyone lived in the properties on either side.

The house sat on five acres, much of it wooded, with the water in the back. Looked like the neighboring properties included at least that much land. Made things nice and quiet. Reporters in '62 described the place as "secluded." I could barely make out the outline of a white-framed house to my right through a thick cluster of pines. The house on my left had an unobstructed view, but from this distance, I couldn't tell if anyone lived there. Both places looked more than fifty years old.

One thing was obvious: both were far enough away that you couldn't hear a little boy scream if he had been shut up in the house. That was something I had wondered about that final day, fifty years ago. As I climbed the three steps leading to the front porch, it dawned on me . . . that wasn't a healthy thing to be thinking about at this point.

Still, there it was.

I tried the front door. Of course it was locked. I glanced through some thin, weathered curtains hung up on the other side of the front door to block the view through the glass window. Saw a worn-out oval throw rug covering a wood floor and the bottom few feet of some upholstered furniture. Right off, I knew this front door had to go if we kept this place. Elaine would never go for company being able to look right into the living room.

As I unlocked the door, I tried to push a strong feeling of being in danger out of my mind. I didn't need to run from these memories; I needed to face them. Like Elaine said, "stare them down." I could tell even through her protests that she really hoped this place would work. She'd be fine here. I was the problem. We hadn't met until 1972, so she'd never been here. We never even talked about the place until I got that registered letter a few weeks ago.

I took a deep breath and stepped into the living room. The house seemed much smaller than before.

I walked down a narrow hallway. A doorway to the right opened to the small galley-style kitchen, which led to the dining area. From there, a wooden door opened into the old screen porch facing the water. I walked through all this quickly. The closer I got to the porch, the more I tensed up. I couldn't help it.

But I couldn't spend the whole week avoiding it. If I was going to do that, I might just as well turn right around and head out the door for good.

I stepped onto the porch and looked to my left. There it was. The door leading to the storage room. The dark place. I remembered how dark just then. When I first opened it fifty years ago, the blackness was so thick you could feel it. It was only as deep as the porch, you could see that now; but in a kid's mind, the darkness could have stretched on forever.

I tried the knob. It was locked, but I had the key. I thought about walking away but felt an even stronger urge to get this behind me. Otherwise, it would keep messing with me all night.

When I unlocked the door, I was shocked to find beams of light shining in. I stepped inside and, what do you know, someone had built a small window just off center, about chest high. The storage room was no longer the scary place I remembered. It was empty. As I turned to leave, something in the shadows caught my eye. It took a moment for my eyes to adjust and focus. There beside the window, tucked behind an exposed wooden stud . . . I couldn't believe what I saw. What was it doing here?

Could it have been here all those years? I slid it out and held it up to the light. My little brother's Spiderman comic book. Almost like new. One of two he'd brought with him that day. I thought it had been lost for good.

This one was his favorite, the first comic book with Spiderman on the cover. I read the title: *Amazing Fantasy*. And the date: "15 Aug." Had to smile at the price: "12¢." Worth a whole lot more now, I was sure. I opened it and began flipping through the pages. My smile quickly disappeared as darker memories of that day began filling my head.

I closed it, set it back where I'd found it, then hurried out to the porch. My heart was beating rapidly. I could feel it pulsing in my temples. I had to calm down. It was fifty years ago.

I sat on a bench and glanced back at the storage room, the door still open. I wanted to lock the whole thing back up and go. Leave everything just the way I'd found it.

It was just a stupid comic book.

But I knew it was more than that. I had to conquer these dark memories. Here and now, once and for all. That was what Elaine was secretly hoping for, and I knew it was what my father, Scott Harrison, would have wanted too, if he were still alive.

3

October 22, 1962
DeLand, Florida

Some said Scott Harrison had movie star good looks. That might've been part of what had gotten him into so much trouble. He didn't care about his looks, no more than other men did. On this day, he didn't care about them at all. He was carrying the weight of the world as he sat out there by the curb on Clara Avenue, eyes fixed on the front door, working up the nerve to go inside. How was he going to face her, the Queen, the Grand Old Lady of the Harrison clan?

Scott's mother wasn't a person to cross.

She always spoke with a civil tongue, but her eyes could get cold as steel if you displeased her, a coldness that went right through you. Enough to make you shudder inside, make you wish you could be anywhere else but there, locked in her gaze. But you couldn't move. You had to just stand there, and that stuck feeling would continue until she looked away.

Scott didn't want to get out, walk down that long sidewalk and up those porch steps, and ring that doorbell. He especially didn't want to tell his mother what he'd come there to say.

But he did.

"Why, Mister Scott, we don't ever see you 'round here this time of day." It was Mamie Lee, the Harrison family's lifelong maid. Scott stepped inside and gave her a big hug, like he always did. Much to his mother's chagrin. But he felt Mamie Lee was really the one who raised him, taught him how to treat people and about the things in life that really mattered.

He always said her place in heaven would dwarf that old Southern mansion he and his brothers had grown up in on Clara Avenue, and that they'd all be lucky if she ever gave them the time of day once God had settled the score. "Mamie Lee, good to see you. Wish I was here on more pleasant business."

"Uh-oh," she said, stepping back. "What kind of trouble you in now?" She was smiling, like she always did. But knowing what he'd come there to say, he couldn't return the smile. "I expect you want me to fetch your mama."

"Is she busy?"

"I guess you could call it that. It's such a nice

day, she wanted to read a book out there on the back porch. Got that nice cross breeze blowing through. Had half a mind to stay out there and join her, when I brung her some fresh coffee just now. You'll find her out there on that wicker chair she likes so much."

Scott walked through the large foyer, trying to keep his footsteps light on the polished wood floor. "I'll just make my way out there and surprise her."

"You know she doesn't like surprises very much."

"I'll be gentle." Scott tried to keep things upbeat and positive with Mamie Lee. No reason to worry her about something she couldn't do anything about. "Might be a good idea if you stay clear of the porch for a while, Mamie Lee. If you get my drift."

"Oh, I do. I can see in your eyes something's troubling you pretty bad." She leaned forward and whispered, "You been troubled 'bout something a good long while. I can tell. Every time you visit lately."

He should've known Mamie Lee would've picked up on the true state of his emotions. No matter how well he'd tried to hide them. But today the hiding stopped. He had been given the afternoon off due to some top-secret thing going on at GE. The whole plant was on lockdown. But his boss said to call in a few hours, in case the situation changed. He rarely got time off on weekdays anymore. This gave him a chance to talk with his mother without his father around.

"There anything I can do for you, Mister Scott?"

"Not a thing, Mamie Lee. Wish there was, believe me."

"That what you came here to talk about, with your mama?"

He nodded.

"How 'bout I just pray?"

"That'll help."

"I been doing that right along. But I'll keep on praying, don't you worry."

He patted Mamie Lee's forearm and smiled. "I know I can count on you for that. Well, I better get out there. Get this over with." Scott walked through the wide hallway past the stairs toward the back of the house as Mamie Lee disappeared through the dining room on her way to the kitchen. The hallway ended in his father's study.

The back and left walls were covered floor-to-ceiling with hardbound books on shelves, and there was a large mahogany desk nearby, but Scott had never seen anyone study in this room. It was mainly the place the men retired to after dinner to smoke pipes and cigars while they talked money and politics. Scott didn't smoke and had little to say about money or politics. He looked toward the other two walls, all of French windows. The wall to the right led to the back porch. There was his mother, sitting with perfect posture by the corner in one of two wicker chairs, a book opened on her lap. Scott eyed the empty chair beside her, deciding whether it was best to deliver his news standing or sitting down.

The French door creaked as it opened to the porch, but his mother didn't look up. He stood beside her, shuffling his feet the last few steps in an attempt to get her attention. "Oh my, Scott. There you are." She said this almost as if she expected him.

"What are you reading?" he said. "Is it any good?" She closed the book, and he read the cover: *The Winter of Our Discontent*. "Steinbeck, eh? Enjoying it?" A delaying tactic, some idle small talk.

"I'm trying to," she said. "It's supposed to be very good." He understood that to mean it was a recommendation from her circle of friends. "What are you doing here on a Monday afternoon? Shouldn't you be working on your rockets?"

"We don't actually build rockets, Mom. Remember? They do that down at the Cape. Gina and I live in Daytona Beach." Daytona was a thirty-minute drive east of DeLand.

"But don't you work on the space program? That's what I've been telling everyone."

"I do, but indirectly. It's complicated. We build test equipment they use to help make sure the rockets work okay. We're not even working on the

Mercury launches going up now. Remember when President Kennedy said last month he wants to put a man on the moon by the end of the decade?"

"I couldn't believe he said that. How absurd." His mother had voted for Nixon. "Kennedy's Catholic, you know," she'd said at the time.

"It better not be absurd," Scott said. "That's what my job depends on. It's called the Apollo program. Don't you remember? I told you all about this a few weeks ago." He had a feeling she hadn't been listening. Scott's father and two older brothers were bankers. She didn't understand what they did, either.

"So, why aren't you at work doing that?" Her face grew serious. "Wait a minute, there's something wrong. Is that why you're here?" She leaned forward in her chair.

Scott decided to sit down. His knee-jerk reaction was to say that nothing was wrong, but that wasn't true. Something was terribly wrong. As wrong as it could be.

"Is it Gina or one of the boys? Are they all right?"

"Well, give me a few minutes to explain. That's why I took the time to drive over here in the middle of the day. So I could explain what's going on, face-to-face. You always said some conversations are important enough they should only be done in person."

"Oh dear . . ."

Yes, oh dear, he thought. "You know that big birthday party you're planning for Dad in two weeks?"

"His sixtieth," she said. "So . . . you're not coming now? Is that what you're here to tell me? The whole family's going to be here. Your brothers, their wives and kids. Uncle Don and Aunt Elizabeth, even some of your cousins are driving all the way over here from Tampa. Your—"

"No, that's not what I'm saying. I'll be there. It's just . . ." He sighed, took a deep breath. "It's just . . . Gina won't be. And I'm not sure about the kids."

"What? Why not?"

"Well, that's why I drove over here in the middle of the day. Why I'm not working on my rockets. There's something I've gotta tell you, Mom, something I know you won't want to hear."

4

His mother stared at Scott for several moments, the confused look on her face shifting to frustration. "Aren't you going to explain?"

Scott took another deep breath. "I will. But you need to let me lay a few things out before you react."

"I won't react, but don't beat around the bush

for the next ten minutes, either." She set her novel on the end table between the two chairs.

"I won't. The reason Gina won't be coming to Dad's party is . . . she and I have separated. We—"

"What? Separated? What do you mean, separated?"

"See? You're reacting."

She sat up straight, got ahold of herself. "Continue."

"Gina left me, quite awhile ago."

"How is that possible? How long ago?"

This next part would be the hardest to swallow. "Last December, between Christmas and New Year's."

"What?" she exclaimed. "Why, that's . . . that's ten months ago."

"I know."

"But the two of you have been here at least a dozen times since then. The kids too. You were just here for our Labor Day picnic last month."

"I know. We were separated then."

"Scott, is this some kind of joke? You and your brothers are always pulling pranks on each other. Is this one of those—"

"It's not a prank, Mom. I would never do that to you. Not with something like this." The truth was, Scott had never pulled pranks on his older brothers, though he had been a victim of theirs more times than he could count.

She gave him a look he couldn't read. He hated this. He should never have let this charade go on so long. But he honestly thought he could get Gina to come around. This would make him the black sheep again. It started when he'd married Gina and then enlisted to serve in Korea rather than finish college. His parents wanted him to stay single, finish college first, and go into banking, not engineering. Then marry Gina. They wanted those things very much. It had taken the better part of the 1950s to get back in his mother's good graces.

"Well, go on. Finish your story. You were just about to tell me you two were separated back on Labor Day."

"Mom, we've been separated this entire year. At every family event, every holiday dinner or picnic since Christmas."

"But you didn't act separated. You looked just as happy as you've always been. That was all an act? Every time I saw you, you were just pretending?"

Scott nodded. "Afraid so. Well, I wasn't pretending to love Gina, I mean. Just pretending we were still together."

"So you do love her?"

"Of course I do. Even more now than before."

"But she doesn't love you?"

Scott looked out toward the backyard. "To be honest, I'm not sure anymore."

"I can't believe I'm hearing this. I can't believe

24

you're saying these things to me. Harrisons don't get divorced. We don't—"

"We're not divorced. We're separated."

"Harrisons don't separate, either. We stay together. We work through our problems."

"That's what I've been trying to do for the past ten months."

"Well, you can't be trying very hard. Sounds like things are getting worse, if she's not willing to even come to a family event anymore."

Scott had to restrain his anger. Getting mad would only make things more difficult. "I have been trying hard to fix this. It's Gina. She's the one who won't reconsider. I'd move back in today if she'd let me."

"Why won't she let you? It doesn't make any sense. You're both Christians. Our church doesn't even believe in divorce. There's only one exception, and I think you know what I'm talking about."

He did. She was talking about unfaithfulness, committing adultery.

"Has she . . . is she seeing someone else?"

"No, as far as I know, she's not."

A look of shock came over her face. "Then it's you, Scott? I can't believe you would—"

"It isn't me. I wasn't unfaithful to Gina."

"Then what is it?"

Scott stood up and took a few steps toward the wooden railing. "She thinks I was."

"Was what?"

"She thinks I've been unfaithful to her. She thinks she has grounds not just to separate but to divorce." He sighed. "And with this new development, I'm afraid she might be taking things in that direction."

"I don't understand, Scott. If you haven't been unfaithful, why does she think that?"

He turned to face her. "Because she saw something back in December that convinced her I was cheating. She believes it, and nothing I've been able to say or do since then has convinced her otherwise."

"What did she see? What *could* she have seen to make her think such a thing?"

Scott sat again, on the edge of his chair. "I really don't want to go into that much detail, if you don't mind."

His mother shifted in her seat, away from him. Now she looked away also. "This is just terrible. I can't believe you're telling me this. What will your father say, or your brothers?"

Scott didn't need to hear that. "I wish I didn't have to be telling you this. But I had to, with Dad's party less than two weeks away."

She didn't look at him for a few moments. Finally she said, "But I don't understand something. The four of you always came in the same car. I remember coming out to greet the boys sometimes when you arrived."

"We'd meet fifteen minutes early in the parking lot of the A&P. She'd move over to the passenger side, and I'd get in to drive."

There was her subtle, disgusted look, then . . . "The kids!" A gasp. "What about the boys?"

She might as well hear all of it, he thought. "They'd be in the backseat like they always are. They're living with her, of course. Gina lets me see them on Saturdays, if I don't have to work, and one night a week, usually Tuesdays."

"That's awful. The poor things." Then another look of shock. "Do the boys know? Of course they know, what am I saying? Oh Scott, what have you and Gina been doing? Making the boys lie all this time? Neither one of them has said a word, for all these months."

"I'm not proud of it, but yes, that's pretty much it. We didn't call it lying, we called it pretending."

"It was lying, Scott," she said sternly. "Plain and simple."

"I said I'm not proud of it."

"What you should be is ashamed, both of you. Lying is a sin. And you forced your boys to sin right along with you. What's the matter with you?"

Scott suddenly felt like he was six years old.

"And you've got to know, Colt and Timmy know the difference between lying and pretending. Colt does, anyway. He's eleven years old, for crying out loud."

Scott realized this, though he never allowed

himself to think too often or too deeply about it.

His mother stood up and walked to the other end of the porch. She stared out toward the far corner of the yard. "I can't believe this. I just can't believe it."

The French door creaked open. They both looked. "Not now, Mamie Lee," his mother said. "We're in the middle of something important."

Still standing in the doorway, Mamie Lee said, "I know that, ma'am. I know if Mister Scott comes over here by himself on a Monday afternoon to talk, it's probably important. But the phone just rang in the house. Guess you didn't hear it out here."

"No, we didn't. Did you answer it?"

"I sure did."

"Well, can't you just take a message? I'll call them back after Scott leaves."

"That's just the thing. The phone call's for him. It's his wife, Gina. She's the one on the phone."

"Gina?" they both said in unison.

"Why would she be calling here?" Scott said.

"I don't know," Mamie Lee said. "But I'll tell you one thing. Long as I've known her, I've never heard her this upset about anything. I think you better come quick, Mister Scott."

5

Scott stood up and hurried toward the telephone.

Following right behind him, his mother said, "Do you think she's mad because you're telling me your secret?"

"No," Scott said, following Mamie Lee down the hallway. "I didn't even tell her I was coming here."

"Then how did she know you were here?"

"I don't know. Maybe she tried to reach me at work. I told my boss where I was going." He stopped and turned. "Could you stay here? I don't want her to hear you over the phone."

"Well, Scott, what difference does that make now? She already knows you're here."

He looked at Mamie Lee. She whispered loudly, "I didn't know you comin' here was a secret."

"You didn't do anything wrong, Mamie." He stood by the table in the hallway, staring down at the phone. *What on earth could Gina be calling about?*

"Aren't you going to pick it up?" his mother said quietly.

So he did. "Hello? Gina?"

"Oh Scott, they aren't here. We've looked everywhere. But they're not here!" She was half yelling, half crying.

"What are you talking about? Who's not where?" He looked at his watch and answered his own question. The boys. This was the time Gina picked them up from school.

"Colt and Timmy. I came to get them like I always do, and they're not here. They always stand by the flagpole near the front steps. Every day. I sat in my car by the curb and waited for fifteen minutes, but they didn't show up. I knew something had to be wrong. I figured one of them might have misbehaved in class and had to stay after to wash the blackboards. Maybe Colt, but not Timmy. He's never gotten into trouble."

"Is there some kind of after-school game they could've gone to, some kind of team practice?" Scott said. "Maybe they told you and you forgot?"

"No, there's no after-school game. I checked. And neither one of the boys is on any team. I told you Colt had tried out for basketball, but he didn't make it."

"Maybe they went home with one of their friends to play. Haven't they done that before? You know, go right from school to their friend's house?"

"I let Colt do it twice so far this year. But not Timmy, he's too young. And Colt would never do that without asking."

"Maybe he did ask, and you just forgot?"

"That's not what happened, Scott. He didn't ask, and I didn't forget. Besides, he wouldn't have left Timmy at the flagpole by himself. Even if I had said yes. He would've known he'd have to wait there until I arrived to pick Timmy up."

Scott didn't know why he was saying these things. Gina wasn't stupid, and Colt would never do anything irresponsible with his little brother. With the five years in between them, there had rarely ever been any sibling rivalry. He and Gina had sometimes joked how Colt reminded them of Wally looking after the Beaver.

"What's going on?" Scott's mother said. "Are the boys okay?"

Scott put his palm over the phone. "I don't know, Mom. They weren't where they were supposed to be when Gina went to pick them up."

"Well, you know boys . . . always into mischief. I'm sure they're okay." But her face was filled with worry.

"Boys are so curious that way," Mamie Lee said. She also looked worried.

"Scott, I need you to stop talking with your mom and Mamie Lee and listen to me. Their teachers said they were never in class at all today!"

"What!" Scott said. "That doesn't make any sense. Didn't you drop them off this morning?"

"Yes, of course I did."

"Did you see them go in the building?"

A slight pause. "Not exactly. I was running a little late for work, so I dropped them off where I always do, right by the front steps."

Late for work, Scott thought. She wouldn't even be at work if she hadn't left him. There wasn't a mother in their neighborhood who worked outside the home.

"We waved good-bye," Gina continued, "and then I drove off. But I'm sure they went inside. Why wouldn't they? The front door was just fifty feet in front of them. The whole sidewalk on both sides was covered with kids. All of them heading into school."

"Then someone must've seen them go in. One of their friends. Did you talk to any of them?"

"I couldn't. By the time I was done searching the hallways and talking with Timmy's teacher, all but a few of the kids were gone. And I didn't recognize any of them."

"Well, something must have happened," he said. "I mean something simple, something we're not thinking about." He thought a moment. "Wait, if the boys weren't in class this morning, and you didn't call in to say they were sick, wouldn't the school office have called you?"

Another brief pause. "They're saying they did call, but no one answered at home. They said they left a message with someone at work, but . . . I never got it. Should I call the police?"

Maybe they'd better, he thought. But crimes against kids were almost unheard of, especially in small towns like Daytona Beach. He was sure they were fine. "We may have to. But listen, I'm going to leave here right now and head there. Why don't you go back inside the office and make a list of all of their friends. Talk to both their teachers before they leave for home. See if the boys have any friends in class we don't know about. Then see if the principal will help you get the telephone numbers for all these kids' parents. I should be there by then. We'll start calling everyone on the list."

"But what if they walked home? If somehow we missed each other, and they walked home? Shouldn't one of us be there?"

"Okay, I'll drive by and check before I stop at the school. Then I'll drive slowly to school, taking the roads they'd use if they walked."

"Okay," Gina said. "But Scott, please hurry."

"I will."

"And pray," she said.

"I'll do that too."

He hung up and looked at his mother. "I've gotta go."

"Well, not yet," she said. "Aren't you going to tell us what's going on?"

"There's not that much to tell." In two minutes he gave them a rough overview of the situation. A look of alarm grew on both their faces as he talked. "Really, I have to go." He hurried toward the front door.

"You call us the minute you hear something," his mother called out over his shoulder.

"We'll be praying, Mister Scott. You know we will."

"I'm counting on it," he said as he flew down the porch steps. Although at the moment, he wasn't feeling too sure the Almighty was listening to his prayers. He'd been struggling with his faith ever since Gina had left him. But he knew God would always listen to Mamie Lee's prayers.

He took some comfort from that.

6

Gina hung up the telephone and looked up and down the hallway. The principal, Mrs. Johnson, had offered to let her use her office phone to call Scott, but Gina didn't want their conversation overheard. She hated all this secrecy about their separation, which was why she'd insisted it had to stop. But she hadn't told anyone at the school yet.

Here, like everywhere else, their charade was still intact.

She wondered if Scott's presence at his parents' house in the middle of the day meant he'd finally worked up the nerve to tell his mother that Gina wouldn't be playing along anymore. Walking back into the school office reminded her of why they had kept up this phony front. This was certainly not the moment to "come clean." People just treated you different if you were separated or divorced. You could almost feel them pull away, like you had some contagious disease.

Respect went out the window.

No one in her family or in Scott's had ever been divorced. No one in their neighborhood was divorced. No one in any of her social circles was divorced. She was certain plenty of them were unhappily married, but at least they were still together. She walked back through a cloud of cigarette smoke in the reception area and knocked on the principal's open door.

Mrs. Johnson looked up from her desk. "What did your husband say?"

"He's very upset. He's on his way here now."

"You can't think of anywhere else the boys may have gone?"

Gina took a seat in front of the desk where she'd sat before and reached for a tissue. "No. They know better than to leave or go anywhere without getting permission."

"While you were gone, I double-checked. We definitely called you at work this morning when it became obvious the boys were absent, to make sure you were aware. First they called your house, and when no one answered there, they called the work number you gave us. I spoke with a woman who made the calls. She said she'd given the message to the receptionist, because you weren't at your desk."

"Oh, I believe you. It's not the first time I didn't get one of my messages." Gina wished her boss would fire that girl at the front desk. All she did was flirt with the salesmen. It was obvious she wasn't there to work but to fish for a husband. "Can I borrow a few sheets of paper and a pen?"

"Certainly."

"My husband suggested I make a list of all of the boys' friends. And he wanted me to ask their teachers if they've made any friends here at school, boys we might not know about. Once I write them out, I may need your help again. We thought you could help us get their phone numbers."

"That's a good idea," Mrs. Johnson said, handing her the paper and pen. "You start working on that and I'll call their teachers on the intercom, make sure I get them before they head home."

For the next several minutes, they busied themselves with their separate tasks. Gina was glad for the distraction. She reminded herself of something Scott had said, that something simple must've happened here, something they just weren't thinking about. Not something sinister. The boys were all right. They had to be.

"Mrs. Harrison, excuse me." It was Mrs. Johnson.

Gina looked up.

"Timmy's teacher will be here in just a minute. But Colt's teacher wondered if you might be able to come to her classroom. She had to keep a boy after class for chewing gum. He's washing all the blackboards, and he's rather mischievous. She doesn't want to leave him alone."

"I understand. I'll go right there after I meet with Timmy's teacher."

"She did have an interesting idea, something I hadn't considered."

"What's that?"

"Has Colt ever played hooky before?"

"What?"

"You know, skipped school to do something fun? His teacher said two other boys had done that today. It's all this military activity going on, it's gotten the boys all excited."

"You mean the caravans of Army trucks going down US-1?" Gina had seen them all weekend, all heading south. Dozens of them, filled with soldiers and equipment. She had no idea what was going on, but the boys got very animated every time the trucks drove by, pointing at them and yelling. Maybe that was where the boys were. She hoped it was something like that. She'd have to ground them for a year, but she didn't care. Anything to find them and get them back.

"That's what I'm talking about," Mrs. Johnson said. "You know how boys are about the military. It's all those John Wayne movies."

"And there's some new show on TV," Gina said, "just started a few weeks ago, called *Combat.*

Timmy's been begging me to let him stay up and watch it with Colt."

"Maybe the temptation proved to be too much for Colt and Timmy," Mrs. Johnson said, "seeing all these military vehicles riding through their town."

Gina wanted to believe what she was hearing, but it was so out of character for the boys to do something like this. She could almost imagine Colt being talked into it, egged on by his friends. But she could never see him taking his little brother Timmy along on such a scheme. "But aren't all the military vehicles across the river, on US-1?" she asked.

"Mostly, yes."

"Have you seen any of them over here on the beachside, driving down A1A?"

"I haven't," Mrs. Johnson said. "Think it's too far for the boys to walk?"

"Kind of," Gina said. "Maybe not for Colt, but definitely for Timmy."

"I'm pretty sure the two boys who played hooky this morning rode their bikes to school."

Just then the office door opened, and Miss Jenkins walked in. She was young and attractive, her hair in a bouffant just like Jackie Kennedy's. Gina thought she must be in her early twenties. Looking at Gina, Miss Jenkins said, "I'm so sorry, Mrs. Harrison. I've been worried sick ever since I heard. Any news?"

"Nothing yet. But I'm wondering if you can help me."

"Anything."

"Can you think of any friends Timmy has made in class so far this year? Maybe some boys we don't know? The only friends we know all live in our neighborhood."

"As you know, Timmy's awfully shy. Occasionally I do see him playing at recess with the boy who sits in front of him. His name is Roy. But I don't believe Timmy could be with Roy. I always stand out by the school busses and watch my kids get on. I saw Roy get on his bus this afternoon, by himself."

"There's no one else that Timmy talks to or plays with?"

"There might be a few others," Miss Jenkins said. "But none that I would call a good friend."

Disappointing news, though Gina didn't put much stock in this solution. There was still a sliver of hope in talking with Colt's teacher, but she had doubts about that too. She just couldn't see Colt bringing his brother along on such an adventure. What was she saying? She couldn't see him doing anything other than waiting there by the flagpole with Timmy like he always did.

Whatever had happened was totally out of character and totally unexpected . . . for both of them.

7

"Timmy," Colt said, "put the comic book down and eat your pie. It cost me twelve cents."

"I don't like it," Timmy said. "The crust is too dry. Mom's is way better."

"Mom's pie isn't here. You ordered it, you eat it. That's all you're going to get till we get to Uncle Mike's house." Timmy ignored his older brother. "Okay, I'll tell you what, you give me that comic book, and you don't have to eat the pie."

That got his attention. "What? No, that isn't fair. This comic book for an old piece of pie?"

" 'Course it's fair. They both cost twelve cents. If you're not gonna eat the pie, you owe me twelve cents. You got twelve cents?" Timmy shook his head no. "Then I'll take the comic book. Or . . . you can eat the pie and keep it."

"I'll eat the pie." Timmy huffed and set his comic book on the seat beside him, then picked up his fork and started poking at the pie. The fingers of his other hand started thrumming to the beat of "Do You Love Me" playing on the radio.

Timmy loved comic books, even more than toys. And he loved this Spiderman one the most. Some brand-new superhero that just came out a couple weeks ago. He must've read it a dozen times already. Colt had read it once. It was okay, but he was more into baseball than comic books. But he had to bring it on this trip; it was the only way Timmy would come. Colt told him to pack light, so he could only pick two. He picked Spiderman and another fairly new one called the Hulk. Some great big green guy who goes around breaking stuff.

Colt had already finished his grilled cheese sandwich, which also cost twelve cents. He could've splurged and bought them both Coca-Colas for an extra twenty cents, but he had to conserve his money, so they drank water instead. Cost almost everything he had for these bus tickets to Savannah, where they were headed now. Uncle Mike and Aunt Rose, their favorite relatives, lived there. Aunt Rose was their mom's sister.

"Do they even know we're coming?" Timmy said. "Uncle Mike and Aunt Rose?"

"No," Colt said. "I couldn't take a chance. If I called them, they might say no."

"What if they say no when we get there?" Timmy was still chewing.

Colt heard his mother's voice in his head, correcting Timmy for talking with his mouth full. "They won't."

"But what if they do? You have enough money to buy tickets home?"

He didn't. He barely had enough left to pay for dinner if the bus stopped again between here and

Savannah. "It doesn't matter, Timmy. They won't turn us away. We're family. Families stick together. They don't send other family members out into the cold."

"It's gonna get cold tonight?"

"That's just an expression. I mean they won't make us go home." Colt glanced at a wall clock. "Now, finish your pie. The bus driver said we only got till three-thirty. That's less than fifteen minutes. Then he wants us on that bus."

He looked out the window, saw their bus parked right where it should be. He didn't see the driver, who was probably still in his seat. The man said this was only going to be a twenty-minute stop. Two other buses were here when they arrived, one pointed north, the same direction they were headed. The other facing south. A few people from the diner had already left and were boarding that bus. He wondered where they were going. Obviously somewhere in Florida; that was the only possibility going south.

"Where are we, anyway?" Timmy said.

"I'm not sure. Somewhere north of Jacksonville. That was that big city we drove through a few miles back."

"That was the biggest city I ever saw."

"Me too. I wouldn't want to live there."

"Me either. Seems like you could get lost in a place like that without even trying." He took another bite of pie. "Savannah that big?"

"Not even close. I heard Uncle Mike telling Dad about it when they visited two summers ago. He said it was just a little bit bigger than Daytona Beach. Supposed to be a neat place. It's got all kinds of Civil War history stuff."

"What's the Civil War?"

Colt didn't feel like explaining. "It's a war that happened a hundred years ago. You'll learn about it a few grades from now. Keep eating your pie. We have to go in a few minutes." He had no idea how Uncle Mike and Aunt Rose would react when he and Timmy showed up tonight. They were always so much fun when they visited. They laughed the most and smiled the most too, of all their relatives. When Colt had decided to run away, they were the only ones he'd thought of.

They had to take Colt and Timmy in.

Or maybe—and Colt thought this could be what really happened—when he told them what was going on between his mom and dad, how they'd split up, how they'd made the boys lie about it to everyone, Uncle Mike and Aunt Rose would be able to get his folks to see how wrong it was, how bad they'd been treating him and Timmy, and get them talking about whatever had made them so angry with each other. Get them back together again.

Colt still had no idea what caused the split. But living like this was horrible for him and Timmy. Their mom was always depressed when she got home. She yelled at them all the time, made them do all kinds of chores she used to do. She complained about everything, how hard her life was now, how difficult it was being a single mom, like nobody understood what she was going through.

What she's going through? What about us, what about me and Timmy, what we're going through? Did anyone understand that? Did she? Did she even care? He wasn't sure anymore. This running away would get him into all kinds of trouble, but he decided it was worth it.

Somebody had to do something.

He reached for his glass of water and took the last swig. Timmy's glass was almost full. He was just about to tell him to start drinking but then changed his mind. They were gonna be back on that bus in five minutes. He didn't want Timmy to drink all that water then have to go to the bathroom ten minutes down the road.

Speaking of going to the bathroom . . . He slid to the edge of his seat. "Hey, Timmy, I've gotta go. Do you?"

Timmy shook his head no. Something caught his eye out the window, and he turned to look. "Colt, Army trucks, look at 'em all." His face lit up as he pointed. "See 'em?"

"I see 'em." They weren't the only ones looking. Everyone stopped whatever they were doing, including the waitresses, and stared out the window. Then something even crazier happened. A train rolled down the tracks across the street. It was pulling tanks, big green Army tanks, on flatbed trailer cars, one right after the other.

"Would you look at that?" a middle-aged man in the next booth said as he stood to his feet, eyes fixed on the scene.

A man wearing a baseball cap at the counter nearby stood and said, "I'm telling ya something big's going on. Something they aren't telling us. And I bet it's got something to do with Cuba. I've been reading rumblings about Cuba in the papers. I was a marine in World War II. All these troops and military vehicles heading south, there's way more than they need for some war game operation. I'm telling ya."

Another man spoke up. "Says here in the paper, they moved a whole fighter wing down to Key West."

"See," the baseball cap man said. "And what's close to Key West? Cuba! I'm telling ya, somethin's goin' on."

Another man, older, in a bright plaid shirt said, "I just heard on my transistor radio here, President Kennedy wants to speak to the entire nation tonight. He's coming on at 7:00 p.m. on all three networks." He looked back out the window at the tanks still rolling down the railroad tracks.

Timmy was now on his knees, totally fixated on the scene. Colt wanted to stay there and keep watching, but he really had to go. "Timmy, you gotta come with me."

"Aww, Colt, can't I stay and watch this? I've never seen real-life tanks before." He was still staring out the window.

"I can't just leave you here."

"Please, Colt. You're just going to the bathroom."

He couldn't see any harm in it. "Okay, you stay there till I get back. I'll just be a minute."

Timmy didn't answer. Colt hurried toward the back where the restrooms were. He glanced toward their table once before heading into the men's room. Timmy and everyone else were still staring at the trucks and tanks going by.

In the bathroom he thought about what that man had said, the one wearing the baseball cap. About something big going on, something they weren't telling us. He figured by "they" he meant the Army, or else the government. Colt wondered if America was going to war. He sure didn't want to be out there on the road riding a bus if war was about to break out and wished there was some way to be at Uncle Mike's house right now.

He came out of the restroom a few minutes later.

What? Where was Timmy! Colt ran back to the table, calling his name. No one even looked at him. They just stood there watching the tanks and trucks roll by. On a radio in the corner, the Beach Boys sang the chorus of "Surfin' Safari" over and over again.

His brother Timmy was nowhere in sight.

8

"Timmy," he called out. "Timmy!"

He looked under their table, thinking maybe his comic book had fallen to the floor. But he wasn't there. The Hulk comic book was still on the seat. But the Spiderman comic book was gone. "Has anyone seen my little brother? Anyone see where he went?"

No one answered. They all just sat there, watching the tanks and trucks go by. He ran outside. Maybe Timmy had gone out there to get a better view. Several other people stood around watching the same thing. But he didn't see any kids.

He ran back inside the diner, into the other half of the building, which was a store. Running up and down the aisles, he called out Timmy's name. He wasn't there. Colt saw a rack of comic books and stopped there a moment. "Hey, mister!" he yelled to the teenager manning the register. "You seen a little boy in here a few minutes ago? Brown hair wearing a red plaid shirt?"

"No, sorry. But an older guy wearing a brown

sweater and a gray fedora bought a stack of comic books about five minutes ago. Said he was buying them for his son. Was that your dad?"

"Our dad isn't here." Colt couldn't stand there yakking, so he ran back to the diner.

He looked at their booth again, half expecting to find Timmy there. He still couldn't believe he was gone. Where could he be? It bothered him that nobody cared. No one even paid attention to him.

"Let's go surfin' now . . ." the Beach Boys sang on the radio. He decided it was time to make a scene.

"Excuse me, everyone!" Colt yelled. Not loud enough. "Excuse me!"

"What's the matter, kid?" someone replied.

A few others looked his way, but still, most of them kept staring out the window. He walked behind the counter, right up to the radio, and turned it off. "Excuse me, I said."

"Hey, kid, we were listening to that!" said a blond-haired guy in his twenties.

"Has anyone seen my little brother?" Colt screamed at the top of his lungs. They heard that. Everyone turned. "My little brother, Timmy, has anyone seen him? He was just here with me a few minutes ago. I went into the bathroom, and when I came out, he was gone. Did anyone see where he went?"

Almost everyone shook their heads no. A few

just stared at him, confused looks on their faces. "You check the store next door?" someone said.

"He's not there."

"How about the bathroom?"

"I just came from there."

"Maybe he went outside," someone else said, "to see everything up close."

"I checked. He's not outside."

"You check by the street, or just up here near the building?"

He hadn't, but he didn't need to. You could see the whole sidewalk area from the front door. "I looked everywhere," he said. "Somebody had to see him."

"We didn't," the blond guy at the counter said. "Now turn the radio back on."

Just then, a waitress came out from the kitchen. "What's going on? What's all this yelling about?"

"My little brother's missing," Colt said, tears now in his eyes. "And no one knows where he is."

"I saw him," she said. "About five or six? Brown hair, so tall?" She set her hand about waist high.

"That's him. You know where he is?"

"He ain't missing. He just left with your dad. They must be waiting for you on the bus."

Colt looked out the window toward the buses. What was she talking about? "That's impossible. Our dad isn't here. He's back in Daytona, where we live."

"Mustn't be the same guy then," she said. "Guess that wasn't your little brother, either. Did you just come out of the men's room?"

Colt nodded.

"Were there any other boys your age in there?"

"No, no one else was in there."

A confused look came over her face. "Then I don't know what's going on. I saw a man walk toward the front door with a little boy, headed toward the buses."

"What did he look like?"

"He was pretty tall, about six feet, I'd say. Wore a gray felt hat, looked like he needed a shave. Not fat but a little thick around the middle."

"That's definitely not my dad," Colt said. Usually when women described him, they'd start off with how handsome he was, maybe compare him to a movie star. He never wore a hat anymore (said if President Kennedy wasn't gonna wear one, neither was he). And he certainly wasn't "thick around the middle."

"Maybe not," she said, "but that's what this guy looked like. He and that little boy went right out the door, headed for one of those buses. He was carrying a stack of comic books."

"Comic books?"

She nodded. "Must've had four or five of them." She looked up. "You better get going. That bus is pulling out."

Colt turned to look. It was the bus heading south, back into Florida. "That's not our bus. Ours is that one." He pointed.

"I don't know," the waitress said. "That's the bus the man and little boy were walking toward."

Panic filled his heart. He ran outside just as the bus pulled onto US-1, heading south. He ran after it, fast as he could. It kept shifting gears. He screamed out, "Wait, stop!" His voice was drowned out by the noise of the bus and loud trucks driving by in the left lane. For a moment, he started gaining on it, closing the gap. When he was just about to reach out and bang the side, it shifted gears again and pulled away.

He screamed again, "Wait, wait! You've gotta stop!" It just kept going; the gap grew wider every second. He moved farther out toward the right and looked up at the windows.

That's when he saw him.

Timmy, a few rows up from the back of the bus, sitting by the window next to a man wearing a gray hat. Colt yelled out his name as he ran, over and over again. But Timmy didn't hear him. He was looking down at something in his hands.

Colt kept running until the bus reached full speed and went through a traffic light up ahead. He stopped in a patch of grass just off the sidewalk, fell to the ground, and cried.

9

After making the thirty-minute drive from DeLand, Scott drove slowly past their house on Seaview Avenue, using the route the boys would normally have taken if they had walked home from school. No sign of them. He pulled into the driveway behind the house, then rushed in through the back door, calling out their names.

There was no reply. He didn't really expect one.

He'd fought off feelings of dread and panic on the way here, tried to remain calm and remind himself what he'd said to Gina. They had lived in this town for years and had never heard of any crimes against children. The boys were somewhere safe; they had to be, doing something stupid and disobedient. Boys just being boys.

But wherever they were doing it, they weren't doing it here at the house.

He hurried back to his car. After backing out, he drove slowly around the neighborhood, three or four streets in both directions. Still nothing. *Where could they be?*

A few of their friends lived nearby, but Scott had never known which ones. Gina did. It was time to head to the school. As he drove south and turned on Grandview Avenue, he saw a little boy who looked familiar, about Timmy's age, walking on the sidewalk and pushing a bicycle. When Scott pulled up beside him, he was certain this little boy had played with Timmy in their house. He leaned over, rolled down his window, and said, "Hi, can I ask you a question?"

The boy glanced at him then picked up his pace. "I'm not supposed to talk to strangers."

"That's a good boy. Your parents teach you that?" The boy nodded and kept walking. Scott moved the car forward to keep up. "But I'm not really a stranger. I'm Mr. Harrison, Timmy's father. Aren't you Timmy's friend?"

The boy stopped and squinted as he looked through the window. "I played with him a few times. We're in the same grade at school, but we have different teachers."

"You've been at our house though, right?"

"I think so. Isn't it on Seaview Avenue?"

"That's right. What's your name again?"

"Scotty. Scotty O'Brien. I live on Nautilus."

"Scotty, that's my name too. How come you're not riding your bike?"

"Can't, got a flat." He pointed to it. "See?"

Scott thought about offering him a ride but quickly changed his mind. "Say, have you seen Timmy today? Or his older brother Colt?"

The boy thought a moment. "I don't think so. I usually see Timmy at recess or at lunch, but I didn't see him today. I hardly ever see Colt. Even when I do, he doesn't talk to me."

"Can you think of any place around here they may have gone to play?"

"No, not really."

"Well, if you do see either one of them, tell them to go right home, okay? Tell them we're looking for them, their mother and I."

"Are they in trouble?"

They certainly were, he thought. But he didn't want to say that. "I hope not. Well, bye." Scotty waved as Scott rolled the window back up.

By the time he arrived at the school, the parking lot was almost empty, hardly any kids in sight. The school wasn't far from where they lived. He glanced at the flagpole by the front steps, where the boys were supposed to have been a little while ago. He sighed as he headed toward the office.

When he walked through the door, he saw Gina across the room at a desk, using the telephone and writing things down on a pad of paper. He could tell she had been crying. She hadn't noticed him yet. He smiled at two women sitting at nearby desks who did. "My name's Scott Harrison. That's my wife over there making the calls."

"Hello, Mr. Harrison," one of them said, her face full of sympathy. "Please, go right over. Your wife is calling a list of the boys' friends right now."

He was about to ask the woman if Gina had any luck but decided to ask her himself. "Thanks."

When he got closer, she looked up then shook her head no. Guess that was his answer. Gina looked back at the phone, crossed through a name on the list. Several other names had been crossed through already.

"Well, thank you, Mrs. Bruckner," Gina said into the phone. "I'm sorry to have bothered you. If you see or hear anything about my boys, can you call me at this number? Yes, it's the school number. Or maybe try our home number if we're not here. What? No, we haven't called the police yet. We wanted to try all their friends first. See if we just miscommunicated with them. When your son Andrew gets home, will you ask him about this? See if he knows anything? Thanks so much. Good-bye." She set the receiver back in place.

He wanted to put his hand on her shoulder to comfort her, but instead he sat on the seat beside her. "No luck, huh?"

"Oh Scott, no one has seen them. None of their friends in school, and so far none of the friends around the neighborhood. I've only got two more names left on my list."

"It's okay. Let's don't jump to conclusions. Go ahead and make the calls. I'll be right here." There was no confidence behind what he'd said; he hoped it didn't show. Being here, so close to her when she was clearly struggling and afraid . . . it was all he could do not to reach for her hand. During the last ten months they had only been to a handful of school events. And, of course, they pretended to still be together for the boys' sake. They'd feign a measure of closeness; he'd open doors for her, put a light hand on her back and the occasional hand on the shoulder. But no real intimacy, and the closeness would always end abruptly the moment they left school property. He'd hated it, and in a way, he was glad they had decided to end this charade.

He watched and waited for the next five or six minutes as Gina made the calls. Both were dead ends.

The principal, Mrs. Johnson, walked out of her office just then. "Hear anything?"

"I'm afraid not," Scott said, trying to sound calm.

"Can you think of any other place they might have gone?" she asked.

Scott shook his head.

"Me neither," Gina said.

Scott could tell Gina was about to fall apart at any moment. But he had to do it. It was time. He reached for the phone, slid closer to her, and picked up the receiver. Slowly, he put his finger in the little round opening and dialed the zero. "Yes, operator, I'd like the police."

Gina began to cry.

10

Scott and Gina sat quietly in their smallish living room on Seaview Avenue. Scott looked around. It wasn't just the living room; the entire house was small. The whole thing could fit in the dining and living rooms of the house he'd grown up in on Clara Avenue in DeLand. But so what? This was their place, paid for without Harrison family money.

Well, it used to be *their* place.

A police officer was supposed to arrive any moment. Scott had called from the school, but the police suggested that since the boys weren't there, it would be better to conduct the interview at the house. After calling the police, he'd called his boss to let him know what was happening.

"I was so hoping the boys would be here when we got home," Gina said. "And this nightmare would be over."

"Me too," Scott said. He repeated the phrase "we got home" in his mind, liking the sound of it. For a moment, it was as if they were still together. Initially, Gina had moved out of the house because Scott refused to. He hadn't done what she was accusing him of; why should he have to leave because she had jumped to the wrong conclusion? But after a few days, when it became

57

obvious she was serious about splitting up, he'd changed his mind and told her to come back. For her sake and the boys', he'd get the apartment. Of course, it was stretching their budget to the breaking point.

Gina stood up, walked over to the window, and pulled back the sheers. "Here he is. A police car just pulled up. What should we tell him?"

"We just tell him what happened."

"I mean about us. Our situation."

"I don't know." He walked toward the door to let him in. "Let's just see what he says and answer his questions honestly. They can't help us if we're hiding things." She gave him a look, and he realized that last remark was kind of an insult, as if she wanted to hide information. Not enough time for an apology. He opened the door. "Hello, Officer."

A short heavyset man in uniform pulled out a pad and pen as he walked up the sidewalk. "Mr. and Mrs. Harrison? Officer Franklin. Can I come in?"

"Sure," Scott said and stepped aside.

Gina walked back to the sofa and sat on the edge. Officer Franklin followed Scott into the living room and removed his hat. Scott sat, but the officer remained standing.

"You called to report your children are missing? Two boys?"

"Yes," Scott said. "Ages eleven and six."

"The eleven-year-old is named Colt, the six-year-old is Timmy," Gina added.

He wrote both things down. "It says you last saw them at school this morning?"

"Yes, I dropped them off. Right where I always do. They kissed me and waved good-bye, like they always do, and I watched them walk toward the front door as I drove off to work."

Scott could tell, she was trying hard to keep her emotions under control.

"But you didn't see them go in."

"No, I didn't. I was running a little late." As she said that, a pained expression came over her face.

Scott said, "I've done the same thing before, Officer, when I've been late."

He didn't write this down. "Did y'all have any arguments or conflicts this morning? Not you two, I mean with the boys."

"Not really," Gina said. "We had a little tension for a few seconds, but nothing major. And the two of them were getting along fine."

He looked at Scott. "How about you, sir? Did you and the boys have any problems this morning, or last night?"

What should Scott say? He hadn't even seen the boys since Saturday. "No, no problems." Gina gave him a look. If he read it right, she was wondering if his answer meant they were keeping their separation a secret. He half-shrugged, not sure if she got the interpretation. Not even sure what message he was trying to convey.

"Can you tell me what kind of things you've done in your search so far?"

Both of them began to answer. "You go ahead, Gina." Scott listened as Gina recounted her efforts on the phone. He described his drive around the neighborhood.

"Do either of you think there's a chance the boys just ran away? Because if not, we're talking about the possibility of a kidnapping."

"Kidnapping," Gina repeated. "I hope not. Please, Lord, don't let it be that." She dropped her face into her hands.

"I'm not saying they were kidnapped, ma'am."

"I'm thinking they're just off doing something stupid," Scott said. "Like boys do sometimes."

"You're probably right," Officer Franklin said. He looked at Gina. "I don't mean to upset you, Mrs. Harrison. Just trying to cover all the bases. You have any recent pictures of the boys? We'll need those. And I'd like a detailed description of both of them, including what they were wearing when you last saw them."

"I'll get the photographs, Gina," Scott said. "Why don't you give him the description?"

Without thinking, Scott walked back to his dresser to get a framed picture of the boys. Then he remembered, he'd brought it with him to the apartment. He looked around the room, noticed a similar picture taken the same day on Gina's nightstand. Grabbing it, he walked back toward the living room. He glanced down at his sons smiling back at him as they sat balancing on a large coquina rock. The picture had been taken almost exactly one year ago at Cypress Gardens, on one of the few days he'd actually taken a Saturday off for the family.

If he had only known then what he knew now, he'd have taken off every Saturday and been home every night for dinner at five-thirty. And he'd have turned down that big promotion he'd gotten at GE a month after this picture had been taken, which required even more time away from his family. But would it have been enough? Would it have kept Gina from believing that he had been having an affair with Marla, that redhead who had kissed him at the office Christmas party last year?

Then he realized that if he hadn't taken that promotion, he'd never have met Marla. They had worked in two totally separate buildings in two different parts of town. But none of this matters now, he thought as he stepped into the living room. You can't go back in time and fix your mistakes. The best you can hope for is to learn from them and not make the same ones ever again.

But would he get that chance . . . with Gina? Or with his boys?

"Is that a picture of your sons?" Officer Franklin asked.

Scott looked down at it again. *Lord,* he prayed, *please let them be all right.*

11

Gina watched Scott's face as he handed the picture of Colt and Timmy to Officer Franklin. She could see the strained expression he tried to hide, but it was clear. He was deeply worried.

The police officer looked at the picture a few moments then said, "We'll get this back to you soon, after we make some copies. This is recent, right?"

"Last year," Scott said. "They look pretty much the same, both just a little taller."

"Timmy's hair's a little shorter," Gina said.

The officer looked at it some more then looked up as if he had something else to say but stopped himself.

"What is it?" Scott said.

"I'm trying to understand the situation, that's all. What we're dealing with here. We don't have a lot of experience with kidnapping, thankfully. But from everything I've read, kidnappers don't usually go after two children, not unless there's a lot of money in the deal." He looked around their living area. "Y'all have a nice place here, but . . ."

"No, you're right," Scott said. "We don't have a lot of money. I've got a pretty good job, but we don't even have a savings account. Used up most of it when we bought this house."

Gina thought about Scott's parents. They had quite a lot of money and that huge house over in DeLand. Some might call them rich. She wondered if she should mention it.

"Something bothering you, Gina?"

She looked at Scott. "I was just wondering about your folks, whether that could be something."

"What about them?" the officer asked.

"They're pretty well-off," Scott said. "My dad and two brothers are bankers over in DeLand."

"Well, the point I was raising is, I find it hard to believe that a kidnapper would've been able to get two boys into his car, especially when one of them is eleven. Maybe the six-year-old—what's his name?" He looked at his notes. "Maybe Timmy," he continued, "but I can't see the older boy going along with this."

Gina couldn't either. "I think Colt would have made a terrible fuss if someone tried to get him or his brother into a car."

"I agree," Scott said. "I can even see him kicking and punching anyone who tried to mess with him or Timmy. He definitely wouldn't have gone quietly."

"And there weren't any reports of any altercations in front of the school this morning? No reports of anything unusual?" Officer Franklin asked.

"No," said Gina. "It was just a very ordinary day."

The officer shook his head. "See, that's got me thinking that this ain't a kidnapping. Something else happened here, some reason the boys had for walking away from the school on their own. They waited there until you drove off, then they walked away to pursue whatever scheme they had conjured up."

Gina was relieved to hear him talk this way. She looked over at Scott; he seemed to feel the same way. It didn't make things a lot better, but if all they had done was run away, at least they were safe somewhere.

"So that brings me around to what I was getting at before. I'm not trying to pry into you folks' business, but I really need to ask these questions if we're going to figure out what happened here."

Gina tensed up; she knew where this was heading. Her eyes fell on Colt's baseball glove and ball sitting on the hutch, still wet from being left out on the front lawn all night. Flashes of the conflict she'd had with Colt that morning came to mind. He was so irresponsible with his things. She had specifically reminded him to bring it in last night, but there it was when she went out to get the newspaper this morning. She thought about the second argument after breakfast. The boys seemed so distracted; they just wouldn't get it into gear. They had to leave for school in ten minutes, and Timmy still didn't have his teeth brushed or his socks and shoes on. Both the boys' lunchboxes were still unpacked.

"You used to do that for us," he'd moaned. "All my friends' moms pack their lunchboxes."

"Maybe you should go live with them," she'd replied. "I can't do those things anymore. Don't you think I'd like to? But I've got to get ready for work myself. It's not gonna kill you to help out a little around here."

Oh no, she thought. Was that what set him off? She didn't really mean it. She was just letting off some steam.

"Is there anything going on around here," the officer asked, "something between the two of you, or with one or both of them that you're not telling me? I don't mean something small and petty—the ordinary parent-kid stuff—but something big enough that the boys might want to escape from?"

Scott looked at her, then nodded. Was he wanting her to bring it up? Was he planning to? He shook his head. Now what did that mean?

"Possibly," Scott said.

"Possibly?" Officer Franklin repeated.

She heard Scott inhale deeply. How was he going to handle this? Would he blame it on her?

"Well, there is something going on. I don't

know if it has anything to do with the boys being gone, but I guess it could have."

"Go on . . ." Officer Franklin had his pen and paper ready.

"My wife and I have been separated for the last ten months."

"Oh, well . . . that could certainly make a difference," he said. "Who's living where?"

"The boys are here, living here with their mom. We thought that would be the easiest, or at least less stressful on them. The only apartment I could afford in a decent area would have put them in a different school zone."

The policeman wrote that down. "And how often do you see them?"

"Not enough," Scott said, with an edge. "Just Saturdays and—"

"When you're not working," Gina added.

"I do work some Saturdays, but not as much as I used to."

"Is that true?" the officer asked Gina.

"I guess it is."

"Just Saturdays and Tuesday evenings," Scott said.

"Are you and the boys close?" the officer asked him.

Scott looked down at the terrazzo floor. "Not as close as I'd like."

"But he's not just referring to now," Gina added. "I mean, since the separation. He means in general. The boys have always complained about not getting enough time with their dad."

"So how do you fix that?" Scott said. "By only letting me see them twice a week?"

"It's more than you used to see them when you lived here," she said.

"Okay," Officer Franklin interjected, "I get the idea. This how the two of you talk when the boys are around?"

It wasn't how they used to talk, she thought. They hadn't talked very much at all. Before she'd caught him with that secretary last Christmas, he was hardly ever home. For the first twelve years of their marriage, she had played the dutiful wife, the perfect homemaker like June Cleaver or Margaret Anderson on *Father Knows Best*—take your pick. *Yes, dear. No, dear. Whatever you think, dear. Can I get you anything while I'm up?* Always trying to get him to notice her, always doing everything for him.

Him, him, him.

"I'm afraid we do talk this way sometimes with the boys around," Scott said. "Certainly not all the time. Half the time I'm just dropping them off or picking them up. Gina and I might not say any-thing to each other for a week."

"Sometimes he just sits out in the car and won't come in," she said. "If I need to give him a message, I'll tell Colt."

Officer Franklin sighed.

"What's wrong?" Scott asked.

"Nothing," the officer said. "It's not my place to judge."

"What do you mean?"

"It's just . . . all this pretty much confirms what I said about them running away. We're not in the clear, but it's certainly better than a kidnapping situation."

It definitely was, but it depressed Gina to think that she might have driven the boys away. Could it really be that bad around here? Bad enough for them to want to run away?

Officer Franklin started inching his way toward the front door. "I think I've got enough here to make a report. And I need to get back to the station and start disseminating this information, put out an APB, get our guys to start keeping an eye out for your boys."

"What should we do?" Gina said.

"Well, one of you needs to stay here at all times. There's a good chance after they miss a few meals or it gets dark, they might give up on this scheme. And stay by the phone. If anyone else calls, keep the conversations short."

"Should we tell anyone else what's going on?" Scott said. "Seems like if more people know, more people can help us look."

"That's up to you," the officer said. "You may just want to wait a little while before spreading the word, in case they come home in a few hours. But if they don't, and we still don't know where they are tomorrow, then by all means, get the word out. That happens, and we'll be doing the same thing."

He opened the front door then turned. "You folks heard about President Kennedy talking to the whole country tonight?"

"No," Scott said. "Why? What's going on?"

"I don't know," he said. "Heard it over the radio on my way here. Must be something big. The buzz is it's something to do with the Russians, or maybe Cuba."

Gina didn't care about the news. Her boys were gone. Nothing else mattered. Not Russia or Cuba or anything the president had to say on TV.

Nothing.

12

Colt didn't know how long he had lain there on the grass crying. Probably just a few minutes. When he stood and looked down the road, the bus with his brother was long gone. And it was all his fault. He didn't know what to do. It had all happened so fast.

A loud clicking noise caught his attention. Off to his left, the last tank-carrying railroad car had just passed by. The end of the Army caravan of trucks was also in sight. Back toward the diner, a small line had formed by the door of the correct bus. He ran back to talk with their driver. Maybe he could do something. The driver stood by the door, nodding to people as they boarded. "Help me!" Colt shouted. "Someone just took my little brother."

Everyone looked at him. "What?" the bus driver said. "What did you say?"

"My little brother, Timmy. He just left on that other bus, the one that was right over there. The one that went that way." He pointed down the road.

"You mean he got on the wrong bus?" the man said.

"No . . . I mean yes, but not by himself. A man took him. A man wearing a gray hat."

The driver's face showed instant concern. He squinted as he looked down the road.

"You can't see it anymore," Colt said. "I ran after it, but it was going too fast."

"Why do you believe a man took him? Maybe your brother just made a mistake."

"Because he did!" Colt yelled.

"You sure it wasn't your dad?" a lady asked.

"Yes, I'm sure! Besides, the bus was going the wrong way. And I know the man took him because of what the waitress in the diner said."

"What did she say?" the bus driver asked.

"I was in the bathroom, and when I came out, Timmy was gone. She said our father came and took him. But our dad isn't with us. We're traveling alone. My dad's in Daytona Beach, at work. We were going to Savannah to visit our aunt and uncle. A man took him, I'm telling ya!"

The bus driver looked down the road again, then at the line of passengers. Everyone stared at him.

"You know where that bus is going?" the same lady asked.

The bus driver shook his head. "I don't have all the routes memorized, just mine. I only got this job a few weeks ago." He looked down at Colt. "Do you know where that bus is headed? Did you get the bus number or license plate, even part of it?"

"No."

"You better call the police," the lady said.

"When are we gonna get back on the road?" a man asked.

"In a few minutes," the bus driver said. "The rest of you go on and board. I'm gonna go inside and call the police, get this little boy situated. I'll be right back." He started walking toward the diner and said to Colt, "C'mon. The police will know what to do."

Once inside, the bus driver asked Colt to point out the waitress he had talked to, the one who'd seen the man leave with Timmy. She saw them talking and came right over. "Ma'am, this little boy's saying some guy ran off with his little brother."

"I know, I feel awful about it." She looked

down at Colt. "I had no idea. I thought he was your father."

"Well, I need to get my bus back on the road. I didn't see anything anyway, so I don't know how I can help the police. Can you call them for me? I mean, for him? The only thing I can verify is that I do remember him traveling with a little boy. He's not making that up."

"Oh, I know he's not making it up," the waitress said. "I saw them over there in the booth. Your little brother was eating a slice of apple pie, right?"

Colt nodded.

"Great," the bus driver said. "So, can you take care of this? I gotta get back on the road."

"I suppose," she said. "You have any suitcases?" she asked Colt.

"Just our book bags. They're sitting on the seat."

"Well, hurry back and get them. And I'll call the police, get them headed this way."

Colt ran out the door toward the bus. "Excuse me," he shouted to the people in line. "I need to get my stuff off the bus." People by the door stepped aside. He ran in and down the aisle, found their book bags, and grabbed them. They were mostly filled with clothes, not books, so they were light. He ran out and passed the bus driver heading back toward the bus.

"I hope you find him," he said. "Sorry I can't stay and help you."

Colt said thanks and kept running toward the door. When he got inside, the waitress was already on the phone near the cash register. After she got off the phone with the police, she walked Colt back to the booth, and he sat down. People stared at him the whole way.

"Why don't you have a seat until the police get here?" she said.

But he couldn't eat.

Within ten minutes, a single police car pulled up to the diner, lights and siren flashing. Two officers got out and hurried through the door. The waitress met them and pointed in Colt's direction. All three of them came toward his table. Everyone, including those outside, stopped whatever they were doing to look.

Five minutes had passed since the bus that was supposed to take Timmy and Colt to Savannah had pulled out of the parking lot. It was all Colt could do not to start crying again as it faded from view.

"You the one who lost his little brother?" the older and shorter of the two policemen said.

Colt hated how he put it. "I didn't lose him. A man took him."

"How do you know that?"

"Because Timmy would never leave me, not with a stranger, unless he was tricked somehow. We were on our way to visit our uncle and aunt in

Savannah. I just went into the bathroom a minute, and when I came out, he was gone."

"We were told he left on a bus."

"He did, but the wrong bus."

"You sure it was the wrong bus?"

"Of course I'm sure. I know which bus was ours."

"You think your little brother did?"

Colt thought a moment. "I think so, but that's not the point. The point is, he left with a strange man. I told him to wait right there till I came out. But for some reason, he didn't listen. Instead he got up and followed this man."

"I saw the man he's talking about," the waitress said. "He had a bunch of comic books in his hand. The boy was staring at them as he walked away."

"That's how he did it," Colt said. "Timmy loves comic books."

Finally, the cop started writing this down. He looked outside, through the glass windows. "All the buses are gone?" he asked the waitress.

"Last one just left a few minutes ago."

"Do we know where this bus was headed? The one carrying your little brother?"

"No," Colt said. "I asked my bus driver, but he didn't know. I know it was going south, back towards Florida."

"We're still in Florida," the younger cop said.

"I mean, he was heading south. Aren't we close to Georgia?"

"Yeah, but we're not there yet. But if he was

heading south, there's a good chance his destination was somewhere in Florida." He looked at the older officer. "Can't we just find out where this bus is headed? Have someone waiting there at the next stop to pick them up?"

"It's not that easy," the older officer said. "He's probably already in downtown Jacksonville by now. There's a dozen different ways he could turn from there. I've had lots of cases involving Greyhound buses. There's hundreds of different routes and bus stations all over the state. We don't have the manpower to put a guy on each one. And besides, this sounds like a kidnapping. That means we have to get the FBI involved. They're gonna want to run point on something like this."

"Why's that?"

"It's federal law. Ever since the Lindbergh baby got kidnapped thirty years ago, the FBI's got jurisdiction on kidnappings."

The FBI? Kidnapping?

Just hearing him use those words, Colt thought he was going to be sick.

13

For the last half hour, Colt had been sitting in the booth at the diner. He didn't understand why no one had started looking for Timmy yet. He could be anywhere by now.

During the wait, another caravan of Army trucks had driven by, generating a whole new flurry of stares and speculation from a whole new group of customers. Now everyone was talking about President Kennedy coming on the television tonight, trying to guess what he might say. They all seemed to be in agreement that, whatever it was, these caravans of trucks and tanks were part of it.

All he knew was, the police were not looking for his brother, and they weren't letting him leave the diner. He had been told to "stay put." The older officer had gone back out to his car and made several calls on the radio. His partner appeared to be walking around outside talking to the people standing around. After a few moments listening to him, they took turns shaking their head no.

Meanwhile, his brother was sitting beside a total stranger, getting farther and farther away.

Finally, the older policeman left his squad car and walked toward the younger officer. As he talked, the younger man nodded. They both looked in Colt's direction then started walking his way. Everyone's eyes now followed them, not the truck caravan. The policemen walked up to the waitress, who stood behind the counter about fifteen feet away. "We've got to go. There's been an accident a few minutes south of here. Some idiot ran a red light, smacked right into the side of an Army truck."

"What about the boy?" the waitress said.

"It's like I said, it's a kidnapping, the FBI's jurisdiction. I was just told they've been notified and they're on their way."

"Here?"

"Of course here."

"Hey, Syd, shouldn't the boy's parents be told? They been called yet?" It was the younger police officer. The older officer looked at the waitress.

"I don't know if they've been called," the waitress said. "I don't think so."

"Well, look, we gotta go. Can you make sure that happens? Hey, kid," the younger cop said, looking at Colt. "Give her your telephone number."

The cops turned and hurried out the door. Moments later, the squad car sped off, sirens wailing and lights flashing.

The waitress came over to Colt. "The FBI is coming. They'll know what to do. Here . . ." She handed him her pen and pulled a napkin out of the holder. "Can you write your telephone number down?"

He certainly didn't want anyone calling his parents. Not yet anyway. They'd kill him if they knew what he had done. "They're probably not home. They both work during the day. How about I call my Aunt Rose? They're the ones we were taking the bus to go see. They live in Savannah."

"I suppose that'll be okay," she said. "Just make

sure they call your parents as soon as they get home from work."

"I will."

She looked down at the empty table. "Still not hungry?"

"No."

"How about something to drink?"

"I don't have enough money."

"It's on the house."

"Maybe a Coca-Cola then."

"You want me to make that a cherry Coke?"

"Yes, ma'am."

"Coming right up." She walked away.

He reached down on the seat and picked up his brother's Hulk comic book, opened up the first few pages. He'd read it maybe twice already, mainly looking at the pictures. But he was glad for anything to occupy his mind.

"You like comic books?" The waitress set down his cherry Coke.

"What? No, this is my brother's. I like them okay, but I'm more into collecting baseball cards."

"Really? My nephew does that. He's about your age. Who do you got?"

He knew she was just trying to be nice. He didn't really feel like talking. "I got a whole shoe box full of them under my bed. Got two or three of the best players."

"How'd you get so many?" she asked.

"We buy 'em every time the ice cream truck

comes by. For a nickel you get five cards and a piece of Bazooka gum. I keep the good ones in that shoe box and the ones I wanna trade in a cigar box. When my friends come over, we got this game we play on the patio. My mom says it's gambling, but my dad says it's not really, so we keep doing it." Maybe he didn't mind talking about it, after all. And it was getting his mind off the bad things going on.

"I think my nephew plays the same game," she said. "You toss them across the patio, see who gets closest to the wall."

"That's it. The closest one wins them all. I always try to get leaners."

"Leaners?" she asked.

"Yeah, if you do it just right, they flip up just as they get to the wall and lean against it. If the other guys can't knock it down, it's an automatic win."

"You pretty good at that?"

"Better than anyone else on my street," he said.

"Hey, Doris, we got paying customers over here. You gonna stand there all day yapping?"

Colt looked up toward the deep voice. Looked like the cook. He'd come out of the kitchen wearing a T-shirt and a dirty white apron.

"I'll be right back," Doris whispered. She walked toward the man. "Have a heart, Ed. The boy's having a bad time." She was talking quietly, but Colt heard every word. "His brother's missing, some guy took him on one of those buses

79

that was here awhile ago. I'll only be a few more minutes. FBI's on their way. Besides, Sadie and Joan said they'd cover for me a few minutes."

The cook looked at the two other waitresses. One was refilling a cup of coffee by the counter, the other wiping down a table.

"Anyway, we're in a lull till the dinner crowd starts to show up."

"Not if another bus pulls up."

"Oh . . . get on back into the kitchen. You're fussing over nothing."

He made a face, then started to turn around but stopped. Something out the front window had caught his eye. "Looks like they're here."

She turned to look, then Colt did the same. A large black car had just pulled up. Two men in dark suits and dark hats got out. Both wore white shirts and thin black ties. They headed right for the front door of the diner. Instantly, he tensed up. They looked just like the FBI guys in the movies, serious faces, eyes looking straight ahead.

When they got a little closer, he could see little wrinkles around their eyes. Both men looked older than the police officers.

Doris walked up to them. "You guys from the FBI?"

Everybody stared at them now, but some looked back and forth, first at them, then at Colt. He heard the agents say yes, they were. Both showed her their IDs. He could see the blue FBI letters clearly from his seat. "I'm Special Agent Victor Hammond," the first one said. "And this is my partner, Nate Winters."

Then they both looked right at Colt.

14

Special Agent Victor Hammond had a gut feeling about this when they had gotten the call. In his experience, most kidnapping cases were nothing more than short-term custody battles between divorced parents. Usually the culprit was a dad fed up with how little he got to see his children under the new arrangement. And usually, once she got her kids back, the ex-wife didn't want to press charges. If her ex-hubby went to prison, the alimony and child support would dry up. And the fathers, facing life in prison on a kidnapping charge, would suddenly have a change of heart and promise to behave from now on.

But this situation felt different.

Vic glanced over at the boy sitting in the booth. A scared look in his eyes. Vic leaned over to his partner Nate, who was smoking a cigarette, and whispered, "Let's go easy on him."

"Sure, Vic."

He and Nate had worked together off and on since the forties, during the war. Vic trusted no one more.

"Wow, you guys got here fast," the waitress said. "Isn't your office downtown?"

Vic nodded.

"That's thirty minutes south of here," she said. "The police couldn't have put in the call more than ten minutes ago. Were you already in the neighborhood?"

"That's classified," Nate said. He liked to give that answer to nosy questions.

"Something to do with all these Army trucks and tanks?" she asked.

"Something like that."

"What's the boy's name?" Vic asked.

"Sorry, I never asked."

They walked over to the boy. "Mind if I sit down?" Vic asked, pointing at the empty seat across the table.

"No."

Vic took off his hat and sat in the booth. "Pull up a chair, Nate." He did his best to sound friendly and at ease. "I understand your brother has gone missing?"

"He isn't missing. Some man took him. They drove off in a bus together a little while ago, and no one's even started looking for him."

"And you definitely didn't know this man?"

"I never saw him before. He wasn't even on our bus. They got on a bus going south, back toward the city. Our bus was going north, toward Savannah."

"Who's in Savannah?" Vic asked.

"Our aunt and uncle," the boy said.

"Where are your parents?"

"Back in Daytona, where we live." The boy shifted in his seat.

This seemed a little strange to Vic. And the way the boy was tensing up just now, he was giving off signals that he was hiding something. "Mind if I ask what you and your brother were doing traveling on a bus, on a Monday? Isn't this a school day?"

A long pause. The kid was trying to think up a good one.

"It . . . usually is. But we got the day off. Just today, to visit Uncle Mike and Aunt Rose."

"Why?" Vic asked. "Why didn't your parents send you on Friday, when you'd have two whole days to visit? Don't you have to be back in school tomorrow?"

The boy looked away. He was about to cry any minute.

"What's your name?" Vic asked gently.

"Colt," he said. "My little brother's name is Timmy."

"How old are you, Colt?"

"I'm eleven, Timmy's six."

He needed to press harder, pull on these threads a little more. "Your parents know what happened? About your brother, I mean?"

He shook his head no. "They're at work. I

haven't called them yet. They wouldn't be home if I did. I guess my Uncle Mike was supposed to call them once we got to Savannah."

"So, have you called them, your aunt and uncle?"

"Not yet. I was going to just before you got here."

"You sure they're home?"

"Aunt Rose is. She's a housewife. She's always home, like my mom *used* to be."

He said this with a pronounced sadness, even looked down as he finished the sentence. If Vic's hunch was correct, a story was taking shape. He glanced at Nate, who nodded. Nate was probably thinking the same thing. "You and your brother go to the same school?"

"Yeah," the boy said. "But just for one more year. Next year, I start going to junior high. But . . ." He took a deep breath. "Why are you asking me all these questions? Shouldn't you be out there looking for my brother? Figuring out where that bus is going?"

Vic wished it was that simple, but he had worked several cases involving Greyhound buses. There were so many routes and so many different stations, just in Florida alone. To make matters worse, he'd already been told almost every available agent in the South was going to be pulled off regular duty because of this business with Cuba. Something the whole country was going to find out about tonight, after the president went on television.

Normally, a little boy getting snatched at a diner by some creep would take precedence over anything else. But not now, with maybe the whole world being blown to bits. That was the buzz around the watercooler downtown. All the secrecy surrounding these troop movements heading south. The special agent in charge of their field office in Orlando had hinted that some kind of D-Day invasion of Cuba might happen before the week was out.

Vic couldn't fathom it.

"Look, son," Nate said, "this is a little more complicated than that. The information we got said the bus driver who left you here didn't even know which bus it was or where it was going, except it was heading south. Isn't that right?"

"Yes, sir," Colt said.

Vic wished Nate would lighten up a little. The boy was definitely hiding something, but his little brother really was missing. "And I'm sure you've seen all those tanks and trucks going by today," Vic said. Colt nodded. "They're causing all kinds of problems, car accidents, traffic jams, all kinds of things. A lot of law enforcement officers have their hands full right now. We might be handling this case without a lot of help. So, we need to ask these questions so we know what we're dealing with. You understand?"

Colt nodded again. "I guess." He glanced out the window. "You know what's going on out there? Are we going to war?"

"Let's not worry about that now," Vic said. "I got just a few more questions, then we can call your aunt. What was her name again?"

"Rose."

"Right, Rose. Okay . . . so what time did your mother drop you off at school this morning?"

"The same time she always did."

"But didn't you just say," Nate interjected, "your parents gave you the day off school to visit your aunt and uncle in Savannah?"

"What? Oh yeah," Colt said. "They did. I meant what time they dropped us off at the bus station."

"C'mon, Colt. Be straight with me," Vic said. "You were telling the truth the first time, weren't you? Your mom dropped you and your brother off at school this morning. Then you guys left school for some reason and got on a bus going to Savannah. Isn't that what really happened?"

Colt's mouth hung open. Tears filled his eyes.

"I'll bet your folks don't even know you got on that bus, you and your brother. Do they?"

Colt shook his head no.

"Did your aunt and uncle even know you two were coming for a visit?"

Again, he shook his head no.

Vic leaned forward on the table, tried to form a gentle look on his face. "Why, Colt? Were you guys running away? Is that what was going on here? Some problems at home between your mom and your dad?"

Colt put his face in his hands and burst into tears.

Vic hated being right about stuff like this.

15

At this point, Colt just wanted to run. Go anywhere, be anywhere but here.

But how could he? The two FBI agents were standing right behind him. Somehow, they had figured out his whole scheme. It was shot to pieces now. Nothing had gone the way he'd planned. He should've listened to Murph, his best friend. Murph lived across the street. He'd told Colt not to do this, said it could never work. Colt thought he was just being negative. He could be that way sometimes.

This time Murph was right.

Colt looked at the telephone. How could he tell Uncle Mike and Aunt Rose what he had done? He was supposed to show up there with Timmy. They would've been upset at first, because of the surprise, maybe even get a little angry. But he figured since they were so nice, they'd get over it quickly and shift their focus to the reason he and Timmy were there. They'd start asking them questions about how bad things had gotten at home between Mom and Dad. The way they were treating them now, and had been for months. Colt's parents would be the ones getting in trouble.

But now Timmy was gone, and it was all his fault.

"You know the number?" It was the FBI agent who smoked, the meaner one.

"I wrote it down." Colt pulled the napkin out of his pocket, unwrinkled it, and set it on the counter next to the telephone.

"Take your time," Vic, the nicer one, said. "You know how to reverse the charges? Want me to handle that?"

"No, I can do it." Colt dialed the operator, told her what he was trying to do, gave her the number. A few moments later, he heard her and Aunt Rose talking on the phone. As soon as she heard it was him calling, she instantly said she'd accept the charges. The operator connected them.

"Colt, that you? What's wrong, honey? Why are you calling?"

"Yes, it's me, Aunt Rose." He was about to say everything was all right, but it wasn't. "It's kind of a long story, Aunt Rose. Mom and Dad are separated and—"

"What?"

"Mom and Dad are separated. They're not getting along for some reason. They won't tell us why. It's been going on since last Christmas."

"Last Christmas? That's almost a year. They've been separated all this time?"

"Yeah, and see, the thing is, they've been making Timmy and me lie about it, all this time, to everyone. Folks in the family, in our neighborhood, even at our school. Timmy and I were getting really tired of it. And the way they were treating us. We were so unhappy, all the time."

"I'm so sorry, Colt," she said. "Little boys shouldn't have to deal with things like that."

No, they shouldn't, he thought. But that was something he wanted to hear her say with him standing there in her living room, him and Timmy. Wait till she hears the rest of what I have to say, he thought.

"You better get to the main point," the smoking FBI agent said. "It's long distance."

"Give him a minute, Nate," Vic said.

"Listen, Aunt Rose, that's not why I called. Something's happened. Something bad."

"What's the matter?" she said.

"It's Timmy, he's . . ." Colt started to lose it. He couldn't say the word. Vic, the nicer agent, took the phone from him as he started to cry.

"Ma'am, I'm sorry, but Colt is pretty upset. I better explain, at least what I know. Give him a minute to calm down." Vic reached over on the counter for a clean napkin and handed it to Colt.

"Who are you? What's going on?"

"I'm Special Agent Victor Hammond, with the FBI."

"FBI?"

"Yes, the FBI. You already heard Colt talking about the problems he's having at home. Apparently, he and Timmy decided to run away this morning. After their mom dropped them off at school, they hopped on a Greyhound bus heading for Savannah, intending to visit you and your husband. Are you . . . what's your relationship to Colt's parents?"

"I'm his mother's younger sister. Mike and I had a feeling something wasn't quite right in their relationship, Scott seemed so—"

"Scott's his father's name?"

"Yes, Scott and Gina. That's my sister's name. But I don't understand . . . you said they took a Greyhound bus to Savannah. Where are they now?"

"We're about thirty minutes north of Jacksonville, in a diner off US-1."

"A diner? What are you doing there? Did Colt and Timmy miss their bus?"

"I'm afraid it's much worse than that. But listen, you better just let me explain. You keep asking questions and this phone call's gonna cost you a fortune."

"Okay, I'm sorry. Please, continue."

"The bus stopped here for people to get a snack and use the restroom. During that time, Colt went to the bathroom by himself. When he came out, Timmy was gone."

"I told him to stay put," Colt said. "But he didn't listen."

"Gone?" Rose said. "What do you mean, gone?" She sounded frantic.

"It appears that someone took him, a man wearing a gray hat."

"Oh Lord . . . no."

"A waitress saw him—this man—leading Timmy out the door of the diner while Colt was in the bathroom. It looks like he lured him away with comic books."

"Oh no, please, God."

She was crying, but he had to continue. "Colt ran outside in time to see Timmy and this man riding south on another bus."

"Where?"

"We don't know where right now. It was heading toward Jacksonville, but once it got there, we have no idea which direction it went. This all just happened about thirty minutes ago."

"Can't you do something? We've got to find him! We've got to get Timmy back!"

"We're going to do everything we can. Right now, I need to get word to his parents. Colt said they're both still at work. He knows his own number but doesn't have those numbers memorized, said they're written down on a pad next to the telephone at home. Do you have those numbers by any chance?"

"I believe I have Gina's work number, but not Scott's. This is terrible." She was crying again. "Excuse me, I have to get some tissues."

"Ma'am?" She was gone. He heard noises on the other end.

"I found Gina's work number," she said when she returned.

She gave it to him, and he wrote it down.

"Can I ask you a favor?" she said. "Would you let me try to reach her first? I understand you need to talk with them yourself, but I'd rather she hear something like this from family. It's going to be horrible no matter who tells her, but it might be a little less painful for her if she hears it from me first."

"I guess we can do that, but I will need to talk to her right after. Call me when you're done."

"Okay. Is there anything you want me to ask her?"

"We're going to need a recent picture of Timmy to put out over the wire."

"How's she's supposed to get the picture to you?"

"My partner Nate and I are gonna drive Colt down there now. It might take us a few hours, with all the traffic. Tell her to have it ready when we get there. We'll be contacting all the bigger police departments in central and northern Florida, see if they can get some squad cars to patrol the bus stations. Maybe we'll get lucky. But it'll be a lot better if we have a picture to work with."

"I don't understand," she said. "What do you mean by *some* squad cars? A little boy's been kidnapped by a strange man. What could be more important than that? Every policeman in every city should be out looking for him."

How could he explain this? "I agree with you, ma'am. They should be. But something big is going on in the country right now. I'm not sure if you're seeing anything in Savannah, but we're seeing them all over the place here in Florida."

"You mean the Army trucks and soldiers?"

"Yes," Vic said. "President Kennedy's getting on television tonight to explain what's going on. I don't know everything. But I do know this, it's making life pretty crazy for law enforcement right now, on every level. But I promise you, we're going to do everything we can to find Timmy."

There was a long pause. Vic heard her quietly crying on the other end. Finally she said, "How's Colt holding up? He must feel terrible about this."

Vic looked at the boy sitting in the booth, staring at the floor. "He's holding up okay, I guess. But he's very worried about his little brother." At that, Colt looked up at him. Tears filled his eyes.

"But please tell him for us, for his Uncle Mike and me, that we love him and we're going to pray nonstop that God protects Timmy and brings him home safe. And also tell him that we're gonna drive down there tonight, to Daytona Beach, to be with him and his folks."

"I'm sure he'll be glad to hear that," Vic said.

"Is there anything else I need to know?" she said.

"I'll take care of anything else. You going to call her now?"

"As soon as I get off the phone with you."

"Then we'll wait here at the diner a few minutes. Have her call me here after you've talked with her. She won't be able to reach me once we get on the road."

"Okay, I'll do that."

He gave her the number to the diner then heard Rose start to cry again and say, "What am I going to tell Gina?"

16

The black-and-white cityscape appeared on the small square screen of her television set, accompanied by the soothing voice of the network commentator: "And now. . . *The Edge of Night*, brought to you by . . . Tide. The one that works the hardest to get your clothes the cleanest clean there is." She waited as the familiar piano and organ music finished playing the theme song.

Gina hadn't been able to watch her stories for so long.

She sat back in her chair, knowing this show couldn't take her mind off her missing boys. Nothing could. But maybe some noise would help to fill the empty space.

She glanced out the front window. Scott had left the house five minutes ago, said he couldn't sit there anymore doing nothing. He was going to drive around, see if he could find the boys. Since the policeman had left, the two of them had tried to stay out of each other's way. It felt hopelessly awkward. There was so much to talk about, so much that needed to be said. But now just wasn't the time. It would only end in another fight, and a big one. Half her thoughts were about blaming Scott for creating the situation they were facing in the first place, by cheating on her with that secretary. And for the ongoing neglect of his sons since he'd moved out. The other half were even worse: flashes of memories—too many of them— of her yelling at the boys for little things that seemed like a petty overreaction now. She'd never used to do that; she wasn't a yeller. But now she did it so much, Colt and Timmy felt the need to run away.

To escape from her.

The TV characters blurred as tears filled her eyes. The phone rang. She jumped and hurried to turn off the television. She stood by the phone, took a deep breath, wiped the tears from her eyes, and picked up the receiver. "Hello?"

"Gina?"

It wasn't them. It sounded like her sister, Rose. And she sounded upset. "Rose? Is that you?"

"It's me, Gina. So, you're home? I thought you didn't get off till five."

"I don't, normally. Why are you calling? Is everything okay?"

"Up here it is. How are you doing?"

Could she know? "Not very well, to tell you the truth."

"Because of the boys?"

"You know about the boys?"

"I've spoken with Colt."

"You've talked with Colt! When? Are they with you?" *Please say yes.*

"No, they're not. I wish they were."

What did she mean by that? Gina heard her inhale deeply over the phone. "Rose, when did you talk to Colt?"

"Just a few minutes ago. He's with some agents from the FBI."

"The FBI?"

"I'm afraid so."

She felt instant relief. But why did Rose say "I'm afraid so"? "Then they're safe, right? The FBI has them?"

"Gina, listen . . . there's something I have to tell you."

"What, Rose? What's the matter?"

"Colt's all right. He's a little shaken up, but that's all."

"What about Timmy? Where's Timmy?" A too-long pause. "Rose, where's Timmy? Isn't he with Colt?"

"Gina . . . something's happened. Is Scott there with you?"

"Scott? No, Scott's out looking for the boys. Rose, tell me. What's the matter?" She heard Rose begin to cry on the other end. Her legs began to feel weak. She sat in a hardback chair.

"Timmy is missing," Rose said. "He's not with Colt."

"What do you mean, missing? Why isn't he with Colt? Colt would never leave his little brother."

"He didn't mean to. He only left him a few minutes while he went to the bathroom. Apparently, some man lured him out the door with comic books. They were at some bus stop or diner, a little north of—"

"No!" Gina screamed into the phone. "He can't be missing. Oh God, no!" She let go of the receiver and dropped to the floor. She couldn't believe what she was hearing. It seemed like her whole body was sobbing. How could Timmy be missing? Taken away by a strange man? This couldn't be real. She pulled her knees close to her chest and buried her face as she cried.

A few moments later, she heard a faint voice

calling her name over and over through the receiver. She didn't want to, but she picked up the phone.

"Gina? Gina, please pick up the—"

"I'm here," she managed somehow.

"I know," Rose said. "This is horrible. I can't believe I'm having to tell you these things. I wish I didn't."

"You said they were at a bus stop," Gina said. "Where was this? Were they on a bus?"

"Colt and Timmy took a Greyhound bus this morning. I guess their plan was to come here, to see Mike and me. Really, I don't know what's going on, but Colt said you guys are having some problems and you've been separated awhile. I guess whatever's happening was really starting to bother them, and for some reason, they thought coming here might help the situation. Or maybe they were just trying to escape. I don't know. The bus stopped awhile at this diner, and that's when . . . that's when Timmy and Colt got separated."

She pulled herself back to her feet. "So Timmy took a bus somewhere? Is that what you're saying?"

"Looks that way. I don't have that many details. The FBI agent wants to talk to you. He said they're going to leave in a few minutes to take Colt back to Daytona."

"But what about Timmy? What are they doing

to find him? Do they know which way the bus went? Where it's going?"

"I don't think they do. He said something about there being too many buses and bus stations all over Florida and not having enough people to search them all, because of all these Army trucks."

"Army trucks? How can that be more important than finding a little boy?"

Rose started crying. "I don't know, Gina. It's not. I don't know what's going on. But listen, Mike and I are gonna drive down there to be with you guys. I called him before I called you. He's on his way home from work right now. We'll leave as soon as he gets here."

"Thanks, Rose. That means a lot."

"I don't know what we can do, but we'll help any way we can. I'm gonna call that FBI agent as soon as I hang up. His name is Vic Hammond. He's supposed to call you in a few minutes."

"I'll be here. I'm supposed to stay right by the phone."

"Gina, Mike and I are going to keep praying that God will protect Timmy. Don't give up hope."

Gina said she would try not to, but that was just something to say. What little hope she had been clinging to had just shattered.

17

Scott decided to make one more stop before heading back to their house on Seaview Avenue. He hadn't found the boys or even a trace of them. But then, he hadn't really expected to. There was at least a chance he could have been successful, and it had gotten him out of the house for a while. The tension between him and Gina was too much to bear.

He had stopped and asked several children playing throughout the neighborhood if any of them had seen Colt or Timmy. None had. He wasn't looking forward to this last stop and didn't really expect to find the boys here. But there was a chance, so he had to make the effort.

Old Weldon lived four doors down from them, and Scott had always considered him something of a wacko. An overly talkative, thoroughly boring wacko. But Scott knew the boys—particularly Colt—loved to play in Weldon's bomb shelter. Weldon didn't allow it, but Colt and his friends occasionally snuck in his backyard when he wasn't home to use it as a fort when they played army.

The last time they had—at least, the last time Scott knew about—was a month ago. Weldon had found Colt, Murph from across the street, and one other boy whose name Scott had forgotten, hiding inside. He had about blown his stack. The boys' moms, including Gina, heard him yelling at them from inside their homes. They wouldn't put it past old Weldon to take it upon himself to start spanking them with a paddle. So the three moms had run over there to rescue the boys.

Colt had told Scott about this the following weekend when he picked the boys up. He had to laugh as Colt mimicked his mother's part in the shouting match that ensued. Weldon considered his bomb shelter to be serious business, life or death serious. He'd spent almost fifteen hundred dollars having it built two years ago and wasn't about to let it become some kind of playhouse for a bunch of spoiled brats running loose all over the neighborhood.

Scott pulled into Weldon's driveway to find him unloading boxes from the back of his station wagon. Weldon lived on the corner lot, so his garage faced the adjoining street. And Weldon's home was the only one on the street that actually had a real hill. The entire east coast of Florida was notoriously flat. But in Daytona Beach, a handful of homes built within a block of the ocean had sand dunes on their property. Weldon's was one of them. It was a matter of some pride for him, since it allowed him to save tons of dirt being shipped in when they'd built his bomb shelter. He used the savings to add an additional three feet of living space to the dungeon he and his aging wife planned to live in, all alone, should the "big one" come.

Gina had said she'd rather be vaporized by an atom bomb than face that fate.

As Scott got out of the car, Weldon turned to face him, his arms still filled with boxes. He snarled a moment before shifting to a fake smile.

"Afternoon, Mr. Weldon. Could I talk to you a moment?"

"Can I set these boxes down first?"

"Sure, can I give you a hand?"

"Not with these, but there's three more just like them in the back of the car there. Could you get those for me?"

"Sure, I can do that. You want me to bring them into the house?"

"Not the house, the fallout shelter."

"Really?" Scott said as he opened the back door of the station wagon. "That's actually what I'm here to talk to you about."

Weldon stopped walking, set the boxes on the hood of his car. "Finally gonna take my advice and put one in? Afraid it's too late, my friend. I think the big one's just around the corner now. I'm sure you're seeing all these military trucks and tanks driving through toward south Florida."

Scott stood up behind the car, the boxes stacked, ready to be picked up. "You think we're going to war with Cuba?"

"Not Cuba," Weldon said. "We could crush them like a bug if we wanted to. That Bay of Pigs fiasco last year, Castro only won that 'cause he was fighting a bunch of other Cubans. Our Marines had gone in there, or even just a few of our jet fighters, Castro would be gone by now. I think we're about ready to go to war with the Russkies."

"The Russians?"

"Don't you read the papers?" Weldon pulled the cigar out of his mouth, flicked the inch-long ash on the driveway. "That's what Kennedy's gonna be talking about when he gets on TV tonight. Mark my words, it's the Soviets. They've been sending all kinds of weapons to Castro ever since we invaded the Bay of Pigs. It's all about to hit the fan, my friend. That's why I'm stocking up supplies in the shelter. The big one could come any day now. When it does, Sarah and me will be ready. Looks like we'll be the only ones, at least on this block."

"I would have liked to put one in," Scott said. "We just didn't have the money. I think that's why most of the people on the street don't have one. President Kennedy urged everyone to get one last summer."

"That's because he knows secret things they never talk about on the news," Weldon said. "Classified things. He wouldn't tell everyone to build shelters unless he thought we needed 'em.

He said the same thing in *Life* magazine. *Life* magazine," he repeated, as if that made it more official. "The big one's coming, and that's a fact."

"Maybe so," Scott said, "but everyone can't afford to have one built like you did. And the do-it-yourself versions they're selling are just junk. I checked them out. I'm an engineer. People who get them don't stand a chance in a nuclear attack."

"You might be right," Weldon said. "But I think it's a matter of priorities. People spend money on what they think is most important. You got money for a car, don't you?"

"Yeah, but—"

"A good shelter costs about the same. What good's a car in a nuclear attack? Can't take shelter in that."

Scott realized this conversation was going nowhere. He needed to change the subject. "Mind if I take these boxes into the shelter ahead of you?" He picked them up and started walking toward Weldon.

"Mind if I ask why?"

"Well, it's just . . . there's a slim chance my boys are hiding out in your shelter again."

"What?"

"I'm not saying they are, just saying they might be. They played hooky from school today, and we haven't found them yet. I've been all over the neighborhood, talked to all their friends. No one seems to know where they are. I know the boys liked to use your shelter for a fort."

"They better not be in there. They know they're not supposed to—"

"They're probably not," Scott said. "I just thought if they were, it might be better if I go down there first. And believe me, if they are down there, they'll be severely punished. You have my word on that."

"Well," Weldon said, "I suppose that's okay. You know your way?"

"I think so. It's in the backyard, right? In that hill beside the pool?"

"That's it." He leaned against the fender to let Scott pass by. "You said you're an engineer, right?"

"That's right. I work at GE."

"Engineers travel a lot?"

"Some do, why?"

"It's just I never see you around anymore. Used to see you all the time. Thought maybe you became one of those, you know, traveling sales-men."

"I did change jobs," Scott said, "but I stayed within the company." That's about all he was going to say on the subject. He'd been promoted recently, but it didn't involve more travel. Weldon was just fishing for gossip. Turning around, Scott headed toward the backyard. The boxes were fairly heavy, sounded like they were full of cans.

He followed the walkway around the side of the house, then set the boxes down for a moment to open the wooden gate that led to the pool area.

There was the pool to the left and the rising grassy mound to the right. The sand dune had been re-formed into a makeshift fallout shelter. As he got closer, Scott saw the door that led down a short set of cement stairs. He set the boxes beside it. Should he knock or just walk right in?

He hoped they were there, even at the cost of sitting through Weldon's angry outburst.

18

They were making good time heading toward Daytona Beach. At the moment, and for at least twelve more miles, Vic and his partner Nate were sailing down a section of the new interstate highway called I-95. It wasn't completed yet, not even close. The plan was for it to stretch all the way from Maine to Miami someday.

Today, well . . . even twelve miles was something. No red lights, no traffic jams, no getting stuck behind someone driving half the speed limit and being unable to pass. Just a straight shot traveling at eighty miles an hour (an FBI perk). Then it was off the interstate near Flagler and back on US-1 for the rest of the journey. Vic adjusted his rearview mirror to check on the boy in the backseat. Colt hadn't said a word the last fifteen minutes.

He wasn't asleep, just sitting there staring out the window.

The last thing he'd said was a question, asking if he could roll the window down a few inches to get some fresh air. Nate's cigarette smoke had been gathering like a small cloud in the backseat. Vic had quit last year, to make his wife happy. He'd been after Nate to quit the last few months. Partly to be free of the temptation but also to be free of the smell, especially in close quarters. It had never bothered him all the years he smoked, but now he couldn't stand it.

"Did you ever smoke those?" Nate said.

Vic looked to where Nate was pointing out the window. It was a billboard for Tareyton cigarettes showing a bald guy with a fake black eye, smiling and smoking. Next to him, the caption read "Tareyton smokers would rather fight than switch."

"I tried 'em once," Nate said. "Hated 'em. I'd fight anybody who tried to make me switch." He smiled at his own clever play on words. Nate smoked Camels, nothing fancy. No high-tech carbon filters, no menthol. The same cigarette he'd smoked since they started working together during World War II.

"My mom smokes Tareytons," Colt said.

Vic looked back at him through the rearview

mirror. Colt was still looking out the window.

"She just started smoking this year, after my dad left," he said. "I hate it. I used to sit close to her on the couch watching TV, but now I can't. The smoke from her cigarette always finds me. It can be going in any direction, but as soon as I sit down, it turns and comes right after me. Gets me right in the eyes." He let out a sigh. "So now we can't sit together."

"I know what you mean, Colt," Vic said. "Nate's cigarettes do that to me sometimes."

Nate turned around, looked at Colt over his shoulder. "But kid, we never cuddle on the couch."

Colt laughed out loud. Vic almost did. What a revolting thought. Vic wondered if he could keep the boy talking. "When did your folks split up?"

"They haven't split up," Colt said. "They're just separated, that's what my mom said."

"I know. So when did they separate?"

"Around New Year's. First my mom moved out, then a few days later she came back and my dad moved out. And he's been gone ever since."

"You mind me asking what you hoped to gain by running away?"

Colt wasn't smiling anymore. "It was a dumb idea. I know that now. But I thought it might work."

"What do you mean . . . *work?*" Vic said.

"I thought it might get my parents back

together." He was looking out the window again. "They've been hiding it all this time from everyone. And making us lie and pretend everything is fine. Lying's a sin, you know. A big one. One of the Ten Commandments, even."

"I know."

"So's the seventh commandment," Nate added. "Know which one that is, kid?"

"Nate," Vic scolded. "Never mind, Colt."

"What?" Nate said.

"You know what." *Thou shalt not commit adultery.* That was the commandment Nate was referring to. They had both already figured out that was probably the reason why Colt's parents had split up. Usually was. And seeing as it happened right after New Year's, Vic guessed Colt's mom had caught his dad cheating on her over the holidays.

"That's all right," Colt said. "I don't know all the commandments, not all ten of them. And I don't remember them all in order."

"That's a good thing to work on, Colt. Memorizing the Ten Commandments. It'll keep you out of lots of trouble." Vic still remembered them from when he was a kid in Sunday school. He'd never figured Nate to be one who'd remember them, though. "You ever go to church? Your folks ever take you?"

"We used to go most of the time when my parents were together. We still go sometimes with just my mom, but not every Sunday. Sometimes she's too tired. That's what she says anyway."

"So how did you think getting your aunt and uncle in Savannah involved would help your parents get back together?"

"I don't know," Colt said. "I thought maybe the shock of us running away would get them to start paying attention to us. Maybe they'd listen if other adults talked to them. They sure won't listen when I try, either one of them. They say things like it's too complicated, or I just wouldn't understand, or maybe I'll understand when I'm older. Sometimes they say they just don't want to talk about it, and they look away like . . . *end of discussion*. But I know what they're really saying is they don't want to talk about it to me, 'cause I'm a kid."

"That's gotta be hard," Vic said.

"It is . . . hard."

Vic could hear his voice breaking up.

"I do understand, a little, why they want to hide it," Colt continued. "I see how people treat you different when you're divorced, like there's something wrong with you. Not just adults, but kids do it too. There's only one kid in my whole class whose folks are divorced, and everybody treats him different. He's always getting into fights. People say he steals from stores. Some parents won't even let their kids play with him. I don't want to be like that kid. Why should I get punished because of something my parents did?"

Vic wanted to keep asking Colt more and deeper questions before they reached Daytona. Kids often just didn't know better and would answer a lot more honestly than adults. Once Colt's parents were in the picture, honest information would be a lot harder to come by. People who had been living a lie for ten months were all about hiding things, and they'd probably become very skilled at making up phony answers to curious questions.

But he had to be careful. Colt was in a vulnerable state right now, and he didn't want to exploit that. Especially if this thing turned sour and they weren't able to find his little brother alive, or at all.

19

Scott had left Mr. Weldon's property fifteen minutes ago, after searching his fallout shelter. There was no evidence Colt and Timmy had ever been there. Had they tried, they would have soon been caught by Weldon anyway. Scott had to sit through another of Weldon's ten-minute tirades citing the many evil intentions of those "nasty commie scumbags."

Once again, he'd proclaimed that President Kennedy would be declaring war on the Russians tonight, saying that was the real reason he had blocked off time on all three networks. Scott didn't argue, partly because he wasn't sure Weldon was wrong on that point, but mostly because he wanted the conversation to end as quickly as possible.

Scott got out of his car after pulling up to a 7-Eleven at the corner of A1A. He'd come there to use the telephone booth outside. Of course, there was a phone at the house, and it was only four doors down from Weldon's. But Gina was there, and he didn't want her to overhear his conversation. It would just make her upset. She'd start laying into him about calling work at a time like this. How could he even consider such a thing? He was always climbing the corporate ladder of success. Never satisfied with the status quo. *"Your job, that's all you ever talk about, your job."* His family, always getting the leftovers.

Scott walked up and got inside the phone booth, closed the door.

Gina didn't understand. He was doing all this for her, her and the boys. Not for himself. It had always been for them. That's what it took to get ahead these days. He hadn't been doing anything more than every other man at GE. She hadn't worked a single day outside the home since the day they got married, up until ten months ago when she kicked him out.

And what was she now? Some clerk at a midsized insurance firm, still mostly dependent on his income. She could never understand the pressure he was under at a company like GE, working on the most sophisticated technology being developed anywhere in the world. They were trying to get a man on the moon before this decade was out. That's what the president said. How could she understand anything about the kind of work he did, what it took to pull off something like that?

He dialed his boss's number from memory, shaking his head. He couldn't think of one other husband at work who had to put up with a wife like this. Wives were supposed to be supportive of their husbands, to stay at home, to cook and clean, take care of the kids, be there with dinner ready when he got home, or keep it warm in the oven if he had to come home late.

Okay, in the last few years that had happened a lot. But he wasn't out gallivanting around, chasing women or spending happy hour with the boys at the bar. He was working, and working hard.

"Hello, Mr. Finch's office, Marianne speaking. How can I help you?"

"Hey, Marianne, it's Scott, Scott Harrison. Just checking in. I told Mr. Finch I'd call this afternoon."

"Oh, Mr. Harrison. Have you found your boys yet? Mr. Finch told me what happened."

"Not yet. They'll probably turn up soon. Either by dinner or before it gets dark."

"I hope so. You want to speak with him?"

"Please."

"I'll put you right through."

A few moments later, "Hey, Scott, Finch here. How did you make out? The boys safe and sound?"

"Not yet, Mr. Finch. Still looking for them." He knew Finch wouldn't like the sound of that.

"Hmm, that's not good. I hope you find them soon. Really counting on you to supervise the setup of that big shindig down at the Castaway Beach Motel, our part of it anyway. The lockdown on the main plant shouldn't affect things going on at the Castaway. You know there's over a thousand coming to this thing now. Scientists and CEOs and engineers from all over the US. They've even decided to open it to the public here in Daytona, sort of a goodwill gesture. Let them hear all about our big plans for the future."

"I know, sir. I'm sorry. I thought we would have found them by now. Mark Mitchell's there now. I briefed him on everything this morning before I left."

"Mitchell's good, but he's not you. This is your baby, Scott. A lot of good PR can come out of this, if it's done right. It's done wrong, the opposite can happen."

"I know. I know, sir."

"Can you at least stop in before the day's out? Make sure everything's on track for tomorrow?"

Scott looked at his watch. "Sure, I can do that."

"Great. Let me know if I need to get involved."

"You know I will," Scott said. "But I'm sure everything will be fine. I've been working on this for weeks."

He hung up and got back in his car, decided he better stop in at the house and see Gina before he stopped at the Castaway and checked in on Mitchell's progress.

Hopefully, she'd be there and so would the boys, and they'd have a chat about a fitting punishment for pulling such a stunt and giving them all a scare.

Where was he? Scott was never there when she needed him.

Gina felt like she was losing her mind. She was sick with worry. Where could her little Timmy be? She would cry some more, but she was all cried out. She looked at the telephone again, willing it to ring. She stared at the phone every few seconds, hoping another call would come and erase the terror of that first call: the one from her sister saying Timmy had been stolen.

The FBI agent had told her some things to get ready to assist them in their search. She mentioned they had already given the best photo of Timmy to Officer Franklin. The FBI agent—she had forgotten his name—said not to worry, he'd get the photo himself, or have the Daytona police wire a copy to the FBI.

Since the phone refused to ring, Gina walked outside again and down the sidewalk, trying to get a glimpse of Scott's car. Where could he be? He said he was just going to drive around the neighborhood some more, looking for the boys. How long could that take?

No sign of him. She walked back in the house and let herself drop onto the sofa. How could they expect her to just sit here by the telephone? Did they really think the kidnappers would call with ransom demands? If they did, she could show them a stack of bills. The money in their bank account wouldn't even cover them. If they wanted Scott's family's money, why didn't they kidnap one of them? The kidnappers obviously hadn't done their homework. Scott was sort of the black sheep of the Harrison clan. Why kidnap her little Timmy? Scott's brothers were the wealthy ones; they followed their father into the banking business. Why hadn't they taken one of their kids?

She sat up and buried her face in her hands. What was she saying? She didn't want that either. She loved Colt and Timmy's cousins.

She soon discovered she had at least a few more tears as she heard a car pulling into the driveway.

20

As Scott turned the corner onto his street, his stomach involuntarily cringed. He'd skipped lunch, but it wasn't that. "Please let the boys be here," he said aloud. He looked down the road and picked out their place, just in time to see Gina walk inside the front door.

She was alone.

A few moments later, he pulled into the driveway. He sat in the car, staring at the house, not sure what to think or what to do. A man was supposed to protect his wife and children. It was his job. No, it was more than that; being the protector was part of a man's calling, something ordained by God. His father had always said that.

But Gina had made it impossible.

He got out of the car and walked toward the house. He'd just have to face whatever came and make the best of it. After opening the door, the first thing he noticed was the sound of Gina crying.

Not good.

She was sitting on the edge of the sofa, her head buried in her hands. As soon as she saw him, she stood and ran into his arms. "Oh, Scott . . ." was all she managed to get out before she collapsed into his chest and sobbed even harder.

He put his arms around her and held her tight. It was the first time they had touched this way in almost a year. He stroked her head gently and patted her back. Was she releasing some pent-up anxiety that had built up over the day, or was there some terrible new development? When appropriate, he asked, "What's wrong, Gina? Is there any news?"

She pulled back and looked up at him. Total heartbreak in her eyes. Before she spoke, he braced for something awful.

"He's gone, Scott," she blurted out. "Timmy's gone. Somebody took him. A strange man stole him and took him away on a bus." Tears flowed down her face again.

For a moment, her words did not penetrate. Scott was still mostly focused on comforting her. But when he realized what she said, his legs became weak.

About ten minutes later, Scott and Gina were sitting beside each other on the couch. Scott had a need to know everything she had learned so far, and she had a need to say it. But neither one wanted to utter the words. They were just too awful.

Scott decided to take the lead. First, he blew his nose. He had done some crying too. He couldn't stop it. "So Colt is definitely fine?"

Gina nodded. "He should be here with the FBI agents in about thirty minutes."

"These are the same agents you've already talked to?"

"I only talked to one of them," she said. "His name was Hammer or Hamilton. I don't remember."

"And they're the ones who found Colt?"

"No. I don't think anyone found him." She explained the rest of the story, as much as she knew.

"Colt knows better than to leave Timmy by himself. What was he thinking?"

"Don't go there, Scott. The FBI agent said he already feels terrible about all this. You're only going to make it worse if you start down that road."

Scott stood up and began to pace. "But it's his fault, Gina. You don't think Timmy came up with this scheme, do you?"

"Of course I don't."

"So who else should get the blame, if not Colt?"

"Well," she said, "for starters, how about you?"

"Me?"

"And me," she added quickly. "Both of us. We're equally to blame."

He stopped pacing and turned to face her. "What are you talking about? How are we to blame? If Colt and Timmy had simply stayed in school this morning, like they were supposed to, none of this would have happened."

"That's true. But I've been thinking. Why did

they feel they had to run away? Why did they feel they couldn't talk to either one of us about why they're so unhappy living here?"

She had a point, Scott thought. And not a small one.

"And blaming Colt won't bring Timmy back," she said, "or help us find him."

"You're right," he said. "You're right."

"I am?"

"You are. I've hated what's going on between us these last ten months. I guess I didn't realize how miserable it's been for Colt and Timmy." He sat on the edge of an upholstered chair.

"I had no idea they were so unhappy," Gina said. "I've been so busy working, feels like all the time, then I come home, try to keep up with everything around here. I haven't had time to pay attention to them."

"You said they were heading to Mike and Rose's place?"

She nodded. "But I'm sure they didn't have anything to do with this."

"I wouldn't think that," he said. "Mike and Rose are just fun to be around. Every time they're in town we're mostly laughing and enjoying ourselves. Mike's always cutting jokes at family gatherings. You can always hear Rose's laugh from any room in the house. That's the place I'd have picked if I were going to run away."

"Did I mention they're on their way here now,

Mike and Rose?" Gina stood and walked toward the kitchen, then turned to face him. "Would you like some coffee?"

"No you didn't, and yes I would," he said as he followed her.

"How long does it take to get here from Savannah?" she asked.

"I'd say maybe four or five hours."

"I was just trying to see if I should plan dinner for them."

"I don't think so, Gina. I'm pretty sure they'd get something to eat on the way. Speaking of dinner, what time's it getting to be?" Scott looked at his watch.

"Why, are you going somewhere? Colt and those FBI guys are gonna be here in a little while."

"I know, but I have to take care of something just up the road on A1A. I should be back before they get here."

"Scott . . . what could be more important than being here when your son gets home?"

"I'll be here."

"No, you won't. You say you'll be here. And you may want to be here, but you won't. Something will come up. It always does."

Scott walked toward her, as close as he dared. "Gina, that's not what's gonna happen this time. I'm involved in this big Technology Expo at work. It's been in the paper. Have you heard about it, at the Castaway Beach Motel?"

"No, I don't get much time to read the paper these days."

"There's supposed to be a thousand people showing up. All kinds of scientists, executives, and engineers from all over the country. They're coming here to learn about the space program, and I'm in charge of GE's part in it."

"How wonderful for you." Said in her typical sarcasm. She didn't even look at him when she said it.

Up until this afternoon, he had been thinking it was a pretty wonderful thing for him. But now, it didn't matter. He just wanted Timmy back. "You're wrong, Gina. I care way more about Timmy. But I've got a ton of people depending on me, and I've got to head over there for just a few minutes, let some key people know what's going on. Then I'll be right back, I promise."

"Can't you just call? I don't want to be here by myself when the FBI guys come with Colt."

"I can't do it over the phone." How could he explain this? He thought a moment. "I wish I could explain why, but I just can't. It's too complicated. But I won't get stuck there this time. I'll be back before Colt gets here. I promise."

She didn't say anything. She wouldn't even turn to look at him, just kept setting up the coffee percolator. Finally, she said, "Guess you better go then."

21

"The boy won't come in," Vic said.

"What do you mean, he won't come in?"

It was the husband, Scott Harrison. Vic had already committed both their names to memory. The guy looked to be in his early thirties, dark hair, about six feet tall. Strikingly handsome, Vic had to admit. "Nothing to worry about. He'll be fine for a few minutes in the car. My partner, Nate, is watching him."

"But I want to see him," his mother said.

"Well, he doesn't want to see you at the moment. Neither of you. He's afraid you hate him, said he can't bear to look at you right now, wouldn't know what to say. He feels totally to blame for what happened to his little brother. That's the best I could put together through all his crying. He's settled down a bit now, but I'm sure it'll start right up if either of you go out there. Might be better to leave him be for a little while, let him settle down. Might be a good idea too, if we could talk a little without him here."

"All right," Scott said, "we'll do it your way." He backed up and opened the door the rest of the way to let Vic in.

It was already getting dark outside. Vic turned and tipped his hat to Nate before going in the

123

house. The lamplight in the living room revealed a cozy place, nothing fancy. Basic furniture but clean and tidy. With a closer look, the lighting also revealed how puffy the eyes of both parents were, especially Gina, the mom. He noticed a box of tissues on the coffee table and a brown paper bag filled with tissues lying next to it on the floor.

"What took you so long?" Scott said. "From what you told Gina on the phone, we thought you guys would be here a half hour ago."

"It's almost seven o'clock," Gina said. "We were worried sick. I thought, now I've lost both my boys." Her eyes filled with tears.

"I'm very sorry, ma'am, Mr. Harrison. Couldn't be helped. Ran into a major traffic jam up near Flagler, near where I-95 ends."

"But you're the FBI," Scott said. "Couldn't you just turn on your siren, make everyone move out of the way? I'd think a kidnapped little boy should rate something like that, don't you?"

Vic took off his fedora, tried to remember these folks had had the worst day imaginable. "I certainly would have turned on our siren, sir, if it would've done any good. The problem was, we were backed up on the new highway overpass, up in the air, blocked in by cars on every side. As soon as we got through that mess, we did turn on our siren and beat a path here as quick as we could."

"I'm sorry," Scott said. "We're both just so upset. Please come in and have a seat."

Vic looked at his watch. They still had a few minutes to talk before the president came on TV. He didn't want to miss that. They'd have to watch it here.

Better get right to it. Scott Harrison sat next to his wife on the couch. Vic didn't know if they were pretending, but they didn't seem to be at odds with each other. He took a seat on a tan, squarish chair. "I'm guessing there've been no developments on your end," he said.

"No, nothing," Scott said. "Would you be expecting anything?"

"Not exactly," Vic said. "More like hoping."

"Hoping for what?" Gina said.

"Well, Mrs. Harrison . . ."

"Please, call me Gina."

"And call me Scott."

"Okay, I'm Special Agent Victor Hammond, and my partner outside is Nate Winters. But you can call me Vic. I'd be hoping you might have gotten a phone call with a set of demands."

"You mean like a ransom amount?" Scott said.

Vic nodded. "At least then we'd know what we're dealing with. But to be honest, we weren't really expecting it."

"Why not?" Gina said. "I wasn't expecting that kind of call either. But why weren't you?"

"The evidence points to a crime of opportunity,

125

not a planned event. It's not as if the perpetrator was tracking your boys, looking for the right moment to nab him. He wasn't even on the same bus. He would have no way of knowing your boys were stopping there at that time. It was all just a terrible coincidence. We think he saw Timmy there by himself in that booth, saw the comic books, and decided right then to snatch him. We learned he'd purchased a stack of comic books at that same time from the little general store connected to the diner, and somehow lured Timmy outside. Probably promised him he could have those and a bunch more, if he'd only come out to the bus to get them."

Both parents' faces fell at the sound of this.

Vic didn't want to go on, but he knew he had to. They had to come to grips with what they were facing, or at least could be facing in the days ahead.

"But how did he get Timmy to ride away with him on the bus?" Scott asked. "I can see the first part, Timmy getting tricked to follow him out to the bus. He really loves comic books. But how could this man, this stranger, get him to stay put and ride off with him like that?"

"I'm not sure, Scott. It's hard to know a thing like that. Most likely, he threatened him somehow. We don't know that, but it's one of the things these guys do, take advantage of the kids' fears. All Timmy would have to do is scream bloody

126

murder, and the bus driver would instantly stop and all the passengers nearby would've turned around and confronted this guy. But that's not what usually happens. Usually the kids get terrified and just clam up and cooperate. I'm guessing you never rehearsed something like this with him?"

Scott shook his head no, looked down toward the floor.

"We never even thought about doing something like that," Gina said, reaching for another tissue.

Vic wasn't trying to make them feel guilty. Things like this hardly ever happened. It wasn't something you'd ever expect as a parent. "Well, let me fill you in on what's happening so far. Another agent and a sketch artist are working with the guy who sold the comic books to the kidnapper, and the waitress at the diner. Both of them got a good look at the man. We've already notified the Daytona Beach police that we've got jurisdiction on the case now. They've wired your son's photo to our Orlando office." Or at least they should have by now, Vic thought.

"So you don't need me to find you another one?" Gina said.

"Not right now. We plan to get Timmy's picture and a sketch of the kidnapper wired to every police department and sheriff's office in Florida as soon as possible. We already sent out an APB on this, asking for any squad cars who can to drive by any of the bus depots, keep on the lookout for a man in his late thirties with a gray hat and a dark coat, escorting a little boy wearing a light blue jacket, dungarees, and black sneakers."

At that, Gina just lost it. Maybe Vic had gone too far. He thought it might comfort them to hear that the APB included an accurate description of what Timmy was wearing, but all it did was conjure up a picture in a mother's mind of a scared and lost little boy.

Vic waited a few moments to let Scott comfort his wife. He was again struck by the level of affection they were showing each other. For a moment, he'd forgotten that this whole thing had begun because the two of them couldn't get along and had made life at home so miserable that the boys felt the need to run away.

Finally, Gina composed herself.

Vic looked at his watch and said, "Might be a good time for someone to go out to Colt. The state he's in, I can see him wanting to sit out there all night unless one of you can make something happen. Which of you two is in better shape to talk to him?"

"I don't think either one of us is," Scott said. "But I'll go."

Vic stood and opened the front door for Scott. "Please," he whispered, "be as gentle as you can. See your wife over there? I'd say Colt's in even worse shape than she is."

Scott nodded as he walked past. Vic got the strongest urge that more needed to be said, so he followed Scott out. "I'll be right back," he said to Gina. Scott made a beeline for their car and his son. "Scott, hold up a sec. Mr. Harrison."

Scott stopped and turned.

Vic walked up and quietly said, "I need to say one more thing, man-to-man. I wouldn't say something like this in front of your wife, but . . ."

"What is it?"

Vic almost looked at Colt in the backseat but caught himself. "We all hope this situation turns out well, and Nate and I will do everything in our power to see that it does, but . . . you just never know with a thing like this. What you say right now . . . well, it just really matters. If we get a happy ending here, then . . . all will be forgotten, maybe in a matter of months. This situation ends badly, what you say in the next few minutes may haunt Colt to his grave. So, be careful."

Scott took a deep breath as he looked over at Colt. "Thanks, Agent Hammond. I think I needed to hear that."

22

She'd already missed her bus ride home, so there wasn't any need to be rushing around.

Mamie sat at the little dinette table in a corner of the Harrison kitchen, where she normally took her meals, poking at the meatloaf and mashed potatoes she'd made for the Harrisons. That was before she knew Mr. Harrison wasn't coming home for dinner. Some big thing going on down at the bank, he'd said. Called five minutes before he normally arrived home, leaving poor Mrs. Harrison all by herself to worry 'bout her grandbabies.

For that matter, Mamie had a mind to lay into Mister Scott next time they talked, leaving his poor mother in the dark all day 'bout his missing boys. Mamie had raised him better than that. After she prayed on it, she felt the Lord nudging her to give him some leeway, seeing how worried he must've been himself. Those boys were usually well behaved, least they were whenever they came visiting around here. She guessed Mister Scott and Miss Gina weren't used to them running off like that.

But still, at some point during the day, someone should have called, let Mrs. Harrison know her grandbabies were okay now. So she could stop worrying, her stomach could settle down, and she could eat this fine meal Mamie had worked hard all afternoon to make.

Of course, not like it would go to waste. Meatloaf seemed to improve with age. For a few days anyhow. She'd wrap it up good in tinfoil for sandwiches over the next few days. But that wasn't the point.

Mamie slid her chair back quietly and stood. She tiptoed across the kitchen floor and pushed open the door to the dining room a few inches. At the end of the long mahogany table, all dressed for dinner, sat poor Mrs. Harrison. She had her fork in her dainty little hands, resting on the edge of her china plate, a small chunk of meatloaf balancing on the edge. Mamie stood there a few seconds watching, quiet as a mouse.

Mrs. Harrison didn't move. Just stared out the dining room window. Couldn't be seeing anything but her own reflection, since it was almost dark outside. The poor thing. No one to talk to, no one to share her fears with. Here was Mamie, not thirty feet away, walking that same road as her. She cared every bit as much about Colt and Timmy, since she'd raised their daddy like he was her own. But poor Mrs. Harrison would never think of stepping outside that high-and-proper wall she lived behind to let someone like Mamie in.

Did she even let God in to help? Mamie

wondered. She knew Mrs. Harrison went to church every Wednesday and Sunday. Knew the Harrisons prayed a proper prayer before every meal. But somehow she could never imagine Mrs. Harrison talking to Jesus heart-to-heart, like she did. Like she had already done several times today. Only way she knew to keep her peace of mind at a time like this.

But Mamie also knew the value of talking heart-to-heart with good friends. She had plenty of 'em in her neighborhood and at church. God meant for friends to help carry heavy burdens. Didn't mean for any of us to carry them all by ourselves.

Like poor Mrs. Harrison over there at that table. She'd seen the kind of friends she had in her life. Mostly uppity types. Noses high in the air. Dressed all fancy and proper, even for a cup of tea or a game of cards. Not the kind of friends Mamie'd want anything to do with. Made her nervous just being around 'em. Judging each other over every little thing they said or did, talking bad 'bout each other behind their backs.

Seemed like the kind of people to weigh you down further, not lift you up.

Mamie eased the door back into place, stepped away from it, leaned up against the counter. She had to do something to ease Mrs. Harrison's troubled mind. Several times today, Mamie had a thought she should just call over there to Mister Scott's house herself, see what was going on.

But she knew she never would. Such a thing just wasn't done.

Then she got an idea. Probably wouldn't work, but she had to do something. She walked over to the icebox and pulled out the pitcher of iced tea. She gave it a good stir, grabbed a fresh drinking glass, then walked out to the dining room. When she got close enough so she wouldn't be shouting, she said, "You been out here a good while, ma'am. How 'bout I refresh your tea?"

At first, she didn't reply. Then she noticed Mamie standing there. "I'm sorry, did you say something, Mamie Lee?"

"Your iced tea, ma'am. All the ice has melted. Want me to pour you some more?"

Mrs. Harrison looked at her glass. "Thank you, Mamie. That would be nice."

She said it with a kind tone, but Mamie could hear the sadness in her voice. She was definitely worried something awful about them boys. At least there was that; Mamie could always count on Mrs. Harrison treating her nice when she was fretting 'bout something. Mamie set the glass down and poured her tea. Then she picked up the old glass. Normally, at this point she'd just head back into the kitchen. But she decided to say what she thought to say. "I don't suppose you've heard anything more from Mister Scott?"

Mrs. Harrison looked up at her. "Now, Mamie Lee, you know as well as I do he hasn't called.

You're the one answers the phone most of the time."

"That's true. I thought maybe he might have called this afternoon while I was out in the backyard hanging laundry."

Mrs. Harrison reached for her glass. "No, he didn't call. Wish he had, but he didn't."

"Hopefully, no news is good news," Mamie said.

Mrs. Harrison glanced up at the wall clock hanging above the antique country sideboard. "What are you still doing here? Haven't you missed your bus?"

"I did. But I had some things needed tending to. It's a beautiful night out, so I thought I'd just walk home, enjoy the breeze and night air." Mamie turned, as if heading back toward the kitchen. Then stopped and said, "Mind me asking, ma'am, why don't you call Mister Scott and ask him about Colt and Timmy? He probably just got busy and forgot to call. I'm sure everything is all right."

Mrs. Harrison shook her head. "I can't call over there."

"I sure would," Mamie said, "he were my boy. And I'd give him a piece of my mind at the same time, making his mother worry all day like this."

Mrs. Harrison smiled. She actually smiled. Mamie half expected a scolding for being so bold. "I could call him, if you want me to. I've called over there a few times before."

"No, Mamie Lee. We'll just leave well enough alone. He'll call when he's ready. If I haven't heard anything by the time Henry gets home from his dinner, I'll have him call."

"Yes, ma'am. Whatever you think is best. You still eating that dinner, or want me to take it away?"

"No, you can take it. I'm not hungry."

"I'll be right back to get it. Shortly after that, I'll be heading home." Of course, Mamie thought, she could wait around for Mr. Harrison to call when he got home. But that could be hours from now.

That would make it too late for her to hear anything about the boys tonight. And that wouldn't do.

No sir, that wouldn't do at all.

23

Colt was alone in the car, huddled in the corner of the backseat. He wanted to open his eyes, but he was afraid to look. He knew they were home. Mr. Hammond, the nicer FBI agent, had already told him that.

He had pulled his knees up to his chest and buried his face in between them. Held on tight, as if by ignoring his circumstances hard enough, he could will himself to be somewhere else. Reality was too painful. He was not with Timmy in

Savannah, enjoying the sympathy of Uncle Mike and Aunt Rose. He was in the backseat of a dark FBI car in his own driveway, and Timmy was gone. Maybe forever. And it was all his fault. Why did he think this idea would ever work?

For several moments, nothing happened. He could hear the muffled voices of men talking just a few feet away. The backseat door opened on the other side of the car. He tensed up, waiting for . . . he didn't know what.

"Colt?"

It was his father's voice, speaking gently. He pretended not to hear.

"Colt . . . it's Dad. Please come here. You're home now, son."

He didn't move.

A few more moments passed in silence. "Colt, I . . . *we,* your mother and I, don't hate you. We love you, as much as we ever did." It sounded like he was choking up. *Is Dad crying?* "I know you feel bad about this, about what happened. You know you did wrong running away like that. But we don't blame you. We know . . . you never meant for any of this to happen."

That did it.

"I didn't, Dad." Tears poured out of Colt, and he turned to face his father. His dad reached for Colt across the seat. "I'm real sorry," Colt said through his tears. He wasn't sure if his dad heard him because he was crying too.

They clung to each other for a good while. He cried a long time. Finally, he heard Agent Hammond say from outside the car, "Scott, could Nate and I watch President Kennedy's address on your television?"

They stopped crying, or at least his dad did. Colt tried, and was at least able to start calming down. They slid out of the car together and faced Agent Hammond. "I'm sorry, what did you say, Vic?" his father said.

"The president's about to go live in a couple of minutes," Vic said. "He's gonna talk about Cuba. We really don't want to miss it, if that's okay with you."

"No, that's fine. Let's go back in the house. Are you okay, Colt?"

Colt stood in front of his father; his father rested his hands on Colt's shoulders. "I guess so," Colt said. But now he had to face his mom.

"Lead the way, Vic," his dad said. And they headed toward the house.

The front door opened before they got there. His mom was in the doorway, tears coming down her face. She opened her arms and said, "Colt, I'm so glad you're home." He ran into them, and the crying started all over again.

Five minutes later, they were all sitting around the television in the living room.

It was an odd sight for Colt, one that anchored

the memory in his mind even more firmly than it would've otherwise been, given the historic nature of what they were about to witness. His mom and dad were sitting where they usually sat when the TV was on, but joining them were two strangers in dark suits, FBI agents no less. All of them with eyes glued on the president, John F. Kennedy, who was about to speak.

As odd as it was, Colt was glad for the distraction.

The president looked straight into the camera. The atmosphere in the living room instantly changed.

Good evening, my fellow citizens. This government, as promised, has maintained the closest surveillance of the Soviet military buildup on the island of Cuba. Within the past week, unmistakable evidence has established the fact that a series of offensive missile sites is now in preparation on that imprisoned island. The purpose of these bases can be none other than to provide a nuclear strike capability against the Western Hemisphere.

Colt liked President Kennedy, but he talked funny.

Upon receiving the first preliminary hard information of this nature last Tuesday morning at 9:00 a.m., I directed that our surveillance be stepped up. And having now confirmed and completed our evaluation of the evidence and our decision on a course of action, this government feels obliged to report this new crisis to you in fullest detail.

"Wow," Nate Winters said, breaking the silence. "You hear that? He just called it a crisis. That's saying a lot, coming from him."

The characteristics of these new missile sites indicate two distinct types of installations. Several of them include medium range ballistic missiles, capable of carrying a nuclear warhead for a distance of more than 1,000 nautical miles. Each of these missiles, in short, is capable of striking Washington, DC, the Panama Canal, Cape Canaveral, Mexico City, or any other city in the southeastern part of the United States, in Central America, or in the Caribbean area.

"Cape Canaveral," his mother repeated. "What's that mean, Scott? Is he saying—"

"He's saying the Russians have nukes on Cuba," his dad said, "capable of reaching Washington and every city in between, including the Cape." He patted her knee, an attempt to end the conversation.

The president went on to say that other missile sites on Cuba, ones that weren't finished yet, would give the Soviets the ability to launch missiles twice as far, all the way north to Canada and all the way down to Peru. Then the president started talking about some treaties the Soviets were breaking and, it sounded like, some lies they were telling about what they were up to. Colt didn't understand everything.

His eyes kept switching back and forth from his parents' faces to the FBI agents, then back to the president on TV. He had never seen adults look more serious about anything than the four of them did that night. The president finally began to say some things Colt could understand, except one word, *quarantine.*

Acting, therefore, in the defense of our own security and of the entire Western Hemisphere, and under the authority entrusted to me by the Constitution as endorsed by the Resolution of the Congress, I have directed that the following initial steps be taken immediately:

First: To halt this offensive buildup a strict quarantine on all offensive military equipment under shipment to Cuba is being initiated. All ships of any kind bound for Cuba from whatever nation or port will, if found to contain cargoes of offensive weapons, be turned back. This quarantine will be extended, if needed, to other types of cargo and carriers. We are not at this time, however, denying the necessities of life as the Soviets attempted to do in their Berlin blockade of 1948.

"He's really talking about a naval blockade, Vic," Nate said. "Isn't he?"

"What's that mean?" Colt's mom asked, a frantic look on her face. She was gripping his dad's leg.

"The Soviets might see this as an act of war," he replied. "It means an invasion of Cuba. It means old Weldon was right."

"That's what all those tanks and truck caravans are all about," Nate said. "Getting ready for a D-Day–like invasion."

As President Kennedy kept talking, Colt thought about a conversation he'd witnessed between his father and grandfather last year, on the twentieth anniversary of Pearl Harbor. His dad was eleven when Pearl Harbor was attacked, Colt's age. His grandfather reminded his dad about something he'd said when they first heard the news coming in over the radio. *Pay attention, Scott. You're going to remember what happened today for the rest of your life.*

Was that the kind of moment Colt was experiencing now? Was this as bad as Pearl Harbor?

Third: It shall be the policy of this nation to regard any nuclear missile launched from Cuba against any nation in the Western Hemisphere as an attack by the Soviet Union on the United States, requiring a full retaliatory response upon the Soviet Union . . .

"Oh my Lord . . ." Colt's dad was rubbing his temples.

"What?" his mother said.

"He's talking about starting World War III, Vic," Nate said.

"Nuclear war," his dad said. Dread all over his face.

Colt instantly remembered something else, something a kid in his science class had said, during one of those drop-and-cover drills. *These drills don't work. You know that, right? My dad said if we ever go to war with the Soviets, it's pretty much the end of the world.*

24

Mamie Lee was a bit shaken up. "Dear Lord, is this it? Is this Armageddon?" She was walking under a streetlight toward home, seeing as she had missed the bus. Along the way, she'd walked through part of the downtown area, right past an appliance store. A bunch of people were standing around the front window watching a television, so she stopped to see what all the fuss was about. It was the president talking. She stood there in the back, listening as best she could.

She didn't understand everything the president said, but she understood enough. And then to hear all the people talking after, the things they were saying . . . 'bout scared her to death.

One of the men, who talked with great certainty, said there was no way the Russians would tolerate this ship blockade the president was setting up. Another man said now we knew where all those Army tanks and trucks heading south were really going. They were headed straight for Cuba! He said just you wait, see if we don't invade Cuba before the week is out. The first man said, when that happens you can be sure nuclear missiles will start firing off in the sky, blowin' everything up. New York City, Philadelphia, Washington DC . . . even Cape Canaveral, just a ways south from here. And of course, the US will blow up Havana, Moscow, and Leningrad.

When Mamie left those people, they were still talking about one bad thing happening after another. She had to get away, 'fore she had no peace left at all in her heart.

It was all too hard to fathom. She had all the worry she could handle right now with her grandbabies missing. Listen to her, like they were *her* grandbabies. Felt like it sometimes, close as she felt to Mister Scott, their daddy.

Up ahead on the corner she saw a telephone booth under the streetlight. That thought came again to call Mister Scott, see if the boys got in all right, give their daddy a poke to call his mother right away, so she could have some peace too 'fore this night was over.

When she got under the light, Mamie reached in her purse to make sure she had plenty of change. It was long distance to call from DeLand to Daytona. But she was fine; she always kept plenty of change in her purse for emergencies. 'Course, she could've just called their house collect. Once a couple of years ago, when she'd got caught walking home in a bad rainstorm, she'd called Mister Scott, who came to her rescue right away. After dropping her off at the house, he'd gently scolded her for not calling collect. So sweet, what he'd said after she thanked him. *"Mamie Lee, you're like my mama. You don't ever have to pay to ask for my help, you hear? Anytime you need to call me, you just call collect, and I'll come as quick as I can."*

About brought a tear to her eye. But still, it didn't feel right calling collect when she had plenty of change in her purse. Anyway, she wasn't calling for help. Wasn't a cloud in the sky. Had a beautiful full moon to light her whole way home, and a nice breeze besides.

She slid the booth door closed and dialed his number.

Scott was the first one to get up when the president finished speaking. He walked over and turned the television off. "I don't think my brain can absorb one more bad thought in a single day."

No one said anything for a moment, then the two FBI agents stood. "I know all that sounds terrible," Vic said, "and it is, but it's about what I expected the president to say, based on what Nate and I have been hearing around the office."

Scott had known something was up too. Everyone did, watching all this military traffic going through town. There was also a lot of buzz at GE. Especially from the guys who worked at the Cape. But for some reason, he had never imagined something this bad.

Not World War III, not a nuclear holocaust.

But the full impact of this news was muffled by the far greater impact of losing his son. "Do you think what the president said will affect the search for Timmy?" Scott looked over at Gina. She looked back and forth between the two agents. She had the same question.

"I can't see how it won't," Nate said. "Normally, a kidnapped little boy would take priority over everything."

"But now it won't?" Gina asked. "I don't understand. My little boy is out there with some strange man." Tears began welling up in her eyes. "How can anything else matter?"

"Finding Timmy will still be a high priority," Vic said. "For Nate and me, it will be our *top* priority. But you have to understand, Mrs. Harrison, what President Kennedy just said involves national security. Our whole country is in grave danger. Probably more danger than we were in during all of World War II."

"Yeah," Nate added, "as long as these nukes remain in Cuba, there's no safe place anywhere in the US."

Scott instantly looked at Colt, who got up from the floor and stood by his mom.

"Mom," he said quietly, "are we all going to die?"

Gina put her arm around him and drew him close. "No, honey, I don't think so. We'll be okay." He didn't look reassured. She turned to the FBI agents. "But you're talking about the danger we *might* be in. Timmy is in danger right now. I don't understand why every agent and every police officer in Florida isn't stopping every Greyhound bus on the road, or at least every bus as it pulls into a terminal. They should've been doing that right away, as soon as we knew he was taken by a man on a bus."

"Ma'am, I know it's hard to understand what I'm saying, but the truth is, there are hundreds of buses and bus routes involved. We have no way of knowing which bus they're on. And the Cuba crisis has made things ten times worse for every law enforcement officer in the country, not just in this state."

"Maybe we shouldn't talk about this anymore tonight," Scott said, looking at Colt's face.

"Agreed," Vic said. Both agents grabbed their hats and began walking toward the front door. Vic turned to face the family. "I want you all to know, Nate and I will do everything in our power to find Timmy. And we're going to work hard to get as many law enforcement personnel involved in the case as possible."

"When will his picture get in the newspapers? And the sketch of the kidnapper?" Scott asked.

"I'd get it in there tomorrow morning," Vic said. "But we have to leave a little time to make sure it's not a typical kidnapping for ransom."

"You don't want a lot of publicity on something like that," Nate added. "Could make the kidnapper angry."

"But you don't think that's what we've got here," Scott said. Both agents shook their head no.

"How will we know if it is?" Gina said.

"Because that phone will ring," Vic said, "and a man on the other end will say they have him and start spelling out demands."

At that moment the telephone rang.

Scott looked at Vic. "What should I do?"

"Go ahead and answer it," Vic said. He quickly moved toward the phone, taking out a pad and

147

pen. "If it's the kidnapper, just talk normally. I'll write down any important information."

"But what if they say don't involve the police?"

"Scott, just answer it," Gina said, "before they hang up."

Scott lifted the receiver. "Hello?"

"Mister Scott, is that you? It's Mamie Lee calling."

Scott was instantly relieved to hear her voice, though part of him wished it had been the kidnapper. "It's me, Mamie Lee." He looked at Vic and then the others, shaking his head. "Can you hold on one moment?"

"I can," she said. "But this is long distance."

"I'll get right back to you in a second." Scott put his hand over the phone. "It's my parents' housekeeper calling from DeLand. I guess you guys can go."

"Okay," Vic said, "but we'll be in touch in the morning. I'm going to lay my card down here on the table. You call the number on that card if anything develops. Anything at all."

"Will do," Scott said, then turned his focus back to Mamie Lee. "I'm back."

"I'm just calling to see how you made out today," she said. "You never called your mama back to let her know. She been worried something fierce all day. Me too, for that matter. Any news about the boys? You find them okay?"

Scott took a deep breath. "Not exactly, Mamie. Colt's here. He's okay. But I've got some terrible news to tell you about . . . Timmy." Just saying his name to Mamie brought up a swell of emotion. He could hardly say the next few words. "We don't know where he is."

"Oh Lord, no," Mamie said.

25

The FBI agents had left about an hour and a half ago. Colt was already in bed, but only after Scott and Gina had agreed Scott would stay overnight and sleep in Timmy's bed, so Colt wouldn't face the night alone. Under normal circumstances it would have felt awkward having Scott in the house overnight, but right now Gina was too exhausted to care.

At the moment, she was straightening up some things in the kitchen. Scott was in the hall bathroom, brushing his teeth and getting ready to turn in for the night. Rose and her husband, Mike, had called a short while ago to say they were in town, asking if she'd like them to stop by tonight or wait till the morning. That was easy; they would come in the morning. Tonight they'd stay at the Howard Johnson's Motor Lodge, a few blocks north on A1A.

Before that, Scott had made two phone calls: a

very difficult one to his mother, and another to some guy at work.

Gina turned off the sink and dried her hands just in time to hear him rinsing his mouth in the bathroom. Her bedroom—their old bedroom—was at the end of the hall, so there was no way to avoid intersecting with him if she wanted to go to bed, which she desperately did. She decided just to get it over with.

He was coming out of the bathroom as she walked by. "Turning in for the night?"

"Yeah," she said. "I'm exhausted."

"Me too," he said. "But if it's okay with you, I'm going to stay up for a while yet. I won't turn the TV on."

"That's fine. Mike and Rose said they'll be over tomorrow morning around nine. They want to make us breakfast."

"I doubt that I'll feel like eating," he said.

"Me neither." She was about to turn and head for the bedroom, then decided to ask, "How did your mom handle the news?"

"Not good. She didn't say much, but I could hear her trying not to cry the whole time we talked. Knowing her, she'll do her best to bottle up her emotions, only let them out in private. Of course, she wanted to know what was being done."

"I heard what you told her. Makes me so angry. Those two agents seem like fine men. But there are just two of them, Scott. What are we going to do? How will we ever find Timmy unless we get more help? A lot more help." She didn't mean to, but she started losing it again. Scott reached for her, to comfort her, and she fell into his strong arms. He didn't say anything, which was so unlike him. Normally, when she'd get upset—upset enough to cry—he'd immediately start talking her out of it, try to straighten out whatever he imagined was wrong in her thinking.

But tonight, he just held her. After a few moments, she understood why.

He was crying too.

Ten minutes later, Gina was safely behind her closed bedroom door. Scott stopped crying before she did, and when she had finished, he'd simply said softly, "Well, good night."

She quickly walked through her get-ready-for-bed routine. For a little while, sheer exhaustion kept dark thoughts at bay. Right up until she turned on the lamp on her nightstand and saw a children's book on the pillow, on the far side of the bed. She'd forgotten about it until then. Last night, Timmy couldn't sleep, so he'd slipped into her room carrying this book. It was called *My Good Shepherd*.

"You forgot to read to me tonight," he'd said. "Colt's already asleep, but I can't fall asleep. Can you read this to me?"

"Of course I will. Hop up here and snuggle next to me." Right then, he seemed more like three years old than six. He fit so comfortably under her arm. She opened the book and started to read. Sometime before she finished, he'd fallen asleep. She closed the book then leaned it up against the pillow and gently carried him back to his room.

Looking at the book now . . . she didn't want to move it, didn't want to touch it, didn't want to do anything to dispel the sweet memory of his presence in that spot last night.

Where was he now? It was way past his bedtime. Was he asleep? Was he safe? Why wasn't he here, where he belonged? She picked up the book, read the words of the cover aloud. "My Good Shepherd." Then she had a thought. A bad one. She wasn't going to say it but decided she might as well. God knew what she was thinking anyway. "But you're not a very good Shepherd, are you?" she said. "You don't look after your little lambs like this book says!" She remembered a picture of Jesus carrying a little lost lamb around his shoulders as he walked it back to the safety of the pasture. "It's just a lie. Just a stupid children's story!"

She was just about to throw the book across the room, but she stopped.

No, she couldn't turn her back on God. She was angry with him now, and he may have let this happen to her Timmy, but Jesus was still the only one who could make this nightmare go away. She clutched the book and cried, "Please, Jesus, don't abandon us. A wolf has stolen my little lamb—*your* little lamb. Please go after him. Please bring him back. Please . . ."

She couldn't think of anything more to say. She lay back on her pillow and pulled the book close.

He hadn't been following a preconceived plan, but a plan was coming together just the same. It was almost as if the Man Upstairs was helping him, things were going so smoothly. August hated having to threaten the boy to keep him in line, but it couldn't be helped. He was sure after a few days of settling in, he would quiet down and begin to mind. Wouldn't do to start using the wooden paddle on Bobby so soon. But he'd do it if he had to.

He leaned his ear up against the closed door. Sounded like the boy had finally gone to sleep. Must've been all that walking and the excitement of being in a new place. August was pretty tired too. For a while, it seemed like he'd never get home. Or else his legs would fall off first.

But it had to be done this way. Couldn't take a chance of riding the bus all the way home. The police would be asking questions before long. So he got out two stops early. Then they took a cab. Couldn't ride the cab all the way home, either, so he had the driver drop him off three miles away.

Lots of walking after a long day. A long, emotionally draining day.

But tomorrow promised better. They had made it back, safe and sound. And Bobby was back in his bedroom, where he belonged.

26

Gina had awakened the next day feeling mostly numb and confused. She'd decided to spend a little extra time preparing herself to face life beyond her bedroom, remembering that Scott was in the house now and that Mike and Rose would be coming by to make breakfast.

They did come, right on time.

The greeting had been difficult but not as traumatic as Gina had imagined. She was just too exhausted to produce the proper amount of grief and tears for the occasion. She was sure her tank would fill back up again before long. Her sister and brother-in-law had put the whole breakfast together, and as they ate, they did their best not to dwell on the two overwhelming topics hanging in the air: Timmy's kidnapping and nuclear annihilation.

It was oddly comforting just to be able to make it through a plate of scrambled eggs and bacon. She let Mike and Rose carry most of the conversation during breakfast. That sensation of normalcy didn't last long, however. As promised, Special Agent Hammond had called to verify there had been no phone calls or other developments since he'd left the house. Scott had taken the call, assuring him there had not. After he'd gotten off the phone, Scott had asked Colt to go get dressed and brush his teeth, so he could brief them on the call.

"So what did he say, Scott?" Mike asked, leaning against the kitchen counter. Gina and Rose were still sitting around the dinette table.

"He said he and his partner Nate had discussed the situation with their supervisor. Everyone agreed that if the kidnapper has not made contact by 1:00 p.m. today, they'll start handling this as an abduction case, not a standard kidnapping."

"By standard, you mean asking for ransom money," Mike said. Scott nodded. "So what's that mean exactly?"

"It means they'll release Timmy's picture and the artist's rendering of the kidnapper to the press. We should see the story start to appear in the late afternoon and early evening newspapers throughout the state."

"Well," Rose said, "at least that's some progress."

"I wish they'd just do that now," Gina said. "We don't have any money. It's obvious what kind of kidnapping this is."

"I'm with you, hon," Scott said. "But they've gotta follow protocol."

Gina wondered if the "hon" was an unintended slip or if Scott was trying to keep their separation hidden from Mike and Rose. He must know Mike and Rose already knew the truth.

"He did ask something I didn't know the answer to," Scott said. He looked at Gina. "Vic asked us to think about whether we'd be open to answering a few questions from reporters once the story breaks. He thought it was a good idea. It could help to generate interest and sympathy from people, hearing from us. Might make them work harder at searching for Timmy or reporting suspicious things to the authorities."

"Then we should do it," Gina said. "We should do anything that might help, even a little."

"But he also said reporters can be pretty aggressive going after stories, ask really insensitive questions, get pushy. Depending on how big the story gets. He thought this whole Cuba thing might cut down on some of that, because it's such a big story by itself."

Gina noticed Colt had walked in from the hallway and stood next to his Uncle Mike. Mike put his arm around Colt's shoulder. "I've got an idea. I saw them do this on a kidnapping case last year in South Carolina. After the child's parents made a public appeal, most of the rest of what the family had to say came through a family spokesman. I could do that for you guys, if things started getting crazy. Answer the phones, take questions from reporters."

Scott walked farther into the kitchen to pour himself another cup of coffee. "I appreciate that, Mike. Especially if you'll do that for Gina when I'm not here. But I think when I am here, I can handle it. I've actually been dealing with the local press a good bit with my new job at GE. Nothing like this, but—"

"I'd really appreciate that, Mike," Gina said. "If things do get kind of crazy. But I really want to talk to people if it will help find Timmy. I'll go nuts if all I do is sit here."

"Well," Rose said, "let's just wait and see what happens. We just want you both to know—you too, Colt—that we're here for you. Mike took the whole rest of the week off and we reserved our motel room through the weekend. So let us handle anything we can while we're here."

"I hope Timmy is back long before the weekend," Gina said.

"If the world will still be here by the weekend," Mike said quietly.

Rose shot him a look.

Colt spoke up for the first time. "You don't think they'll find Timmy before the weekend?"

"We hope they do," Scott said. "Once they put his picture in the paper, all kinds of people will be looking for him. Somebody's bound to see a man with a little boy that's not his."

"They're gonna put Timmy's picture in the paper?" Colt didn't look too happy about that.

157

"Well, yeah, son. I forgot you were in the bathroom when I said it."

"When?"

"Might be today, in time for the—"

"Today?"

"Yeah, but not until the evening edition," Scott said. "But this is a good thing, son. The more people who know about it, the more help we'll get finding your little brother. Right?"

Colt's shoulders slumped. "I guess."

Gina could tell having Colt with them through all this was going to be a problem. She just wanted Timmy back and life to return to normal, but they weren't there now, and they needed to be able to talk about "adult" things with Mike and Rose. But she could see the pain on Colt's face. He felt totally to blame for what happened, and as they talked, she could see him sink further into a pit of guilt. For him, the more people found about the kidnapping, the more people would blame him.

Mike seemed to pick up on this. He turned and bent down to Colt's level. "Hey, Colt, how would you like to come back and check out our motel room? It's right on the beach."

"Which one is it?" Colt asked.

"The Howard Johnson's. It's even got a swimming pool. Maybe we can go for a swim."

"I think the water might be too cold," Colt said.

"Well, we can see. If it is, we can take a walk on the beach, maybe build a sand castle. Or we could get some ice cream. Howard Johnson's makes the best. Would you like that?"

Colt nodded.

"You want to come with us, Scott?"

"I don't know. Maybe I should stick around by the phone, so Gina and Rose can visit."

"We'll visit better if you go," Gina said. "You and I both know the kidnapper isn't going to call here, and reporters won't start calling till the story breaks. Why don't you spend time with your son?"

Scott gave her a look, like that last remark stung a little. She meant for it to sting. Why wasn't he the one picking up on how Colt was doing, thinking up something to take his mind off things? Mike, on the other hand, was wonderful. He'd already taken off the entire week.

She wasn't even sure Scott would stick to his promise and take off the rest of today.

27

The guys were gone, leaving Gina and Rose alone in the house. Rose had insisted Gina let her clean up the kitchen. Gina pulled rank as the older sister, telling her "no chance." Besides, Gina could use the distraction.

They had chatted mostly about lighter things as they worked. Gina had filled Rose in on her job at the insurance firm. Rose seemed to find it fascinating; she hadn't worked outside the home since she had gotten married. Even then, it was just as a cashier in a grocery store.

As they talked, Gina got a sense both of them were stalling, avoiding bigger topics. When they were done cleaning, Gina suggested they take their last cup of coffee to the patio out back. It was such a beautiful October morning.

"Don't you need to stay by the phone?" Rose asked.

"We've got the windows open, we can hear it fine out here as long as we leave the radio off. You don't have any desire to hear what everyone's saying about the world blowing to bits, do you?"

Rose poured her coffee. "Not really. It doesn't seem real to me anyway."

Gina poured her coffee too, then pulled the plug on the percolator. "Me neither. I suppose I'd care about it more if my life wasn't so upside down right now."

Rose walked toward the patio door. "Right out here?"

"Right out there." As she stepped through the doorway, Gina inhaled the crisp sea air. "If we're quiet enough, you can hear the waves breaking on the beach from here."

"Really?"

"It's only about a block away," Gina said.

They sat in the patio chairs and listened a few moments.

Rose looked across the yard. "I'd forgotten about your cactus bushes over there along the back fence. They've gotten so much bigger."

"I guess they have. Scott never messes with them. He tried once, when we first moved in. That was all it took."

"You know," Rose said, "I think those are the only cactus plants I've seen in Florida."

"Maybe the previous owner of this house came from out West," Gina said. "They seem to grow well here." She took another sip of coffee. "Okay, Rose, how about you just ask me the questions you're dying to ask me? Probably starting with, 'How come you and Scott are separated, and how come you never told me?' "

Rose offered a sheepish grin. "I guess those are good ones to start with. I'm sorry, I didn't know if you wanted to talk about that. And I didn't want to add any more to your stress. We don't really talk at that level anymore since I moved to Georgia, and long distance is so expensive."

"I know," Gina said. "And that's really why I didn't tell you. That and the fact that the real reason we're not together is so painful . . . and humiliating."

Rose's face grew instantly serious. "It's not because . . . he cheated on you, is it?"

Tears welled up in Gina's eyes as she nodded.

161

"No . . ."

Gina nodded again.

"When did this happen?"

"Last Christmas, at an office Christmas party."

"I can't believe it."

"I wish I didn't have to."

"How did you find out?"

"I walked in on them."

Rose's face turned to shock. "Oh Gina, no."

"Well, it's not like they were . . . you know, doing *that*. But they were making out. Scott and this young redhead."

"Oh Gina, I'm so sorry. It's so hard to believe Scott would do something like that."

"Unfortunately, it wasn't that hard for me to believe."

"Why? Have you caught him being unfaithful with other women?"

"No, but you can tell when your husband has lost interest. He'd been coming home late from work almost every night for months. Even longer than that. And when he was home, he was constantly preoccupied with his job, always talking about work, never taking an interest in me . . . or the kids. Guess I know why now."

"Did Scott admit to it, after you caught him?"

"No, he acted like nothing was happening between them, like what I saw was just some big misunderstanding."

"A misunderstanding?"

"Yeah. Like it was just some Merry Christmas kiss between co-workers. It didn't mean anything at all."

"Is that possible? Maybe they had a little too much to drink?"

"Rose, what I saw wasn't some Merry Christmas kiss. She had her arms around him, and he had his hands on her waist, and he was kissing back. Put that together with all the months of eating dinner by myself with the boys at home and the lack of romance in our relationship the last few years . . . that's proof enough for me. Besides, the girl told me they were in a relationship and they were in love. She was sorry I had to find out that way."

"When did she say that?"

"Right then, that night. With Scott standing right there. He acted shocked and totally denied it, said it wasn't true. But of course he'd say that. What else could he say? I'd caught him with her." Gina stood up. She didn't know why, or where she was going.

"I'm sorry to get you talking about this. Look how upset you're getting. That's why I started talking about things like your cactus bush and—"

"No, it's all right, Rose. We needed to talk about it. You needed to know. We're sisters. There's never gonna be a good time to have a conversation like this."

"I guess, but still . . ."

"I just feel so bad for the boys," Gina said.

"They don't understand what's going on, and I can't tell them. Listen to me . . . tell *them*. Oh Lord, where is Timmy?" She sat back in her chair, folded her knees up to her chin.

Rose got up and hugged her.

It was apparently time to cry again. Gina let it go as her little sister Rose rubbed her back softly.

After a few minutes, Gina regained her composure and Rose returned to her chair. "It must've been terrible keeping something this big a secret all that time. Not having anyone to confide in."

"Don't feel too bad for me about that. It was a stupid idea, and I wish I'd never agreed to it. To make it work not only did we have to lie to everyone, we made the boys do it too. Can you imagine such a thing? Parents forcing their kids to lie? What kind of Christians would do that? What kind of parents would? I'm sure that's the reason Colt and Timmy ran away, or at least a big part of it."

Rose sat back in her chair and made a face Gina couldn't interpret. But it was obvious she agreed with what Gina had just said. "Just say what you're thinking, Rose. It can't be any worse than what I'm thinking about myself right now."

"I wasn't thinking anything bad. Just that what you said is true. The lying part, I mean. Colt did tell me on the telephone that was a big part of why they ran away. He didn't want to have to keep lying about what was going on here."

Gina sighed. For some reason, hearing Rose confirm it made it even worse. They really were to blame, her and Scott, for Timmy's disappearance. They were the adults, the ones who were supposed to do the right thing and teach their kids the right thing. But instead, so they wouldn't look bad and their reputation wouldn't get soiled, they had broken one of the Ten Commandments. Not just once, but over and over again for months.

Was that why this happened? Was God punishing them for all the lies?

28

August didn't like people as a rule. Had no use for them.

Couldn't think of one who'd ever done him any good. Nothing but a bunch of users and takers. Couldn't trust anyone to do what they said they'd do. Not a single one. People letting you down was like a scientific law, like the laws of motion or gravity.

Starting with his pa, a no-good drunk who beat him every chance he got, and his ma, who watched him do it. Then she up and died, leaving him alone with that man to take all he had to dish out until August could finally take no more. At sixteen, he hit his dad back, then got the better of him. Knocked him out cold then ran off to join the Army.

People in the Army treated him no better. Maybe even worse. Would have gotten out except that the Korean War started up, and there he was, stuck in the middle of it. Like a foretaste of hell, that place. The only upside was, he had to kill these Chinese and North Koreans for Uncle Sam. Finally found something he was pretty good at, and he had to admit, he took some pleasure in it.

None of his bosses since the war were any good. Every single one had treated him badly. Every co-worker too. Then finally came Bobby's mom. Thought she might be the one person on earth to treat him different. Seemed that way for a while, a good while. Then she started drinking and going out. Said she'd made a mistake, wasn't ready to be nobody's wife or ma. It was a good day when she left for good, 'cause he'd have wound up in prison for killing her.

Bobby had been his only bright spot.

Like most kids, didn't listen half the time. But at least it was only half. The rest of the time August liked having him around. A lot. Actually made him laugh, Bobby did, a good number of times, right out loud. All the things he came up with.

Then, for a little while, Bobby was gone. Those were the darkest days of August's life.

But he was back now. His Bobby was back.

"Mister?"

August looked down. He'd been out on the porch, staring at the water.

"Excuse me, mister. I finished eating the cornflakes. Can I go home now?"

What was he talking about, going home? He was home. "You put the bowl on the washboard like I told you?" The boy nodded. "You rinse it out first?" He nodded again. "That's a good boy." August patted him on the head. "Why'd you put on the same shirt you had on yesterday?"

The boy stepped back. "It's the only shirt I got. All my other ones are in my dresser back home."

"Why you keep saying 'going home' or 'back home'? You are home, Bobby. And you got a whole dresser full of clean shirts to pick from back in your room. Now get on back there and put a clean shirt on. Don't matter which one. Everything matches dungarees."

The boy just stood there, a confused look on his face.

"Did you hear me? Go on, get!"

He ran off. August heard him crying as he made it to the bedroom. Had a mind to yell, "Stop that crying, or I'll give you something to cry about." But he didn't. His pa wouldn't have just said it; he'd have come after August with a switch. But August knew better. The boy needed at least a day or two to settle in.

But he'd have to mind. August couldn't have a willful boy messing up his quiet home. He knew what to do with willful boys who wouldn't mind their pa. You didn't have to beat 'em. Not all the time. There were better ways of dealing with such things.

Then August got an idea. Wouldn't do to bring the boy with him. He walked back into the house then over to the hallway, near the boy's bedroom door. Peeking inside, he saw him buttoning up a blue flannel shirt. "You're doing that wrong, Bobby. Got started on the wrong button."

"Mister, my name isn't Bobby. It's—"

"What do you mean, it isn't Bobby. 'Course it is. I don't know what's gotten into your head. Now unbutton those buttons and start over."

"My mom sometimes has to help me with the first button."

"Don't even talk about that woman in this house, you hear?" The boy looked up, startled. Like he was about to cry. "I'm sorry, I didn't mean to yell like that. But I'm the one raised you all this time, put food on the table every night. And if you need help with anything, I'm the one you come to. We clear on that?" The boy's head nodded slowly up and down. "Here, let me get you started on the right one. Have a seat on the bed."

The boy sat, and August reached over, buttoned the first button. "You can do the rest, right?"

"Yes."

August stood, walked back through the doorway, and turned. "Listen, I need to get a few things down at the general store. I won't be gone too long."

"I'm going to be alone?"

"It'll only be for a while. You'll be fine. No one ever comes here. Folks around here keep to themselves. You just sit there on your bed and read your comic book till I get back."

"But where are the other comic books? They were on the dresser last night, but when I woke up they were gone."

"They were just for the bus ride. I'll give them back to you, one at a time, but you have to earn them by being a good boy and doing what you're told."

The boy picked up the one comic book he'd brought with him. "But I've already read this one a hundred times."

"Well, read it a hundred and one." August began closing the door.

"Wait," the boy said. "Can't you leave that open?"

"No, I can't. Can't have you traipsin' all around this house by yourself, getting into who knows what kinds of trouble. I don't want to lose you again. You'll be fine in here with the door closed. I'm locking it for your own good, so you'll stay safe."

Bobby was pouting as the door closed behind him. But it had to be done. "You don't cry,"

August yelled through the door, "and I'll bring you home a Coca-Cola. You like Coca-Cola?"

"Yes," Bobby yelled back.

"Okay, then. I'll sit out here and listen a few moments. I hear any crying, and I'll drink that Coca-Cola myself."

"I'll try real hard not to cry."

August put his ear up to the door. Heard some whimpering, but that was all. A few moments later, he heard the bedsprings creaking. The boy was doing what he was told. August started walking down the hall toward the front door.

See, you didn't have to always beat 'em to get 'em to mind. Sometimes you could just trick 'em into doing the right thing, and it would only cost you a nickel.

Beatings were only for the worst things. A distinction his pa knew nothing about.

29

It had taken August thirty more minutes to make his way home than he had planned. That stinkin' rear tire went flat on him. He'd been eyeing both of them for the last month or so, hoping to squeeze a few thousand more miles before he had to fork over the money for a new pair. The spare he'd stuck on there wasn't much better than the tire that had blown. But it would have to do for now.

The other thing that had slowed him down were all the people out shopping, on a Tuesday morning no less. It was the craziest thing. Worse than shopping on Saturdays. And this town didn't have but a few hundred residents. Seemed like nearly all of them had picked that moment to replenish their cupboards. Only time he'd seen anything like this was two years ago when Hurricane Donna had come through.

He didn't like chitchatting with people, but his curiosity was getting the better of him. He was just about to break down and talk with someone when he overheard a small group of ladies by the produce tables all lathered up about something they heard the president say last night. He'd heard people buzzing on the bus ride yesterday about the president going on TV, but August made no plans to listen to him. Why should he? He'd voted for Nixon in the last election. Since then, he'd noticed how the whole country seemed to go ape over JFK, especially over his wife, Jackie. But August was no hypocrite. Figured he wouldn't pay much attention to politics till '64 when the whole thing started back up again.

But hearing these old ladies go on, you'd think JFK had announced the world was coming to an end. If that was true, he didn't see much good in filling up your kitchen with a month's worth of groceries.

Something was going on with Cuba and the

Russians; he didn't know exactly what. August didn't pay for the newspaper to be delivered every day. The routes didn't come out this far from town anyway. So he'd picked up a paper at the store and put it in the grocery bag to read when he got home.

He was just turning onto his street now, a shady dirt road. Plenty of quiet, few people. Houses spread far apart, just the way he liked it. The neighbor on one side lived up north most of the year. The neighbor on the other side had tried to make friends when she first moved in a few years ago. But there were ways to discourage things like that. People generally got the message you wanted to be left alone if you kept sending it loud and clear.

He started things off right by not even answering the door that first time when she'd brought over some homemade blueberry pie. He made sure she knew he was home too. She had kept knocking a good while, then finally gave up. August had let the pie sit there a couple of hours, occasionally peeking out the window until he was sure she was looking. Then he walked out, picked up the pie, and carried it over to the trash can. He had tossed it inside, making as much noise as he could.

It was quite a sacrifice, especially when he'd realized it was blueberry. But it had to be done. She'd left him alone pretty much all the time after that.

As he drove down his long, bumpy dirt driveway toward the house, he knew right off the bat something was wrong. Couldn't quite place what it was, so he slowed to a crawl.

Then he saw it. The bedroom window. Bobby's window. It was open, the thin green curtains blowing in and out. He knew for certain that window was closed when he'd left for the store. He accelerated the car to the end of the driveway and slammed on the brakes. He got out and ran toward the house, leaving the food, even left his car door open.

There was no way he'd let this happen again.

"Bobby!" he shouted as he ran to the right side of the house. "Bobby, you in there?" There was no answer. He leaned inside the boy's bedroom. No one there. But he knew that already. That was why the window was open. The boy had gotten out! August had been gone so long, Bobby could be anywhere by now. How could August have been so stupid and not checked to make sure the window was locked?

The water.

Boys loved water. Attracted them like bees to pollen. Instantly, he set out running. "Bobby!" he screamed over and over, eyes looking all around. He couldn't lose him. Not again. "Bobby! Where are you, boy?"

When he got to the water's edge, he almost jumped right in. Horrible memories flashed through his brain. But he quickly realized Bobby wasn't there. It was just a memory, a dark, terrifying memory.

Then where was he? He turned and began to scan the property all around the house, but there was no sign of him. He ran toward the neighbor's house on the right side, calling out his name. Maybe Bobby had gone there. This was the neighbor who lived up north. If Bobby tried them, no one would answer the bell.

August ran all around the property but saw no sign of him.

He took off toward the neighbor's house on the other side, which was a good distance away. For a moment, he thought about stopping at his house for his gun. If Bobby had gone to that neighbor, there might be some trouble. But when August reached the clearing, he happened to look down by the water.

That was when he saw him.

A little boy, walking along the water's edge, about halfway around on the south side. Had to be him, had to be Bobby. August hadn't seen him before; that big cluster of bushes must've blocked his view. August moved toward him, but this time he didn't call out the boy's name. Didn't want to take the chance he'd scare him, cause the boy to set off running. He did that, Bobby might fall right into that water and drown.

Besides, he didn't know the people over that

way and how'd they feel about him trespassing on their land. So he decided just to run quiet like, a little ways off the waterline. As he ran, he came up with his plan.

He'd come at Bobby from behind, hide a moment in some palmetto bushes, make sure nobody saw him run up, and snatch Bobby. He'd probably have to cover up the boy's mouth to keep him from screaming his head off on the way back to the house. He didn't want to, but it had to be done.

Of course, if anyone did see him, he could just tell them he was running after his boy and had to carry him like this, because the boy knew the spanking he'd get when they got home. For running off and for playing near the water. Everyone spanked their kids when they misbehaved.

And he had one more thing in his favor . . . none of his neighbors would have any reason to question him about bringing his boy back to the house, since none of them knew what happened the last time.

August kept his eye on Bobby as he rounded the first curve. Bobby was still walking away, in the wrong direction. And he was way too close to the water's edge. August would have to teach him a lesson, one he wouldn't soon forget.

Bad little boys that didn't mind had to be punished.

Bobby would have to spend some time in the dark place. And he'd better get used to it too, because that's where he'd have to stay from now on, whenever August left the house.

30

About three o'clock that afternoon, Gina and Rose left for the grocery store to pick up some food for the next few days. Gina was a little annoyed that the FBI hadn't called back yet. Colt had just left to play with his best friend Murph, who lived across the street.

Scott had initially told him not to talk about the situation with Murph, until Colt explained that Murph already knew the first part, about them running away, and had done his best to talk Colt out of it. He might as well know the rest of the story, Scott decided. Maybe Murph could be some comfort to Colt. Before his son had run out the door, Scott said, "Make sure Murph knows he can talk to his folks about this and that they can call me if they need to."

"I will."

A few minutes later, the phone rang. Scott picked it up.

"Hello, Scott? This is Vic Hammond. Sorry I'm late calling you, but a few things came up."

"Anything about Timmy?"

"We've talked a lot about him, but there aren't any new leads, if that's what you're wondering."

"It is. So, you calling about the decision to start treating this as an abduction?"

"Yeah, we made that call over an hour ago. I was going to call you then, but a reporter was standing right here, so we worked on putting together a press release, which I just authorized to be wired to all news outlets and other law enforcement agencies. Things should start getting a lot more active very soon."

Scott sat in the chair next to the telephone. "Is there anything we can do? Anything at all?"

"For now," Vic said, "just be prepared to take any phone calls from reporters. Most of them are following up on stories related to this whole Cuba situation, but I'm pretty sure some will see this as a big story and try to get an interview with you and Gina."

"Gina and I talked about it, and we are willing to do things like that. We want to do anything that'll help get Timmy back."

"Good, we appreciate that. We're going to try to get coverage on the radio and local television news too, not just the newspapers."

"The radio and TV?" Scott repeated. Mike heard this and took a step closer.

"Yes," Vic said, "lots of people are listening to their radios all day, trying to get the latest on this crisis with Cuba and the Russians. And they'll be watching the TV news every time it's on. In the next day or so, our plan is that everyone in Florida, maybe even in parts of Alabama and Georgia, will hear about Timmy."

"You think there's a chance Timmy's in Georgia or Alabama?"

"Could be. Nate pointed out that once that bus hit Jacksonville, it could have turned west toward the panhandle."

Scott hoped not. The whole state of Florida already seemed way too big a haystack to search through.

"Nate and I will have our hands full shortly, running down every lead that comes in, as well as recruiting more help, so it might be a little hard to reach us. You still have my card?"

"I do."

"Well, just call that number. They'll be able to reach us, and I'll get right back to you."

"Will do," Scott said. "And thanks, Vic, for everything you're doing. You and Nate."

"We'll do all we can," Vic said.

They hung up, and Scott filled Mike in on the details. Just as he finished, the phone rang again. Who could it be? he thought. He picked it up on the third ring.

"Hello, is Scott Harrison there?"

It sounded like Scott's boss from GE. "Is that you, Mr. Finch?"

"It's me. Scott?"

"Yes, sir, I'm here." Finch had never called him at home. Scott wasn't even sure how he got the number.

"Hey, I'm glad I got you. Just wanted to call and tell you how sorry we are about your boy being missing."

Wow, Scott thought, this was unexpected. "Thank you, Mr. Finch."

"But one of them came home, right?"

"Yes, last night."

"Haven't heard anything about it on the news yet. Maybe it's getting drowned out by all this news about Cuba. That was really something, what the president said last night. Mark Mitchell was the one told me about your boys, down at the Castaway Motel."

Mark was Scott's assistant, the one filling in for him today. "I just got off the phone with the FBI, as a matter of fact. You should start reading and hearing about the kidnapping later today. They wanted to wait a little while to make sure this wasn't a ransom-type kidnapping. They didn't think it was, but they had to be sure. That's why I had to stay by the phone, just in case."

Finch didn't reply immediately, then he said, "Things have really started hopping down at the Castaway this afternoon. The Expo's just a few days away."

Well, *now* this phone call was starting to make more sense. Scott didn't reply.

"Talking with Mark there—just got off the phone with him—he seems a bit overwhelmed by it all. Know what I mean?"

Scott did. He wished he didn't. He wanted the illusion that Mr. Finch actually cared about him to last at least a few moments longer.

"This project is really your baby, Scott. I can see Mark handling all the behind-the-scenes aspects, but he doesn't really have your gift of gab. Not even close. I think if he tries to give some of those talks you were planning to give, he'd bore people to tears. And he really only knows about half of what's going on, so I don't see all the Q&A sessions working out too well, either."

Scott couldn't believe this. This was the kind of pressure you applied when a worker was home milking a sore throat or a cold, not when their child was kidnapped. Was he kidding? Of course, Scott knew the answer. He glanced at Mike, who was standing by the coffeepot, pouring another cup. He was pretty sure Mike couldn't hear what his boss was saying, but he had to be careful with his own replies. "I'm really sorry about that, Mr. Finch. But I don't see how I can help. Nobody knows how important this Expo is more than me. I've been working on it nonstop for weeks. But sir, my son was kidnapped yesterday."

"Oh, I know," Finch said. "You need to be available for your family at a time like this."

"With all respect, sir, I don't need to be available *for* them, I need to be here *with* them."

"But I thought you said the FBI cleared up that this wasn't a standard kidnapping, so you don't really have to stay chained to the telephone anymore, right?"

"Mr. Finch, I need to be here."

"I see."

Scott doubted that.

"You don't think there's a chance you could split your time between the two places? The Castaway's only, what, ten minutes from where you live?"

"I really don't, Mr. Finch. At least not the rest of the day, and probably not tomorrow. If the press stops calling after that for a while, then maybe . . ."

"No, I understand, Scott. You do what you gotta do. We're all pulling for you over here. Look, I've gotta go. Got a meeting to attend before I call it a day."

They said their good-byes and hung up. When Scott looked up, Mike was standing there.

"Was that your boss?"

Scott nodded and released a chestful of frustration.

31

Gina couldn't believe the atmosphere at the grocery store or the prices. "Look at that, Rose, hamburger forty-five cents a pound. It was thirty-five cents when I went shopping here three days ago."

"And did you see the pork chops?" Rose said. "Seventy-five cents a pound. That's up over a nickel since the weekend."

"I have half a mind to put all this stuff in my cart back and go to another store," Gina said. "I think they've marked all the prices up because of this Cuba thing."

"Probably gonna be the same everywhere else," Rose said.

"Look at all the people. You'd think the food was gonna run out by tomorrow." Gina walked beside Rose as they made their way down the meat aisle.

"I wonder if it is," Rose said. "You think they announced something new over the radio this morning? Maybe we missed it."

"I don't think so." Just then a middle-aged woman pushed her cart past them. "Excuse me, ma'am," Gina said. "Why are there so many people in the store shopping now?"

The woman slowed but didn't stop. "Didn't you

hear the president last night? Or read the papers this morning? We could be at war with the Russians in a few days. My husband says they could be firing nuclear missiles at us at any moment."

"But they wouldn't bomb here," Rose said. "Not Daytona Beach."

"Maybe not. But they could bomb the Cape, and the fallout could certainly reach here. And what do you think will happen if they bomb all the major cities on the East Coast? People are saying the economy could shut down completely . . . for weeks, or even months." The woman started pushing her cart faster. "Excuse me, I've got to keep going."

Rose and Gina stopped and looked at each other. "You think we should buy some more things?" Rose said.

"I don't know," Gina said. "I can't imagine that really happening. Did you listen to what the president said last night? We had the TV on, but I was so distracted I don't remember most of it."

"We did listen to it, on the radio in the car. It sounded pretty serious, but I didn't think he was saying we were going to war. Mike said he was saying it could happen, not that it will."

"Maybe people are just panicking and over-reacting like they always do. They did it two years ago when Hurricane Donna came through. The grocery shelves were bare."

"You're probably right," Rose said. "But still, maybe just to be safe, we should buy some extra things. You know, just the necessary stuff. Even if they're wrong, all this panic buying could cause a food shortage by itself."

Then Gina remembered. "I can't, I didn't bring any extra money. Just enough for a few things."

"Well, we did, Mike and I. Let me help out."

"I can't let you do that. You're our guests."

"Don't be silly, Gina. This isn't like some planned vacation. You and Scott weren't expecting us. C'mon, I insist."

They stood there looking at each other. "Okay," Gina said. "I guess that would be all right. For now. But I'll pay you back when we get to the house."

Rose started moving the cart forward. "You'll do no such thing."

"Do you want to split up, so we can get done faster?" Gina didn't like being gone from the house that long.

"We could, but then we couldn't talk. And you know what will happen when we get home. The guys will be there, including Colt. And then we'll have to start fixing dinner."

Gina walked back and picked up another pound of ground beef and put it into the cart. "Is there something specific you wanted to talk about?" She hoped it wasn't about Scott's cheating. She couldn't talk about that without breaking down or getting angry.

"Kind of," Rose said. She hesitated. "I told Mike about . . . you know, what Scott did . . . at the party. What you saw."

Gina stiffened up but kept walking.

"I hope you don't mind, but I felt he needed to know. I mean, it sounds like it's the main reason you two aren't together anymore. Which sounds like the main reason the boys ran away."

"Do you two talk about everything?" Gina tried to keep the annoyance out of her voice, but she couldn't help feeling a little betrayed. She had assumed what she shared was just something between them. She walked over and picked up a package of chicken breasts.

"Pretty much," Rose said. "Certainly about important things. I'm guessing you and Scott don't? I don't mean just since he moved out. I'm talking about when you were together. You guys didn't talk about things? You know, how you're feeling, the things that bother you . . . or bother him."

Gina could hardly believe the question. She and Scott never talked like that, and she didn't know any other wives who talked with their husbands about things like that, either. Everyone knew men didn't share their feelings, even with each other. "Let's head down this aisle. I want to pick up some cans of tuna."

Rose waited for a woman to pass then turned the cart to the right. "I guess you didn't like that question?"

"It's not that, Rose. Scott and I didn't have that kind of relationship. We never have. For one thing, we hardly ever got to see each other. For most of our first two years together, he was off in Korea. You knew that. Then when he got home, he wanted to finish college. He got this idea that he had to do it himself. He wouldn't take his father's money and go full-time. His dad even offered to help us with room and board, not just tuition. But Scott said no. Instead he worked full-time and went to night school for seven years on the GI Bill, while I sat home alone trying to be the good little housewife and mother." Look what that got me, she thought. Now they were separated, she was working full-time, and her little boy was—

"Why wouldn't Scott let his father help him?" Rose said.

"He said, for one thing, the help came with strings. His father would only pay if he went into business and finance, like Scott's brothers. Scott wanted to pursue engineering."

"Okay, but didn't he graduate three years ago?" Rose said.

"Yes," Gina said, reaching for the cans of tuna. She waited a moment to continue until a woman with a toddler in her cart got far enough away. "Nothing changed after he graduated. I thought it would. The whole time he was going to night school he promised me it would. But right after he graduated, he started working at GE. Then it was all about climbing up the ladder as quickly as he could. He hated being the low man on the totem pole, having to listen to all these younger guys who went to college right out of high school and graduated several years ahead of him. So once again, he's leaving me alone night after night, getting home late, so he can impress all his bosses and get promotions." Gina pointed to a jar of mayonnaise. "Of course, now I don't even know if that was true."

"If what was true?" Rose put the mayonnaise jar in the cart.

"Why he got home late each night, once he started working at GE. It was probably just a lie, to cover up his affair with that redhead." She looked down the aisle. "We should probably get another loaf of bread, or maybe two. Of course, it'll probably just go stale before we can eat the second one."

"I'm sorry, Gina. I didn't mean to bring all this up. Mike and I just want to help you while we're here, if we can. I kind of knew all the things you just told me, not about the part about Scott cheating but about him being too busy all the time and you being so lonely. I could tell some-thing was wrong every time we'd visit from Savannah. I even talked to Mike about it."

Of course you did, Gina thought. You and Mike talk about everything.

"The only reason I'm bringing it up is, Mike thinks he can help Scott with this. And since it seems to be at the core of your troubles as a couple, we thought—"

"Help Scott with *what,* Rose?"

"Help Scott see how wrong it is, how wrong it's been to keep neglecting you, neglecting your relationship all this time. A few years ago, our pastor back home helped Mike understand some things about a husband's role in the home. He went to a men's breakfast and completely changed after that. Mike's even helped some husbands in our church get to a better place in their marriages. And I thought, maybe—"

"Rose, I appreciate what you're saying and what Mike wants to do. But there's really no point to it."

"No point?" Rose said. "It could change everything in your relationship."

Gina sighed. "No, it can't," she said as tears welled up in her eyes. "Can it take the picture out of my mind of my husband in the arms of that redhead? Or hearing her tell me how much they're in love? Can it bring my little boy home?"

32

"Are there more bags in the trunk?" Scott asked.

Gina and Rose carried their shopping bags past Scott and Mike standing in the living room. "Quite a few," Gina said. "Make sure you carry them from the bottom so they don't rip. The kid who bagged them was in a hurry. He filled some of them too much."

Scott and Mike headed out the door. "I thought you were just gonna get enough for dinner," Scott said.

"We were," Rose yelled. "This is Plan B."

"What's Plan B?" Mike said, stopping at the doorway.

"It's what you do when the world is about to be annihilated," Rose said, "and you're afraid you might run out of groceries."

Mike laughed and so did Scott as he unlocked the trunk. It felt good to laugh, but the feeling didn't last long.

"Colt?" he heard Gina yell from inside the house. "Colt, where are you?"

He'd better get in there, quick.

"Colt!" She sounded more frantic.

"He's okay, Gina," Scott said, running toward the front door. "He's across the street, at Murph's house."

She met him at the doorway. "Are you sure?"

"I'm sure. I walked him over there myself a little while after you left for the store. Thought it would do him some good to get his mind off things."

All the panic left her face. "I wish you had told me."

"I was going to, but you just got home."

She went back toward the kitchen, and Scott headed back for the grocery bags. He and Mike made several trips back and forth, carrying the overloaded brown bags. When they were done, Mike said, "Are you two going to be fixing dinner for a little while?"

"Yes, we are," Rose said. "Why, what do you have in mind?"

"Something Scott just said gave me an idea. I think he could use a little fresh air. Thought maybe he and I could take a little walk on the beach. You up for that, Scott?"

Scott walked into the dining area and faced the two women. "I am if it's okay with Gina."

Gina looked up from a bag she was unloading. "Sure, go ahead. It's going to take us at least thirty to forty minutes to fix dinner. Would you mind checking on Colt first, make sure he's still all right?"

"Sure, I can do that. By the way, the FBI called." Over the next few minutes, Scott updated Gina. As he did, Rose led Mike out to the driveway, saying she needed to talk to him for a moment. When Scott finished filling Gina in, he joined them out front.

Mike pulled out his car keys. "I'll drive, if that's okay with you. I love driving on your beach. I've never seen a beach like the one you've got here."

"I thought you were going to take a walk," Rose said.

"We are," Mike said, "after we drive a little bit. I just want to get down to that section of sand dunes a few blocks north of here."

"Well, keep watch of the time," Rose said.

"And can you pick up Colt on your way home?" Gina said.

Vic and Nate got out of their car in downtown Orlando and hurried into the office building that housed the FBI's Orlando office. Ed Foster, the special agent in charge as well as Vic and Nate's boss, had called them in for a special briefing. Not only them but all the agents who worked out of the Orlando office. They rarely met all together this way, so Vic assumed it was something pretty important.

As they entered the room filled with agents and Vic saw the man standing next to their boss, Vic knew his assumptions had been correct.

"Okay, men," Foster said, "I think everyone's here that's supposed to be. I'll get a memo out to the few agents who couldn't make this meeting. Needless to say, nothing that is said in this briefing can leave this room. You all know the man standing to my left, Associate Deputy Director Stanley Harbaugh. I'll let Director Harbaugh take it from here."

Foster stepped to the side, and Director Harbaugh stepped forward. "Gentlemen, I don't have to tell you very much about the state of affairs we're in at this moment. How many of you listened to the president's speech last night?"

Vic looked around. Every hand was raised.

"Good," Harbaugh continued. "I can tell you that the federal government has been eyeing this missile situation for almost a week now. The president decided to go public last night because things have reached a critical stage. It is no exaggeration to say we are all in grave danger. By all, I literally mean every man, woman, or child living on the planet right now. As of this moment, we have no indication that the Soviets intend to back down and honor this blockade. I mean quarantine. But I am also reliably informed that the president was not saber rattling in his speech last night. He meant every word. The consequences of doing nothing are unthinkable. But as I see it, the consequences of a major confrontation between us and the Soviets is equally unthinkable."

Vic looked around the room. There wasn't a

192

sound other than the director's voice. Every eye was fixed on his face.

"For the first time in my adult life," Harbaugh said, "I believe we are on the edge of a nuclear catastrophe. It could actually happen this time, gentlemen. And we don't have much time. This is not something we can afford to play out over the next few weeks. I've been told the Soviets are just days away from their long-range missiles being ready to launch. The president, along with the Joint Chiefs of Staff and a host of advisors, have decided if the Soviets do not back down before that moment, we must do whatever it takes to stop them."

"So, we're talking World War III?" one of the men said.

Harbaugh nodded. "Yes, we are. Part of the reason I'm sharing all of this with you is because the situation is so grave. We think it's only a matter of time before the general public begins to realize what's at stake, what we're really facing here."

"I think many of them already do, sir," someone said.

"I'm sure some of them do," Harbaugh said. "Our job is to help maintain the safety and security of all our citizens . . . even during a time like this. Agent Foster here is holding a stack of special assignments, security matters we have thought through and anticipated back in

Washington. And I'm sure a host of things will arise we haven't anticipated. Each of you needs to take one and look it over carefully before you leave."

Vic looked over at Agent Foster, who was holding a small stack of paper. His and Nate's names better not be on that list. He'd already been assured they would be staying on this kidnapping case. Foster noticed him looking his way. He pointed to the stack of assignments and shook his head no. Vic interpreted this to mean they were in the clear.

When the assistant deputy director had finished and asked if there were any questions, Vic decided to be a little bold and raised his hand. "Excuse me, sir. Special Agent Victor Hammond here."

"Go ahead, Agent Hammond. You have a question?"

"More like a special request, sir."

"Oh? And what would that be?"

Everyone turned and looked his way. "My partner Nate Winters and I are already working on a kidnapping case, a child abduction that happened just north of Jacksonville yesterday afternoon in a diner."

"I'm sorry to hear that," Harbaugh said.

"Thank you, sir. But as you know, if we weren't in the middle of this major national crisis, this kidnapping would be front and center, and we'd be getting all kinds of help to find this little boy."

"That's true."

"I realize these aren't normal times," Vic continued, "but I wonder if I could make an appeal on behalf of this little boy's family . . . if any of you men find yourselves with any spare time at all in these critical next few days, could you give us a hand? I've got my own stack of copies here. A picture of the little boy named Timmy. He's only six. And a sketch artist's drawing of the kidnapper. Could you take one of these with you as well? I'm hoping they'll be in every newspaper in the state by the end of the day or tomorrow morning."

"We can do that, Agent Hammond," Harbaugh said. "In fact, why don't you come up here and take a few minutes to bring us up to date. And Agent Winters can pass out those sketches."

Vic nodded and handed the stack of paper to Nate as the two of them made their way forward.

"Men?" Harbaugh said. "Do anything you can to help find this little boy. Are there any more questions?"

33

Scott wasn't too sure about this walk on the beach idea.

If anything, the thought of him and Mike, alone, doing nothing but walking and talking on the beach for thirty minutes, made him feel more tense. What was relaxing about that? If Mike wanted to help him unwind, they should head down to one of the arcades at the boardwalk and play pinball. He and Mike hadn't talked about anything, other than the necessary chitchat when planning family visits . . . well, ever.

They were on the beach now, after crossing A1A and heading down the approach. It was a beautiful day, nice and sunny, very uncrowded. Pretty much just them, the seagulls, and after a few blocks, some sand dunes, at least on this stretch of the beach.

"How about here?" Mike said.

"Good a place as any," Scott said.

Mike turned left, pulled the car into a spot just before the line where the sand became soft. Both men got out.

"I'm guessing you weren't thinking about the two of us building a sand castle," Scott said.

"Not exactly."

"You want to talk about me and Gina?"

"Ouch . . . am I that predictable?" Mike said.

"Well," Scott said, as they made their way across the flat sand toward the waterline, "how long have we known each other, Mike?"

"A little over five years, I guess."

"Two things we've never done in that time . . . talk about anything meaningful and take a walk on the beach. Put that together with the fact that I screwed up my marriage in a major way and that I've been expecting God to appoint someone to take me out to the woodshed for quite some time, I guess it might as well be you."

Mike smiled. "I forgot I'm talking to an engineer. You're close, but you're wrong on one thing."

"What's that?"

"I have no plans to take you out to the woodshed. Seriously, that's not what this is about."

Scott looked out to the water. "Well, somebody better do it."

"Maybe somebody will. But it's not gonna be me."

They walked a few steps in silence.

"I just figured with all you're going through, you might need a friend. I know guys don't typically have friendships like that, unless they've been fighting in a foxhole together for a while. I thought I'd take a chance and just jump in, see what happens."

Scott took a deep breath, like he was bracing for something. "Guess you better just jump in then. What's on your mind?"

"Well, not sure exactly where to start," Mike said. "Obviously, it came as a bit of a shock that you and Gina were separated. We could kind of tell, for at least the last year or two, that you guys were having problems. We just didn't know things had gotten this bad."

"If you knew that," Scott said, "you knew more than I did. Until that Christmas party last December, I thought Gina and I were doing fine. At least as good as we've been doing all along."

A slightly bigger wave than the rest rolled in, forcing the two men to scamper out of its way like a pair of sandpipers. "Rose told me about the party, what happened with you and that secretary."

"Then you haven't heard the full story, just Gina's version." Scott stopped walking and turned to face Mike.

"Fair enough. What's your version? She says she walked in on you making out with a young redhead. And that this redhead said the two of you were in love."

Scott felt so frustrated he could scream. "That's not what happened, Mike. Not even close."

"She didn't see you kissing another woman at that party?"

"She did see that, but what she saw wasn't what she saw."

"Okay . . . care to elaborate?" Mike began to walk again.

Scott did too. "She kissed me, this secretary. I didn't see it coming, and she caught me off guard. I could tell she liked me. She had been trying to flirt with me for months. But I never did anything to encourage her." Scott stopped walking again. "Look at me, Mike. Look me straight in the eye. I'm telling you, I wasn't cheating on Gina. This girl and I were *not* in a relationship, on any level."

"What were you doing with her then, alone in that office during a company Christmas party?"

"She told me my boss had some papers I was supposed to take home with me, and she'd forgotten to give them to me. She asked me to come back to his office and she'd get them. It'll only take a moment, she said. I looked around for Gina, to tell her where I was going, but I couldn't find her. I guess she was in the bathroom or something. So like an idiot, I followed this secretary back to my boss's office, and that's when it happened. But it was just one kiss, Mike, we weren't making out. And I instantly tried to push her away. That's what I was doing when Gina walked in."

They started walking again. "Does Gina know all this?"

"Does she know? I've tried to tell her, a dozen times. She won't believe me. Of course, it didn't help that Marla lied to her. Right there, that night. She said we're in love. I said, we are not, as loud as I could. This woman's delusional, Mike. But Gina believed her, and she wouldn't listen to me. That's the reason we're separated right now. And I haven't been able to get her to reconsider, no matter what I've tried."

"Where are things at between you and this girl?"

"There's nothing going on between us. There never has been. She doesn't even work in our office anymore. I told my boss what she did when we got back from the Christmas holiday and he had her transferred to another building."

Scott had to calm down. He hadn't talked about this with anyone for so long, he didn't realize how upset it made him that Gina refused to believe him. "Do you believe me, Mike?"

Mike didn't answer right away. "I do, Scott."

"You do?"

"Yeah, I do. I can see how something like that could happen."

"Then will you talk to Gina? She won't even talk about it with me anymore."

"I can try to, Scott. But have you asked yourself why?"

"Why what?"

"Why she doesn't believe you?"

"I don't know. I guess for starters she saw that kiss, and she's always been the jealous type. Ever since we got married, she's been that way."

"Have you ever given her any reason to be jealous?"

"I don't think so. Gina's the only woman I've ever loved. I've never even been with anyone else. Even when I was in Korea. Lots of guys, even some of the married ones, were playing around. But I never cheated on her. So you tell me, Mike, why she's having such a hard time believing me."

Mike looked at his watch. "Maybe we should turn around now." They did, and started walking back toward the car. "I want to say something to you, Scott. But I don't want to hurt you."

"Just say it, Mike. Whatever it is."

"I'm almost positive, if Rose walked in on me being kissed by a young secretary at a party and I told her it wasn't what it looked like, that she'd believe me."

"Even if that secretary lied and said you were having an affair."

"I believe so," Mike said. "She'd believe me over the girl. It'd be a rough night, but yeah, I know she'd believe me."

Scott had a hard time believing that. But only for a few moments. As they walked together in silence a little while and he thought about what he knew of Mike and Rose's relationship, he had to admit . . . he really could see Rose believing Mike on something like that.

And that really started to bother him.

They didn't say too much until they got a little closer to Mike's car. Scott broke the ice. "Thanks, Mike."

"You mean it?"

"Yeah, I do. And I might regret this later, but right now I'm thinking I'd really like to hear what's going on with you and Rose. What's different about your relationship, why would she believe you if you got in the kind of jam I'm in."

"I don't know, Scott."

"What do you mean, you don't know?"

201

"I don't know if I want to get into that right now. That would be a hard conversation."

"Why?"

"Because it would . . . I've had this same talk before with a few guys in my church back in Savannah. I definitely would like to talk with you sometime about it. But I don't know if now's the right—"

"Mike . . ." They had reached Mike's car. Scott sighed. "I really want to hear it. If it'll help me close this mile-wide gap between Gina and me . . . then I want to hear it." And maybe, Scott thought, it'll finally give them the kind of home life Colt and Timmy would never want to run away from.

34

"What in the world is she doing?" August let the living room curtain slide back into place. He thought he'd heard a strange noise. Wasn't the boy; it came from outside. One look out the window confirmed it. It was his nosy neighbor trespassing on his property, heading right this way. He had to deal with this. Wouldn't do following his old plan of just ignoring her till she went away. Not with the boy in the house.

Bobby was back in his room after spending two hours in the dark place for running off like he'd done. He promised he'd never do it again and begged August not to put him in there. Pitched quite a fit talking about how afraid he was of the dark. But the boy had to be taught a lesson, for his own good.

Now August was gonna have to put him back in there again. And quick.

He rushed back to Bobby's room, found him sleeping, laying right across his bed. He thought about leaving him there, see if maybe he'd sleep right through this upcoming intrusion. But it wouldn't do any good to have him wake up while she was here. Might come right out of his room and surprise them before August had a chance to send her on her way.

For a moment, he entertained the notion of chasing her off with his shotgun. It was sitting right there in the corner, all loaded and ready to go. That would certainly get her moving, but he couldn't take the chance that she'd complain about it to the police. They might come out here to give him a lecture and accidentally see the boy.

He walked over to the bed and shook Bobby awake. Bobby didn't respond. "Bobby, wake up."

"What? What is it?"

"Shhh," August said, holding his index finger up to his lips. "Sit up, right now."

"What's the matter?"

"You need to get out of bed, that's what's the matter. Do it now."

Bobby rubbed his eyes and sat up. "Why? What's going on?"

"Somebody's coming. Stop asking so many questions and do as you're told."

Bobby slid out of bed and stood by it.

August reached out his hand. "C'mon, follow me."

"Where we going?"

"I said stop asking so many questions. Do I need to give you a swat?"

"No." Bobby stepped closer and took hold of August's hand.

August pulled him through the hallway, then the kitchen, toward the back porch.

"Where we going? Where are you taking me?"

As they got to the back door, August said, "You know where."

"No!" Bobby shouted. "Not the closet! Please. I'll be good. I promise."

"Hush!" August pulled harder and squeezed his wrist harder. "It'll just be a few minutes this time, till I get rid of this busybody. But I'll leave you in there another two hours if you make a fuss about it." The boy was still pulling away, trying to dig his heels in, but he found no purchase on the wooden floor. And he didn't weigh nothing, so it was a fairly easy chore getting him across the porch.

"Please don't make me go in there. I promise I won't say anything."

"I can't take that chance." August opened the padlock and flipped open the latch. He swung the door back and pushed the boy inside.

"But it's too dark in here. I'm afraid."

"Well, that's just something you're gonna have to get over. There's nothing in there gonna hurt you. But if you don't hush, I'll put a hurt on you. You keep quiet, I'll be back to get you as soon as she leaves. I might even give you one of those comic books. But you make a racket, and I'll leave you in here all night. You'll get no supper."

As August closed the door, he could hear the boy starting to cry. "You remember what I told you last time. Nobody can hear you crying in there. You're just wasting your time." He locked the door back up and headed toward the living room to intercept his neighbor.

What he had told the boy wasn't exactly the truth. Nobody could hear if they were on their own property. But he had little doubt that if Bobby cried as loud as he had earlier that day and that neighbor was on his front porch, she very well could hear it. That happened, and he might just have to use his shotgun after all. So see, locking the boy up was best for everyone.

By the time August got to the front door, he could already hear that woman's heavy steps across the porch. She was a big woman, probably on account of all them pies she made. He smiled at that thought. He opened the door just as she raised her hand to knock.

"Oh, excuse me," she said.

"Excuse you for what?"

"Guess I was just about to knock on your chest."

"Well, what do you want?"

"Me? I don't really want anything, I just—"

"Then why'd you come over?"

"Now, August, is that any way to talk to your neighbor?"

She lived on the property next door, he thought, but did that really make them neighbors? He decided not to answer. Figured she'd keep talking without his help. He looked at her hair; it seemed a little different from the last time he saw her. More curly and more gray. She had to be what, close to sixty now.

"I just came over to find out if you heard the news. You know, what the president said on television about the Russians and Cuba? I know you don't watch television all that much, but this news is kind of important. World War III could start any day now. That's what everyone's saying."

"You don't say."

"My daughter and her husband live in Cocoa Beach. She's been telling me that all kinds of Army trucks and tanks have been driving down US-1, all heading south toward Cuba. For days now. The president didn't say anything about that, but her husband said they're preparing for an invasion. He said it could happen any day. And if it does, he said you could count on the Russians firing off atom bombs at us. You know, like Hiroshima. And then we'd be firing off our bombs at them."

She stood there looking at him a moment, like all this should matter to him somehow. "Well, I guess if it's the end, then it's the end," he said.

A confused look came over her face. "That's all you have to say?"

"Well, what else am I supposed to say? Not like I can do anything about it, one way or the other." Now she looked frustrated, or was it disgusted? He didn't care either way. He just wanted her gone.

"I just thought I should tell you," she said. "Thought maybe you should be watching the TV a little more over the next few days, or at least turn on your radio. That way if those missiles start firing off, you'll be ready."

Was she serious? How did one get ready for atom bombs going off? Besides, he didn't think they were called atom bombs anymore either. Weren't they made of hydrogen or helium? Either way, none of this was really his concern. If the world was gonna end, it was gonna end.

He was gonna say thanks for coming over, but he didn't want her to think he was glad to see her. "If that's it then, you have a nice day."

She stared at him a moment. He was about to close the door. "Oh, by the way, didn't I see you with your little boy down by the water's edge awhile ago?"

"What?"

"Your little boy, hadn't seen him around for months. But thought I saw him this afternoon with you down by the water. Has he been living with his mother for a while?"

August felt anger rising up inside him. Nosy old biddy. That was probably the real reason she wobbled over here. Not to warn him about World War III. She wanted to get the inside scoop on his personal business. Well, he wouldn't give her the satisfaction. "I'm sorry, but I don't see how that's any of your business. You have a nice day."

With that, he closed the door. Gave it a little shove those last few inches. He stepped away, closed the little set of curtains hanging over the living room door window. Made sure there weren't any gaps.

He waited there a minute, a full minute. Could still see her big shape outlined through the curtains. Get a move on it now, he thought. He walked over toward his shotgun in the corner. Just as he picked it up, he heard her heavy footsteps exiting the porch.

That a girl.

35

Mike and Scott were still at the beach, both leaning up against Mike's car. Mike was just about to honor Scott's request to tell him some of the secrets about how his relationship with Rose was in such better shape than Scott and Gina's. Scott was pretty sure what Mike had to say would also include some of the major screwups and mistakes Scott had made over the years.

Just before Mike began to speak, they were interrupted by a loud roaring sound coming from the sand dunes. The men turned in time to see a WWII-era jeep fly over the top of one of the dunes then bounce and land halfway down the other side, to the great delight of four college kids inside.

As they watched, the jeep went barreling up the next dune, spewing a rooster tail of white sand from its rear wheels, then disappeared down the other side. "That's something I don't get to see much of in Savannah," Mike said.

"Those kids don't seem too concerned about the world ending anytime soon," Scott said. "Were we ever that carefree? I can't remember."

"I think I was," Mike said, "but as I recall, you got sent to Korea when you were their age, so I think you kind of missed out."

"Maybe that's my problem," Scott said, looking down at the sand in front of them.

"You sure you want to talk about all this now?"

"I'm not really sure about anything, to be honest with you. And I'm not really sure if I did everything you're about to tell me that it would make any difference to Gina. I don't think she's ever gonna get over me kissing that secretary, or hearing her say we were in love."

"You might be right about that, Scott. But I think if you work at some of the ideas I'm about to tell you, it could start to turn things around. I think the main reason she didn't believe your explanation was because of all the months and years she felt neglected, like she was playing second fiddle to your career."

Ouch. Scott didn't know what to say.

"See," Mike continued, "Gina had no reserves to draw from when she saw that scene at the party. If she had felt completely loved and cared for and had lots of fresh examples of you choosing her over other things, like your job and the TV, you saying that party scene was all a big misunderstanding would have been easier to believe."

Scott wanted to protest and say how much he *did* love Gina, that everything he was doing, he was doing for her. But Mike wouldn't buy it. Gina sure hadn't.

Right then, he wasn't even sure he did.

"That make sense, Scott?"

"Yeah, I think so."

"Gina was explaining to Rose how detached and lonely she's felt in your relationship, going back years now. It started when you were in Korea, and then—"

"How can she blame me for that?" Scott said. "It was a war. I had to do my part."

"And if that was the only problem, I don't think she would blame you. But what did you do when you got home?"

"I got a job and went to college. Colt was born by then, so I had to work. And if I didn't finish college, I couldn't get a decent job. We'd barely be scraping by. So I went to night school."

"For how long?"

"Seven years," Scott said. "But that's how long it took to finish."

"Right, so for two years you were gone in Korea, then for seven more years you're working all day and either going to school or studying all night. That's nine years, Scott. That's a long time to be left alone in a house by yourself with small children, don't you think? Gina told Rose when they were just out shopping your dad offered to give you guys money to live on while you were going to school so you wouldn't have to work. You could have finished in three years if you'd done that. But you turned him down."

Scott walked away from the car, kicked the sand with his shoes. "That's not the whole story.

All that *help* from dear old dad came with strings. I had to go into banking or finance, like my older brothers. I wanted to go into engineering. Uncle Sam stepped up and offered the GI Bill with no strings, so I took it."

Mike walked over to Scott. "Okay . . . how many times did you get a babysitter and take Gina out during those seven years of night school? Approximately?"

Scott looked away. He was about to say "plenty," until he realized . . . he couldn't think of a single time. But that couldn't be right, could it?

"How about after that magic moment when you graduated? What was that, three years ago?"

"Just a little over three," Scott said.

"Do you remember what you said to Gina then? Really, for the last few years before you graduated. Rose said you kept promising Gina how different it was gonna be once you started work as an engineer. No more night school. The two of you would have all kinds of time together. You'd start going out on dates again, have lots of family outings, right? Wasn't that how it was gonna be?"

Scott walked away, toward the front fender of the car. He didn't know where he was going. A row of pelicans glided by. He wished he could fly away. He hated the sound of everything he had just heard, and how it made him feel. He had said all those things to Gina. Over and over again.

Month after month. But he hadn't made good on any of it. They weren't promises. Just things he said in the moment to calm her down.

Lies, really. Just lies.

"Tell me something, Scott. Think back to how you treated Gina before you were married, how you felt about her then."

"I was nuts about her. I chased her for months, until she finally went out with me."

"And how often did you go out with her, once she finally said yes?"

"Twice a week," Scott said. "But that was only because her father wouldn't let us go out any more than that. I wanted to see her every night."

"You were romancing her."

"I guess you could say that."

"You made her feel like a queen."

You could say that too, Scott thought. He saw where this was going.

"You made her think she meant more to you than anyone or anything else on earth."

"I loved her."

"Right," Mike said. "But did you keep it up after you got married?"

"No, not really. But who could? That's not how life works. The war came, kids came. I had to work, go to school. I still loved her, but . . . the way we were when we were dating? That's not real life."

Mike smiled.

"What are you smiling about?"

"You just said it."

"Said what?"

"The crux of the problem."

"What did I say?"

"See, that's where men and women come at this thing totally different. I'm about to let you in on a secret most husbands never get. I only know it because my pastor told me a few years ago. But I've talked to Rose about it, and she says it's absolutely true."

"What?"

"You know the way most men treat women when they're trying to win them? What we see in all those love stories, hear in all those love songs on the radio?" Scott nodded. "See, women don't know we're only gonna treat them that way for a little while, just as long as it takes till they say yes and they're safely on board. They actually think we mean it, that that's how we feel about them and how we plan to treat them for all time. They think that's what we mean when we say we love them. They think that's what we're going to keep doing when we make those wedding vows."

Scott nodded, his back to Mike. "I get what you're saying."

"Men are so different than women. We're goal setters, we're all about conquest, about taking the next hill. You were willing to do whatever it took to win Gina, and then as soon as she was conquered, your heart and mind shifted to the next goal, the next hill. Finishing school, getting a good job, getting a house, a nice car, moving up the ladder at work as quickly as you could. All the while, Gina's dropping farther and farther down the list. The worst part of it is, she knows it. She could feel it. And there was nothing she could do about it."

Scott felt like he'd just gained a hundred pounds.

"Then on top of all this," Mike said, "she walks in on you kissing a young, redheaded secretary."

Scott exhaled an audible sigh.

"See what I mean?" Mike said. "We're being sold a pack of lies, Scott. About what the American Dream is, what this 'pursuit of happiness' is really all about. Millions of men all over this country are doing the same thing you are, believing the same thing you've been believing, all the while lying to themselves. 'I'm doing all this for her,' or 'It's all for them.' But that's not what our wives want, or what our kids want, either."

No, it's not, Scott thought.

"The truth is," Mike said, "Father doesn't always know best. He should be listening to what his wife has to say a whole lot more. Ward Cleaver and Ozzie Nelson aren't real husbands, and wives don't always smile and say 'Yes, dear' when we're done talking. Millions of wives are frustrated and lonely and tired of being ignored.

Gina's not the only one, Scott. My pastor was talking about this at a men's breakfast awhile back. He said the whole thing's like a boiling kettle about to blow.

"And one of the worst parts about this lie is that it's being presented as something God is okay with. Like this is his idea of church and home. But it's not. My dad told me once that God didn't make Eve to be Adam's little helper, but because he knew men desperately needed the help. God's idea of what it means to be in charge is totally different than ours."

Scott had never heard anything like this before. It sounded almost crazy. And he wouldn't believe a word of it if he hadn't seen it himself. Not just with Gina, but with his mom. She had it all, and she was one of the most unhappy women he'd ever known. He had been raised on a lie. And that lie had cost him dearly.

First Gina. And now Timmy.

Timmy.

Please, God, help us find him. Please keep him safe.

36

Mamie Lee looked out through the screen door on the front porch toward the sidewalk. Paperboy should have come by now, seeing as it was almost five. If she was careful, she could read some of it while she finished cooking dinner. Main thing was to keep it looking fresh and new for when Mr. Harrison got home. He needed to feel like he was the first one to get his hands on it.

She was curious about what they were saying about this Cuba missile thing, but even more so to see if they'd printed anything about little Timmy being gone. A part of her hoped not, even though she realized if they had, it might help get him back home quicker. But she couldn't bear to see the story in print. She knew if she did, it would make it seem too real.

The newspaper wasn't on the sidewalk. Her eyes raked over the porch, then the porch steps. No luck there, either. She scanned the grassy area between the porch steps and the front hedges and finally saw it resting in the flower bed between two petunias. That boy would've gotten a good talking to, had that paper landed six inches either way and crushed her flowers.

She walked out across the porch then almost jumped out of her skin when the screen door slapped shut. She still wasn't used to how quickly it closed, now that the handyman had taken his oil can to it. Coming down the porch steps and onto the lawn, she squinted as she looked up into pale blue sky. Hard to imagine nuclear missiles flying high overhead on their way to who knows where.

She couldn't help thinking about it, after listening to Mr. Harrison talking up a storm on the subject over breakfast. She had never seen him quite so lively. He seemed to be taking the president's speech as seriously as those folks standing around the appliance store last night.

Of course, that all changed once Mrs. Harrison told him about poor Timmy going missing. Mamie had been somewhat surprised to hear him talking about this Cuba matter so forcefully when his poor little grandson had been kidnapped. Then she realized, once Mrs. Harrison started talking, that he didn't know anything about it. For some reason, she hadn't told him when he got home last night.

But once he did hear, he wasn't talking about Cuba anymore.

She had never seen him that angry or upset. He wanted to know every last detail and what the police were doing about it. Poor Mrs. Harrison didn't know the answers to half his questions, and then he wanted to know why that was so. Most of what she said put the blame square on

Mister Scott's shoulders. Mamie had to agree with most of what she'd said, seeing how Mister Scott had kept them both in the dark all day.

Before he headed off to work, Mr. Harrison had said, "Well, you get that son of mine on the phone this morning and tell him I said he needs to call us with regular updates from now on, and find out how much ransom money we need to come up with."

Mamie could see on his face he was more worried than angry, but he wasn't one to let his fears show. Mrs. Harrison had said they were pretty sure it wasn't that kind of kidnapping. With that, he got an even worse look on his face.

All day, she and Mrs. Harrison had waited for the telephone to ring. Maybe Mamie would find out what kind of kidnapping it was exactly. But Mister Scott didn't call, and Mrs. Harrison didn't call him, either. Mamie didn't expect that to happen anyhow. Not like Mrs. Harrison to do such a thing.

Mamie bent down to pick up the paper. Her joints creaked louder than those dang steps. She was feeling mighty stiff all up and down her legs and hips. Guess it was from that long walk home last night in the chilly air. She'd have to rub some liniment on them tonight, maybe soak her feet in some Epsom salt.

She carefully unfolded the paper as she walked down the sidewalk.

"Is it in there?"

Mamie looked up. Mrs. Harrison was standing inside the screen door, looking out. "I haven't checked, ma'am." She climbed the steps. "Wanna look at it?"

Mrs. Harrison started backing into the foyer, to make room for Mamie to come inside. "No, Mamie Lee, you better do it. You know how to keep it fresh for Henry. If I do it, I'll wrinkle it all up."

Mamie opened the screen door. Poor Mrs. Harrison, dread all over her face. Well, Mamie probably looked just the same way. She walked down the hallway with the paper in both hands, intending to bring it to the kitchen, like she always did.

"Where are you going?" Mrs. Harrison asked.

Mamie stopped. "To the kitchen."

"No, come sit with me where there's more light." She walked into the big fancy front parlor and sat in a chair near the front window. Looked right at Mamie Lee, like she expected her to follow. But Mamie had never sat in this room before. "Mamie Lee?"

Mamie Lee looked up.

"Didn't you hear me? I said have a seat." She looked right over at the chair beside her, situated on the other side of a round hardwood end table Mamie Lee must have polished a thousand times. "We can see the newspaper much better here."

Mamie Lee did as she was told, sat right in the chair, taking all kinds of care. She opened the front page and looked it over, up and down.

"Is it in there?" Mrs. Harrison said. "Anything about Timmy?"

Mamie read the biggest headline: "JFK Orders Cuban Blockade, Blasts Reds If Castro Attacks." Noticed a picture under it, looked like a bunch of reporters surrounding somebody at the White House, but it wasn't the president. Under that, another smaller headline: "Havana Declares US Is Preparing Aggression." She looked over the rest of the page. "Nothing about Timmy on the front page," she said.

"Well, skip to the front page of the local section," Mrs. Harrison said. "Maybe they put it in there."

Mamie folded the front section carefully and set it aside. The local section was the next one in order. Soon as she unfolded it, she knew she didn't need to read the page or look at it too closely. There on the bottom half of the page, big as life, was the familiar, beautiful face of Mister Scott and Miss Gina's little Timmy, smiling as though he were having some kind of wonderful day. Beside that, a drawing of some strange man wearing a hat. Next to it the headline: "Local Boy Kidnapped Near Jacksonville."

Tears instantly filled Mamie's eyes. She couldn't help it.

"Oh Mamie," Mrs. Harrison said, standing up. "It's in there, isn't it?" She walked quickly across the room to the fireplace. "My poor Timmy. Put it away. I don't want to see it."

37

"Gina, maybe you should put that away."

It was Wednesday morning, the third day. Gina set the newspaper down and looked up at Rose. She had been holding the morning edition of the *News-Journal*, the local Daytona paper. It had run essentially the same story about Timmy that first showed up in yesterday's evening edition, including the picture of Timmy and the artist's sketch of the man who'd taken him.

She looked down at the picture of the man. He looked so . . . ordinary. "Why would someone take a little boy?"

"I don't know, hon," Rose said. "But maybe we should do something to try to distract ourselves."

"Do what? We can't leave the house. We're supposed to stay by the telephone, in case it rings." They had stayed by the telephone all last evening, but it didn't ring once. Mike and Rose had stayed, trying to cheer them up. The five of them sat around the living room, Colt included. There wasn't anything on about Timmy during the local news. Then Gina had to sit through an entire hour of *Combat* with Vic Morrow, Colt's hero. Colt watched the show spread out on the living room throw rug with his pillow. But all she could think about was not seeing Timmy lying next to him. Usually, when the show ended, it was time for Timmy to go to bed. She'd let Colt stay up another hour, since he was eleven.

She'd walk Timmy back to the bathroom to help him wash his face and hands, brush his teeth. She'd tuck him into bed, sometimes read him a story. Off and on, she'd hear Colt laughing out loud in the living room at some skit on *The Red Skelton Hour*.

None of that happened last night.

Oh, they had finished watching *Combat*, everyone had laughed at the crazy skits on the Red Skelton show, except her. They'd laughed some more watching Jack Benny. Scott even let Colt stay up past his bedtime to watch it. That was a strange moment. Colt didn't want to go to bed at his usual time. He argued that he didn't have to go to school the next day, since they had both agreed to excuse him. Finally, Scott had given in and let him stay up. He had looked at Gina, smiled, and said, "How can I say no, it's Jack Benny?"

It was all so entirely . . . normal.

Was she the only one on the verge of losing her mind over Timmy? How could they laugh at Red Skelton or Jack Benny? Or anything else?

"Gina, are you okay, sweetheart?"

Gina lifted her eyes from the photograph of Timmy in the newspaper. "No, Rose, I'm not okay. I'm not going to be okay until we find Timmy." She started crying again. Rose got up from her chair and came around to give Gina a hug. She didn't say anything, just held her and rubbed her back.

After a few minutes, Rose said, "Mike left a little while ago. Do you know where he went?"

Gina shook her head no as she grabbed for the box of tissues.

"Watching the local news last night gave him an idea. He looked up the addresses of the news stations and said he was going to buy three copies of the morning paper and hand deliver them to each of the local network stations. Make sure they knew about the story, see if he could get them to feature it tonight on their broadcasts. All they want to talk about is this Cuba crisis."

That was good news of a sort, Gina thought. "That sounds like a good idea," she managed to say.

"I saw Scott and Colt heading out the front door this morning," Rose said. "Where were they going?"

"I think just for a walk. Scott told me he had a few things to say to Colt, mostly to apologize for asking him and Timmy to lie about our separation and for making him feel so bad he felt the need to run away to you guys."

"Well, that sounds like a good thing."

It did to Gina too. "I think so. I told him to make sure Colt knew that I was sorry too." She knew she'd have to tell him herself at some point.

"And I couldn't help overhearing what Scott said on the phone this morning," Rose said. "Sounded like he was calling in to take the day off."

Gina heard that too. She had been working up the nerve to ask him to consider that very thing, or at least to take the morning off. "I was glad he did that," she said. It was actually somewhat comforting having him around.

And she'd almost said that very thing to Rose, but thankfully, she caught herself.

38

Colt seemed a little nervous when they'd first left the house. Scott had done his best to reassure him he wasn't in any trouble. They walked down the sidewalk in the direction of the beach, but Scott wasn't sure they'd get that far. He wasn't following a preset plan. Truth was, he'd never done anything like this before with Colt. Taking a walk, just the two of them. Up ahead, the sun was beginning to climb in the sky toward midmorning.

When they reached the first corner, old Weldon's house, Scott said, "I wonder if Mr.

225

Weldon's hiding out in his fallout shelter yet?"

"You mean because of all the stuff on the news?" Colt said.

Scott nodded. "When I was looking for you and your brother on Monday, I came by here to check. You know, since you and your friends sometimes like to use his shelter for a fort."

"It's really cool down there, Dad. Have you ever seen it?"

"I did on Monday. Mr. Weldon was loading it up with supplies, getting ready for 'the big one,' he said."

"Really?"

"You want to go see?"

"You mean go down there?"

"No, we'll just walk by."

"Sure," Colt said.

They turned left and headed down the side street, along the hill that bordered Weldon's property. When they got to the break in the driveway, they heard a radio playing. They both turned to look and were surprised to find Weldon sitting up by his back fence gate, a shotgun across his lap.

Weldon seem startled by their presence but quickly relaxed when he realized who it was. "Out for a walk, boys?" he asked.

"That's right, Mr. Weldon," Scott replied. "Uh . . . what are you up to?"

"C'mon up here and I'll tell you."

"Do we have to?" Colt whispered. "He's got a gun."

Weldon seemed to notice their apprehension and looked down at his shotgun. "Don't worry about this," he said. "This ain't for you boys. It's for everyone else, though."

"C'mon, Colt, it'll be all right." Scott led Colt up the driveway.

As they got closer, Weldon said, "Can't be too careful these days. I'm hearing all kinds of stories on the radio of people looting. Fights are breaking out in grocery stores. People get crazy when they think the world's gonna end."

"There's been looting around here?"

"No. Not yet, anyway. But you gotta be ready. All bets are off once those missiles start firing into the sky. I've heard that happens, and we've got about fifteen minutes before the nuclear blasts start vaporizing everything. Most people are acting pretty calm right now. But that will all change once the fighting begins. I can imagine almost everybody on this street running over here to my shelter, trying to force their way inside."

He looked down and patted his shotgun like a man patting a dog on the head. "But I ain't gonna let that happen. There's just enough supplies in there for a few people, not a whole neighborhood. Won't matter if I shoot 'em. Once that atomic blast goes off, they'll just disappear."

The more he talked, the more Scott felt like

he'd made a bad decision bringing Colt up this driveway.

"But hey," Weldon said, "I'm not talking about you, Scott, or your family. That is, if you find your other little boy before it all hits the fan. Real sorry to hear about him being . . . you know. Saw it in the papers last night and this morning. Couldn't believe my eyes."

"Thanks, Mr. Weldon. It's been pretty awful since Monday afternoon, when we were told."

"Any leads yet?"

"Not really."

"Well, me and the wife are pulling for you. Sure hope you find him."

"Thanks."

"Either way, your family's welcome in our shelter once the shooting starts."

"Thanks, Mr. Weldon. That's very kind. Hope it doesn't come to that, though."

"Don't we all," he said.

"Well, you have a nice day," Scott said. "We're gonna keep walking, enjoy this fresh air."

They nodded to each other. Colt waved as they made their way down the driveway. "That was kind of strange," Colt said.

"Yeah, it was."

"I'm not sure I'd want to be holed up in that dark little shelter with Mr. Weldon very long," Colt said.

"I know what you mean, son."

They walked by a few houses in silence. "Dad?"

"Yeah?"

"Do you really think . . . I mean, could Mr. Weldon be right? You think it really could be the end of the world? People are talking on the news like it might be."

"I don't know, son. I hope not. I hope the men in charge of things, the ones who have their fingers on those buttons, have enough sense not to push them. World War III, if it happened, would be a lot different than World War II."

"You mean like that show *Combat* last night?"

"Right," Scott said. "World War II was bad, and so was Korea, the war I fought in. But a nuclear war . . . well, let's just hope and pray it doesn't come to that."

"But if it does . . . what will happen to Timmy? I don't want to hide out in Mr. Weldon's shelter if he can't be with us."

Scott sighed. He didn't know what to say. "I don't either, Colt." Before they went any farther, Scott really wanted to say what he'd come out here to say. "Colt, hold up."

They stopped walking. "What's the matter?" Colt asked.

"Nothing's the matter. I just want to say something to you, and I want you to look me in the eyes as I say it."

"Am I in trouble?"

"No, you're not."

"What is it?"

Scott rested his hands gently on Colt's shoulders. "I just want you to know—your mom and I want you to know—we don't blame you for running away."

"You don't?"

"No, we don't. We never should have put you in a place where you felt so bad that you had to escape. That's not your fault, that's ours. We were being selfish and not thinking about how all this was affecting you and your brother. We're real sorry about that, Colt." Scott couldn't help it; tears started filling his eyes. Immediately, Colt started crying too.

"And we're real sorry, both your mom and I, that we made you boys lie to everyone so no one would know I had moved out. We should have never done that. Can you forgive us?"

Colt threw himself into his father's arms and sobbed. Scott held on to him until he calmed down.

In a few moments, Colt pulled back, looked up in his father's eyes, and said, "Why can't you and Mom be back together? Why can't we be a family again?"

Scott pulled him close. "I want that too, son. And I want your brother back here where he belongs. I want those things more than anything else in the world."

39

Later that afternoon as they sat at their respective desks in the Orlando office, Special Agents Vic Hammond and Nate Winters reviewed a fresh pile of leads about the Harrison kidnapping. They had all come in either last night or this morning, since Timmy's picture and the drawing of his kidnapper had begun to appear in local newspapers throughout the state.

There weren't as many as Vic would have expected for a case like this, but there was still a good number, considering how distracted people were with this crisis in Cuba. Maybe a dozen of them so far. Still too many for Vic and Nate to run down all by themselves. Usually for a child abduction case, they'd have a good-sized team to share the legwork. They had just divided them into two stacks. Vic thumbed through his.

"Think we got anything here?" Nate asked.

"Hard to say," Vic said. "Did you take any of these calls yourself?"

"A few of them. The ones I did didn't sound too promising. They were from local cops who'd taken phone calls from concerned citizens, mostly moms. Lots of iffy-ness in the language. Nobody's sure of anything. Like this one . . ." Nate held up one of the forms. "Near Tallahassee.

Says a mom saw a strange man with a boy in a car next to her at a traffic light. Man wasn't wearing a hat and he had a thick, bushy mustache. The boy kind of resembled the boy in the picture, although she didn't have the newspaper with her at the time. The officer who took the call wrote a note in the margin here, saying the woman wondered if the mustache was fake."

"Not likely he grew a thick mustache over-night," Vic said. "Just as likely it was his own. For that matter, could just be a dad driving his son to the hardware store."

"Nothing strange about that," Nate said. "I'm afraid we're gonna be spinning our wheels here with most of these."

Vic laid his stack on the desk. "What we really need is someone who can check these out up close and personal. Verify if it's Timmy."

"Since we got his picture, shouldn't be any guesswork," Nate said. "Might be more difficult with the kidnapper, since it's just a sketch. And I'm guessing, based on what the deputy director said at that briefing, we can't be calling on our guys to check these out for us."

"That's the way I read it too," Vic said. "But we can't be driving all over the state, either, eliminating the dead ends. Even if we split up, it would take forever."

"And these are just the leads that came in the last twelve hours, Vic. We asked the papers to keep running these photos until they hear from us. We could get this many leads every day."

The phone rang on Vic's desk. "That could be another one right now." He grabbed his pad and pen and picked it up. Turned out it was.

A woman from a sheriff's office called, somewhere in south Florida. After Vic had confirmed that she had reached the FBI office in Orlando, she said, "Got a possible sighting of that missing boy of yours, the one that got nabbed up there in Jacksonville. I'm looking at his picture here in the paper . . . a Timmy Harrison."

"That's right, ma'am. Have you seen him yourself?"

"Oh no, just passing on a sighting by a tourist passing through. He said he was taking an airboat tour by a man who lives on the edge of the Everglades yesterday, then saw the newspaper at a café this morning. Thought this man looked like your sketch, and he had a little boy with him 'bout the same age as the one in the picture. We're down here in LaBelle, little town in Hendry County, just a ways south and west of Lake Okeechobee."

"Did you say Henry County?" Vic said.

"Close, but you got to add a *d* in there, between the *n* and the *r*. Not important if you forget. People call us Henry County all the time."

Vic had spent quite a few years in Florida, but he had no idea where this was. "Well, why don't you tell me everything you've got?"

She did, and he wrote it all down. Sounded semi-promising. Maybe a tad more than some of the others in his stack. But still, someone had to verify this. Someone had to look at these two people, especially the boy, and compare it to the photograph. When she finished talking, Vic asked, "Have any idea how long it takes to drive to this place from the Orlando area? You know, where the boy was last seen?"

"About three-and-a-half hours, I'd expect. Less if you rode with your sirens on."

"Round trip?"

"No, one way."

Vic sighed. "I don't suppose someone from your office could go check this out for us? We've got about a dozen of these leads to check out already, and they're from all over the state."

"I don't know," she said. "This is an FBI investigation, right?"

"It is, but—"

"Then you'd have to talk with the sheriff about that, or one of his deputies. They're not here in the office at the moment. We're just a small operation here, so I don't know how they'll feel about that."

"Ma'am, I can appreciate that. We're pretty shorthanded up here ourselves, especially with all this stuff going on with Cuba and Russia."

"That doesn't seem to be affecting us all that much down here," she said. "We're a bit overwhelmed just dealing with regular stuff going wrong."

"I understand," Vic said. "But we're talking about a little boy here. We don't know what kind of danger he's in. This guy just took him. Lured him with some comic books when his older brother was in the bathroom. This happened on Monday, and no one's seen or heard from him since."

"That's a terrible thing," she said.

"And see, he can't be in all these places. We've got over a dozen leads, and if my partner and I have to spend hours and hours, or several days, driving all over the state, just to see if we've got the right little boy to start with, we could lose him for good. But if someone from your office can drive out there with his picture from that newspaper—probably take you all of twenty minutes—we can make sure we're not wasting all our time chasing phantoms."

"I see what you're saying."

"We don't care who gets the credit on this," Vic said. "We just want to return this little boy to his mom and dad."

"Well, I'll definitely explain all this to the sheriff. In fact, I happen to know one of our deputies is only about a ten-minute drive from where this man and little boy are supposed to be."

"Now you're talking," Vic said. "Can you call him for me and see what he says?"

"Yeah, I can do that. Let me call this deputy

235

here. I won't call you back unless he says he can't do it for some reason. If he can, I'll call you back after he takes a drive out there."

"That'll be great. I appreciate that so much. What did you say your name was?"

"It's Beth."

"Well, you've been a great help, Beth. My name's Vic, Victor Hammond. When you call back, you can ask for me or my partner, Nate Winters."

"Will do, Agent Hammond."

They hung up and Vic looked up at Nate, who was smiling.

"That worked out pretty good," Nate said.

"Yes, it did. If she follows through."

"I guess that's our strategy then," Nate said. "Work with the locals, see if we can usher in a new era of cooperation."

"That's what I'm thinking. I'm sure you'll get some resistance, but just work the angle that we're talking about a little boy here. Most of these folks are probably parents."

"Got it."

"You start working your stack, and I'll go through mine."

"I'm on it."

"And Nate . . ."

"Yeah?"

"Be extra nice, and if you can talk to a woman in these places—"

"I'm with you, Vic."

40

Gina had tried to shake the gloomy feeling hanging over her all afternoon but with no success. Rose was doing her best to get Gina's mind onto other things, but every conversation, every stray thought always found its way back to one thing . . . where was her little boy? Where was Timmy?

Every few minutes, no matter what else was going on in the room, Gina's eyes locked on to the telephone, as if willing it to ring. Why hadn't anyone called? Not a single reporter from the newspapers or the television news. And they had received no updates from the FBI. Didn't anyone care?

"I know what we can do, Gina."

Gina's eyes shifted from the telephone to Rose. "What?"

"Why don't we start dinner? It's almost time, anyway."

"I guess we could."

Just then, the telephone rang. Gina was about to pick it up after the second ring when Scott came rushing in from the backyard. He, Mike, and Colt had been throwing a baseball back and forth. She was glad, for Scott's sake but especially for Colt. She didn't know what Scott and Colt had talked about on their walk earlier, but it had definitely done Colt some good.

The phone rang a third time. Scott was standing over it. "Do you want to get it?"

"You can," Gina said.

Scott picked it up, said hello, and listened a moment. "Oh, hi, Agent Hammond. Okay, Vic. So glad you called. Any news on Timmy?"

Please say yes, Gina thought. She looked at Scott's face, his eyes especially. He was nodding his head every few moments, as if pleased at what he was hearing.

"Well, that's something, anyway," he said. "Are there any you've followed up on that seemed strong enough to warrant you and Nate driving out there to see for yourselves?"

His eyebrows narrowed at whatever Vic said to that.

"I see. Yeah, that makes sense."

I see what? Gina thought. What makes sense?

Scott continued to listen a few minutes more, then said, "Vic, listen . . . if you need us to do some of this, we're willing. I don't care how far we have to drive. And we don't need any time to get ready. I can hop in the car right now, if you need me to."

"I'll go too," Gina said. Whatever it was, she didn't care.

Scott looked at her, smiled, but didn't respond. "I understand, Vic. But you said it yourself, most of the other agents are off on other assignments. If we did this, we wouldn't actually confront anyone. We'd stay out of sight and just call you or Nate from a nearby pay phone."

What is he talking about?

"I understand. Just keep it in mind. We'll do anything. I mean anything. Thanks for the call. And for everything you guys are doing." He hung up.

By this point, Mike and Colt had come in and joined Gina and Rose in a half circle around Scott. "So what did he say?" Gina asked.

"He said they've actually gotten quite a few phone calls about Timmy from all over the state, and two from southern Georgia."

"Really?" Gina said.

"Yeah, they're coming from police offices and sheriff departments. People who've seen the stories in the newspapers, calling in. Over fifteen so far."

Fifteen, that sounded good.

"But he said only a few actually sounded promising. They're waiting on some callbacks from the local sheriffs to see if he and Nate should drive out to these places and check them out themselves. The problem is, the promising ones are in different parts of the state, several hours away."

"That's what you were talking about," she said, "about you and me driving to some of these places ourselves."

"He's not keen on that idea right now. For all sorts of reasons. But you heard me tell him to keep it in mind. He said he would, and that he'd give us another update call in the morning."

Well, at least there was some progress. More than they had all day. Really, in the last two days.

The phone rang again, startling everyone because they were all still standing around it. Scott picked it up again. "Hello?" The look on his face instantly became sour. "Oh, hi, Mr. Finch."

She knew that name. It was Scott's new boss at GE. She wondered how long it would last, Scott's newfound devotion to his family.

"C'mon, Colt," Mike said. "Let's go finish our game of catch."

Rose said she'd get started on dinner. Gina backed up and sat on the edge of the sofa. She wanted to hear how Scott would handle this.

"Hey, Scott, any news on your boy?"

"Actually, I just got off the phone with the FBI."

"Really? Anything significant?"

"Not really sure. Could be. They're getting all kinds of calls all over the state from the story running in the newspapers. People thinking they've seen Timmy with this guy. But the FBI agent is pretty sure most of these are false alarms. They're going to check into them anyway. We only need one to be the right one."

"That's right," Finch said. He hemmed and hawed a few moments.

Scott figured whatever he said next was probably the real reason he'd called.

"Say, Scott, I just got off the phone with Mark Mitchell over at the Castaway. He said you hadn't been over there at all today. Did I misunderstand something? I thought we had agreed that you'd be splitting your time between there and home today, making sure everything is all set for this weekend. Mark's definitely sounding overwhelmed on his own."

"I guess there has been some misunderstanding, Mr. Finch." Scott took a deep breath. He had already resolved to say what he was about to say next, but still, he felt the tension quickly building inside him. "I never said that I'd do that. You suggested that, and I said I wasn't sure. And I said, as clearly as I could, my place at a time like this is here at home. I know the Expo's important. It's a great PR opportunity for GE. But with all due respect, sir, it doesn't even come close to the serious situation I'm dealing with here at home."

"But Scott, aren't you just pretty much sitting around there all day? You're not actually out driving around searching for your son, right? I would've thought doing a little work might help ease the tension. You know, get your mind off things."

Yeah, Scott thought, that's what you really care

about, easing the tension in my life. "It might, Mr. Finch. But that's not the real issue. The real issue is, my presence here in the house is a comfort to my wife and my other son, Colt. They need me here. More than GE needs me down at the Castaway, getting ready for this Expo."

"Now, listen, Scott—"

"No, Mr. Finch, you need to listen. I didn't mean for this to happen, and I certainly didn't want something like this to happen. But it has. And in a way, it's opened my eyes to some things I wasn't seeing very clearly before." He looked over at Gina sitting on the couch. He couldn't read the expression on her face.

"What are you saying, Scott?"

"I'm saying you better find someone else to take my place down there at the Castaway."

"But there isn't time."

"Of course there's time. This is Wednesday. It doesn't start until Friday afternoon. There were four other guys interviewing for my job. Pick the second guy you had in mind, call him tonight, and tell him you'll give him the job, but he's got to be able to start right away, a baptism by fire, so to speak. Mark can bring him up to speed, and if he's got a good head on his shoulders and some decent communication skills, he should do fine. This kind of job isn't exactly rocket science."

"Scott, you know if I do that, we're not just

talking about the Expo here. You'll be walking away from this job for good."

"Oh, I know that. But I also know the Apollo program has barely started, and from some of the material I prepared for my talks at the Expo, I know GE plans to hire over a thousand more engineers right here in Daytona over the next few years."

"You're gonna go back to engineering?"

"I am. I plan to become just an eight-to-five desk grunt from now on. Do my job right and stay out of trouble."

"You won't move up into management that way. That's not where the real money is."

"I know." Scott surprised himself at how little he cared. "I'm really sorry to put you on the spot like this, sir. But I don't see any way around it. Now, if you'll excuse me, I've gotta go back outside and finish a game of catch with my son."

He hung up, nodded briefly at Gina, then headed out the back door.

41

Mamie Lee did her best to join in the singing, but it was so hard. They were even singing one of her favorites just now, "Nobody Knows the Trouble I've Seen." The lyrics fit her situation like a glove, and that's what made it so hard. Every part of this song was like someone had put a magnifying glass over her troubled soul. The biggest challenge was singing the glory hallelujahs after each verse.

She didn't feel any glory or hallelujah going on inside. Just the part about all her troubles and sorrow.

Sitting next to her at Union Baptist Church was her best friend, Etta Mae, belting it out with the best of them. Almost like she was glowing with that happy look on her face, wearing her bright white dress and big white hat. Mamie continued to sing, glad this was likely going to be the last song before the minister had everyone sit down.

She wanted to sit down now.

One thing she noticed was that nobody else in the congregation seemed down or too concerned about the world coming to an end. Since the president broke the news two nights ago, it seemed like things between the US and Russia had only gotten worse. It was hard for her to even listen to Mr. Harrison's conversation at the dinner table tonight, before she'd left to go home and get ready for church.

But here at the church, it was like nothing was going on at all outside these four walls. At least not anything they needed to be concerned about. God was still on his throne, the devil was still on the run, and Christ had still won the victory.

But she couldn't break through to feel any of this joy. She supposed she could if, like everyone else in here, the only thing she had to fret over was the world coming to an end. That happened, and they'd all meet Jesus together in the air. Nothing too wrong with that. But how could she be happy knowing little Timmy was gone? Mister Scott and Miss Gina must be sick with worry and fear by now. Two whole days and not a word of news about him. Didn't know if he was safe. Didn't know if he was alive or dead. Didn't know what this wicked man took him for or what he planned to do.

The weight of it all proved to be too much. She sat right down on the edge of her pew, put her arms up on the back of the pew in front, and laid her head down. In no time at all, the tears came.

A moment later she felt the warm hand of Etta Mae resting on her shoulder. A moment after that, the singing stopped and she heard everyone take their seats. She lifted her head up and sat back in the pew.

"You poor thing," Etta Mae said and handed her a clean hanky. "It'll be all right. You'll see."

Mamie wiped her eyes and whispered a thank-you. She looked toward the front in time to see the choir taking their seats and their minister, Rev. Ralph Owens, coming to the pulpit. To her surprise, the first thing he did was to hold up the newspaper, the local section with Timmy's picture and the sketch of the kidnapper on the front. Then he said, "Folks, before we go any further in our service tonight, there's something pretty important we need to tend to first. How many of you have read this story in the paper over the last few days, about this little boy who was kidnapped?"

Mamie looked around. Almost every hand was raised.

"And how many of you," he continued, "noticed our sister Mamie Lee not doing too well tonight?"

Mamie noticed all the hands nearby were raised and a few others scattered throughout the church.

"Well, y'all know Mamie is a dear sister. Been in this church since she was a little girl. Way before I got here. And I been here quite a few years. I can honestly say, though I know she's faced a world of troubles in her life before this, tonight is the first time I've ever seen her so low she wasn't able to finish singing a hymn."

Tears welled up in Mamie's eyes again.

"I'm sure the reason is, Mamie's directly connected to the little boy in this story. If you've read it, the story doesn't say how, but I'll let Mamie come up here a moment and explain. Think you can do that, Sister Mamie?"

Mamie nodded. She hadn't been expecting this, but maybe this was what God had in mind. She stood up, started making her way to the center aisle. *Lord, give me the strength to say what I need to and not fall apart doing it.*

"Etta Mae," the minister said, "could you come up with her and stand with her while she speaks?"

"I certainly can, Reverend." She followed right behind Mamie.

Mamie made her way to the front. She had half a mind to bring her fan up with her. About half the ladies in the church were using theirs. It was nearing the end of October, but it had been a warmer-than-usual day, and there was absolutely no breeze blowing through these open windows. As she climbed the red carpeted steps, the minister handed her a box of tissues, which was kind. She held up Etta Mae's hanky to show she was prepared.

She stood next to the pulpit, Etta Mae just to her right. The minister invited her to stand behind the pulpit, but she knew that would make her too nervous. "Can I speak from here?" she said.

"Of course. Whichever one you're more comfortable with."

She looked out at everybody and found the strength for a smile. "Thank you all for your care and concern for me. And thank you, Rev. Owens, for taking time out of the service to let me share. I'm not much of a talker, so I won't keep you long. Some of you know, I've been working for the Harrison family over on Clara Avenue for some time now."

"Some time now," Etta Mae repeated. "The sun been rising in the east for some time now."

Quite a few people laughed. "Okay," Mamie Lee said, "I've been working for the Harrisons for a *long* time now. Long enough for their youngest, Mister Scott, to grow from being a toddler, to a fine little boy, then a teenager, and now a married man and the father of two boys of his own. The thing is, I raised Mister Scott like he was my own. The other members of the Harrison family treat me just fine, but Mister Scott . . ." Now came the tears again. "Mister Scott treated me like family, like we were kin. I love his two little boys, Colt and Timmy, like they was my own grandbabies." It was time to use the hanky.

"That little boy who was kidnapped, the one you read about in the paper, that's Timmy, Mister Scott's little boy." Lots of people reacted now, especially the women. Lots of people reaching for the tissues or their own hankies. "They were on their way to visit their aunt and uncle in Savannah when a strange man kidnapped Timmy while his older brother was in the bathroom at a diner north of Jacksonville. This happened Monday afternoon, and nobody's seen Timmy since. I'd sure appreciate all your prayers for his safe return."

That was about all she thought to say. Rev. Owens said, "Well, we can certainly do that, Sister Mamie. In fact, let's do that right now as a church."

"Rev. Owens?" Etta Mae spoke up. "Before we pray, can I say something?"

"Of course you can, Etta Mae. What's on your mind?"

She looked out to the congregation. "Besides praying for Timmy, and I'm real glad y'all are willing to do that, I wonder if there's something else we could do." She held up the newspaper that had been laying on the pulpit. "Could you all keep a copy of this with you whenever you're out? If not the whole thing, just cut out the part with their pictures and the phone number to call? See, I'm thinking that many of you like me and Mamie Lee clean houses every day. Some of you men are gardeners or handymen, or clean swimming pools. The point is, we're out and about in lots of neighborhoods besides our own, all over this county. Timmy and this evil man are out there too, God knows where. I'm thinking if we keep our eyes open, paying special attention to any little boy you see with some strange man, maybe there's a chance we'll find Timmy. You never know, right?"

Mamie Lee saw heads nodding all over the church.

"That's a great idea, Etta Mae," Rev. Owens said. "As a matter of fact, I think I'm going to call a few pastor friends of mine and ask them if they won't consider bringing this idea before their congregations as well." He stepped closer to Mamie Lee. "I wonder if I could have some folks join me up here as we pray for Sister Mamie and little Timmy. And while we're at it, I'd love it if some of you could join us and pray a prayer of faith over our nation. I'm not exactly looking forward to the whole world blowing up in the next few days. I don't know about you, but when I finally do fly away to meet Jesus in the air, I want to meet him all in one piece."

Mamie smiled at that. First time she smiled all day. Rev. Owens always had a way of lifting her spirits.

42

It was Thursday morning. Colt sat in his bedroom, missing Timmy. Somehow over the last couple of days, he'd been able to stay busy enough to block any really bad thoughts. It was like Timmy was just away on a trip or something.

His father had let him stay up again last night an hour past his bedtime. That's because, once again, they had agreed to let him stay home from school. So Colt got to stay up and watch both *The Beverly Hillbillies* and *The Dick Van Dyke Show* with the adults. He wished those shows came on an hour earlier so he could see them every week. Normally, he had to go to bed by nine on school nights, Timmy at eight. Poor Timmy, there wasn't anything good for him to watch on Wednesday nights, just *Wagon Train*.

What was he saying? Timmy would've loved to be in his own home last night, even if *Wagon Train* was the only show on. If Colt could have Timmy back, he would've even been willing to go to bed at eight and miss out on *The Beverly Hillbillies* and *Dick Van Dyke*.

Of course, most of the time Timmy bugged him. Not in a big way, just little brother stuff. Always wanting to follow him around. Always wanting to borrow his things. Always wanting to play with his friends. Another thing that bugged him . . . Timmy would always stick his grimy fingers in the cereal box, digging for the prize. Even if it was way at the bottom. And his mom never stopped him. It also seemed to Colt that Timmy got away with a lot more things than he did at the same age. All he had to do was whine long enough, and Mom would give in.

Take these bunk beds, for example. When Mom and Dad bought them two years ago, Colt wanted the bottom bunk. He was the older brother. He should get to pick. But Timmy said he was too afraid to be up that high. Afraid he might roll over during the night and fall out. So what did they do? They made Colt take the top bunk, but only for two years. When Timmy turned six, they could switch places.

Is that what happened? No.

Timmy turned six, and he just whined some more. He was still too afraid of falling out. So what did they do then? Colt was looking at their solution across the room. They took the top bunk off and set it on the floor, so that now they had two twin beds instead. Their room was already so small. That was part of the reason his parents had bought the bunk beds in the first place, to give them more room to play on the floor, like on rainy days. Now all they had was a tiny aisle between their beds and a few feet between their beds and the door.

Not enough room to do anything on the floor.

Colt stared at the empty bed, perfectly made by his father that morning before he'd left the room. It was too perfect. That wasn't how Timmy made it. He never got how to tuck the pillow in right, so that it creased all the way across the bed.

Colt got up and quickly fixed the bed the way Timmy would leave it. He stood back to see if anything else was out of place. Bullwinkle. Timmy never put his big stuffed Bullwinkle doll in the center of his pillow like that. He always rested it in the corner against the wall. He said that way Bullwinkle could see the whole room, not just the ceiling. That's right, Colt wasn't supposed to call him a doll. He was a stuffed animal, but a big one. Eighteen inches tall. Colt found it odd that Bullwinkle's size made Timmy feel safer when he went to bed alone every night an hour before Colt.

What difference did it make if he was two feet

or ten feet tall? He was a stuffed animal. He couldn't do anything. Even on TV, Bullwinkle was always messing up and Rocky would have to come in and straighten everything out. But Colt never told Timmy that. Why make him upset?

Then Colt remembered.

Timmy couldn't sleep without Bullwinkle, ever since he got him last Christmas. He was the reason Timmy couldn't bring all his comic books to Savannah. Bullwinkle had taken up so much room in the backpack.

Timmy had spent the last three nights in a row now without Bullwinkle.

Colt sighed. "God, if you'll bring Timmy back, we'll set up the bunk beds again. And he can have the bottom bunk as long as he wants."

"What do you mean, you've never swept floors before?" August stared down at the boy in disbelief. "Ain't nothing to it, Bobby. Just do it like I showed you."

"But . . . you never showed me before. My mom always sweeps the floors. Sometimes my brother."

August grabbed the broom out of his hand. "I told you to never talk about that woman in this house, didn't I? And you don't have no brother, Bobby. Quit making up stories. We never had but one kid, and that was you. Here, I'll show you one more time. But this is the last time, you hear? You don't get this right, and I'll have to punish you."

"Not the dark place again."

"Of course the dark place. Either that or I have to beat you. It's one or the other. And I'm trying to do better for you than my pa did for me."

"I'll get it right," Bobby said. "Show me again, please."

"All right then." August walked the broom down to the end of the hall and started sweeping the corners. "First you get all the dirt out from the edges and corners, like this. After you do that, you start sweeping it from one end to the other, like this. I'm only going to do a few feet here to show you. When you get down to the end, you make a nice little pile. Then you sweep the pile into the dustpan over there. Like I said, ain't nothing to it."

Bobby came down the hallway toward him, his face like a scared rabbit.

"I'm gonna be outside splittin' firewood. You sweep every part of the house that don't have carpet, got that?"

Bobby nodded. "Every part of the house that doesn't have carpet," he repeated.

"Shouldn't take you but fifteen or twenty minutes, if you keep working and don't dillydally. You run into any problems, you come get me. I don't expect you will. Any fool can handle a broom. But if you do, don't come all the way out where I'm swinging that axe. Get your head chopped off. Just yell for me from the back door.

I should hear you fine from there. You got all that?"

Bobby nodded, reached for the broom. August gave it to him and started to walk away.

"Umm . . ."

He stopped at the end of the hall and turned. "What is it, boy? Speak up."

"Aren't I supposed to be going to school? Isn't this a school day?"

"You'll go to school when I say you're ready. Now get back to work."

August walked through the back of the house, out through the back porch, and over to the pile of limbs he'd made a few weeks ago. He grabbed his axe and began chopping away. Felt good to be doing something meaningful with his time instead of babysitting that boy.

He split wood straight through for about ten minutes, then stopped to listen for the boy. He didn't hear him, so he set the axe down and quietly walked back through the porch. When he got to the screen door, he listened in. Okay, he could hear him in there still sweeping. So he returned to his oak pile.

Ten minutes later, he stopped again. Didn't hear the boy this time, either. But he should be done by now. He set the axe down again and headed back for the house. This time, he went inside. Didn't hear the sound of sweeping. He quickly ran from room to room but couldn't find Bobby anywhere. He started to panic. He ran out the front door and almost knocked the boy over.

"What in the world? What are you doing out here?" he yelled. He nodded his head toward his neighbors' properties. "What if somebody saw you?" He grabbed the broom with one hand and a handful of the boy's shirt with the other. "Get in this house," he said through gritted teeth, dragging the boy through the front door.

"But you said sweep everywhere that didn't have carpet."

August slammed the front door and turned to face the boy. "I didn't raise you to be no dummy. The porch gets sweeped every now and then, but it's not the inside of the house. Can't you tell the difference between the inside and the outside of a house? I was talking about the inside of the house, dummy. What if one of the neighbors saw you out there?"

The boy started to cry.

"You want to cry? I'll give you something to cry about." August grabbed him under the arm and started dragging him toward the back of the house.

"No, please. I won't do it again. Please, I didn't know what you meant."

"I ain't raising no dummy," August said. "A boy's gotta be taught to mind."

43

About noon on Thursday, Vic and Nate were just about to get in their car and drive almost four hours south to LaBelle, Florida. The woman who worked in the sheriff's department down there had just called them back about thirty minutes ago. She was a day late and very apologetic about it. The deputy she'd called yesterday had agreed to follow up on that lead about the missing boy, but something had come up and he didn't get to it until after she had gone home.

The deputy had filled her in this morning about his visit with the man in question. He couldn't say for certain whether it was or wasn't the man in the sketch, but it definitely looked like the man to him. He didn't get a chance to see the boy. The man claimed it was his son, and he had no intention of bringing him out for the deputy's inspection. He demanded the deputy get off his property since he didn't have a warrant. The deputy couldn't really do anything. Besides the lack of a warrant, his property was slightly out of their jurisdiction.

She ended the call by saying the deputy felt the man was acting pretty nervous for someone with nothing to hide. And that maybe, since they were the FBI, they could get a little further since they wouldn't have any jurisdiction issues.

It was the first solid bite they'd had since this ordeal began. All of their follow-ups on the other calls so far had proven to be dead ends. Vic was just about to open the car door. "Before we leave, I think I'm going to call Timmy's parents, let them know what we're up to."

"Don't you think we should wait till we see how this pans out?" Nate said. "Could be getting their hopes up over nothing."

"Maybe. But I know from other kidnapping cases we've dealt with, the parents are usually hanging on by a thread. They're not living day to day but hour to hour. Any amount of hope for any amount of time is a plus. I'll emphasize we don't know anything for sure right now, and we won't until we get down there."

"Okay, Vic, your call."

"While I'm doing that, why don't you go make sure this car is all gassed up?"

Nate got in the car, and Vic headed back to the office.

Other than being flatter than a pancake, the landscape during the long drive south to LaBelle was fairly scenic. A slice of Florida neither man had seen before. Vic had noticed at some point it was like they had crossed some invisible line. He was beginning to see all kinds of more tropical-looking palms and vegetation. Even the sun seemed brighter down here.

"I'm surprised we haven't seen more of a military presence," Nate said. "Aren't we getting close to Miami? It's thicker back in Orlando."

"Actually, we're still two hours away from Miami. But it's over there on the East Coast." Vic pointed out the window toward the left. "We're more than an hour inland. All the action's on the coast. This is no-man's-land out here."

"Guess we're pretty safe then," Nate said. "If old Khrushchev decides to start World War III, he probably won't consider alligators and cypress swamps high-value targets."

"I'm sure he doesn't. But to be honest, I'm not sure I'd want to be one of the survivors if things go that way. I read a classified report about it. Sort of the real-life scenario of what survivors of a nuclear war would face." He looked at Nate. "Seriously, I'll take instant vaporization over that any day." He noticed an intersection up ahead. "I think this is our stop up here, better slow down."

"There's his car over there." Nate glanced at his watch. "We're ten minutes early. Mr. Hoover would be proud."

They turned right and pulled off the road in the grass behind the deputy's car. As they got out, Vic looked at the deputy still in the car. He had an odd look on his face and was staring straight ahead at the steering wheel. Didn't even seem to notice them. A young guy, maybe late twenties.

Nate walked up and tapped on his window. "Hey, fella, are you okay?"

The deputy looked up, startled, and quickly rolled the window down. "Sorry, guess I was in a daze. I was just listening to the radio about this Cuban missile situation. Have you guys been listening to the news on your way down?" Nate backed up as the young man got out.

"No," Vic said. "Why, something new going on?"

"I'll say. Our ambassador at the UN—what's his name, Stevenson?—was just having it out with the Soviet ambassador. Pretty much called him a liar in front of the whole world. Of course, he is a liar. All those commies are. Apparently, Stevenson was showing everyone these big pictures our spy planes took of all these missile sites in Cuba."

"Really?" Vic said.

"Yes, sir," the deputy said. "It's not looking good. I don't know what the Soviets are gonna do, but it's really starting to look like we're headed for a fight."

"Hope not," Nate said. "Cause nobody's gonna win that one."

"Listen," Vic interrupted, "we don't have much daylight left. Can we focus a bit here?"

"I'm sorry. Sure." The deputy held out his hand. "Obviously, you're the two agents from the FBI. I'm Deputy Harlan Mason."

Nate shook his hand first. "I'm Special Agent Nate Winters. This is my partner, Vic Hammond."

Deputy Mason pulled a slip of paper out of his back pocket. "I had some time, so I drew you guys a pretty detailed map to this man's house. It's built right on the edge of a cypress swamp. Kind of tricky getting back to it. But at this point, you're really only about ten minutes away. I started the map from where we're standing." He laid it out on the hood of the car. "Does it make sense to you?"

"Looks pretty cut and dry to me," Nate said. He pointed to a spot. "That's this road here, right? The road we're on."

"Yes."

"I think we'll be all right," Vic said.

The deputy walked back to his front door. "I hope so. The guy that lives there seems nuttier than a hoot owl. He had a shotgun on the porch, right next to him while we talked. I stayed by my car. Had a feeling if I didn't leave when I did, he'd have reached for it."

"Thanks for the warning," Nate said. "We'll be ready for him."

44

Vic and Nate followed the deputy's map, which turned out to be a fairly easy thing to do. He'd even written little landmarks in the margins, which was good, since it turned out street signs and even the pavement had soon disappeared. In places, it looked like they were driving through the middle of a swamp. The waterline on both sides of the road came right up to the shoulder.

"I know it's gotta be an optical illusion," Nate said, "but when you look out to the side, the water level looks almost higher than the road."

"That's nice, Nate. But don't look out the side. Okay?" Nate was driving.

"Something else," Nate said. "Don't you think these cypress trees are strange? The way they grow right out of the water? Look at the way the roots stretch up like that. The trunk doesn't start for four or five feet on some of them."

"Nate? Eyes forward?"

They drove in silence, but only a little while. "Can't imagine anyone wanting to live so far back here," Nate said. "It's gotta be a twenty- to thirty-minute drive, one way, to the nearest store."

"My guess is, people out here mostly live off the land," Vic said. "Well, more like live off the water. I heard they eat alligator tail, snakes, turtles, and of course, all kinds of fish."

"I could go for some fried fish about now. Think this guy might fix us some?"

"Don't get your hopes up," Vic said. "The better question is . . . will he shoot us? That deputy had it wrong, thinking we might get *more* cooperation from him because we're with the FBI. He's either not from here or hasn't read much about local history."

"Why's that?"

"If this guy we're coming to see is old enough to have a son Timmy's age, he's probably a first-generation descendent of moonshiners. Moonshine was big business down here during Prohibition. The FBI wasn't a friend to the local economy. He's probably grown up hating guys like us. We need to go in there ready to shoot, if necessary. Especially if it turns out he's got Timmy."

"So no fish fry then?"

"Don't think so." They passed by a few houses spread far apart.

"What's that up ahead?" Vic said. "Some kind of sign."

Both men looked. If it were possible, the road appeared to narrow even more. A large hand-painted sign was nailed to a tall fence post on the right. Big red letters. Big and sloppy. As they got closer, they could see that the sign said: "Russell's Airboat Tours."

"Think Russell is his first name or last?" Nate said.

"I have no idea. Looks like we're about to find out."

As they rode past the sign, the rutty dirt path curved to the right in between two large cypress trees. Beyond that, they arrived at a clearing about the size of a small parking lot. At the far end was a toolshed that leaned much too far to the east. On the left side of the property, sitting out on the water and held up by wood pilings, was a wooden house with a rusty tin roof. It was connected to the land by a rickety dock. The whole property was surrounded by a mossy cypress swamp. Parked at an odd angle next to the toolshed sat an old Ford pickup truck, looked to be from the late forties. It was a dull red, or was it just rust?

"I'm guessing no airboat tours today," Nate said. "No other cars here. The guy probably owns that truck, don't you think?"

Vic nodded. He looked toward the house, saw two wicker rockers on the front porch and some faded life vests hanging over a rail. In between the rockers, the shotgun the deputy had mentioned leaned against the wall. "But I don't see an airboat anywhere. Maybe it's docked behind the house."

"Or maybe he and the boy are out catching dinner."

They pulled up near the entrance to the house

and got out of the car. The next sound was a slapping screen door, followed by the cocking of a shotgun. He moves quick, Vic thought.

"You two Feds can turn right around and get back in your car," the man yelled.

He wore the full hillbilly outfit, complete with overalls and a straw hat. But, Vic thought, if you took off that straw hat and replaced it with a gray fedora, he did look a lot like the man in the artist's sketch.

"How'd he know we were Feds?" Nate whispered.

"Must be the ties," Vic said.

"I know a pair of Feds when I see 'em," he said. "And you might as well talk straight to me. I can hear better than a bat. Besides, I had a feeling I'd be getting more company after that deputy showed up here. Haven't had any lawmen out here in months. Why you harassing me all of a sudden? I ain't done nothin'."

"Mr. Russell, please lower the shotgun so we can talk." Vic couldn't believe this guy had gotten the drop on them.

"I ain't got nothin' to say to you men. It's a free country. This is my property. And I ain't done nothin' wrong to give you cause to trespass on it. Now get back in that shiny black car and drive on out of here."

"We will, Mr. Russell," Nate said. "But you need to do something for us first. Soon as we take care of the reason we came out here, we'll be on our way."

"Have to do with my boy?"

"Well, yes, sir, actually it does."

"What y'all want with him? That deputy wanted to see him too. He ain't done nothin' wrong, neither."

How could Vic explain this? "No one is saying he did. We just need to see him a minute. After that, we'll be on our way."

"Why you need to see him? He's just a boy."

"How long has he lived here with you?" Vic said.

"His whole life. What do you expect? I'm his pa. He ain't hardly ever been off this property."

"Is Mrs. Russell around?" Nate said. "Could we talk with her?"

"She's been gone since he was two. Been just me and the boy ever since." He lowered the shotgun slightly but still kept it aimed in their direction.

"Mr. Russell, please call your son," Vic said.

Russell scratched his chin. "No, I don't think so. I think you men should just turn around and go back the way you came. I don't want to upset my son any further. He struggles with nightmares as it is. Won't help he sees you men in your dark suits, asking him all kinds of questions."

"Think maybe living out here with alligators and snakes might be a bigger cause of those nightmares," Nate whispered to Vic.

"I heard that," Russell said.

"Mr. Russell," Vic said, "we're FBI agents investigating a kidnapping case. We can't leave until we see the boy."

"What . . . kidnapping?" Russell tightened his grip on the shotgun and pointed it right at them.

Vic put his hand on his pistol.

"What's that have to do with me? I ain't kidnapped nobody. There's just me and my boy here. No one else."

"That may be," Vic said, "but we still need to see him. The kidnapping involves a little boy."

"That's ridiculous. You think I kidnapped my own boy?"

"Mr. Russell, we need to confirm he is your boy. The reason we're out here is because some witnesses saw a man take a little boy. Our artists made a sketch of him, and we've been running that sketch in the newspapers the last couple of days."

"That's not my concern," Russell said.

"You look a lot like the man in that sketch," Nate said. "And you've got a boy in there about the same age as the missing boy."

Nate took out his pistol and aimed it at the man's head. Russell saw this and aimed the shotgun at him. "You want to shoot me, G-man? I think I got the edge with this here shotgun."

"Now hold on," Vic said. He wondered what Nate was up to, why he was escalating things.

"I don't want to shoot you, Mr. Russell." Nate reached in through the open car window and pulled out the newspaper. "I've got an idea that should clear this all up pretty quickly. If that little boy is your son, then you've got nothing to worry about from us. Let my partner walk this newspaper to you so you can see the picture of the little boy's face, the one we're looking for. You'll know right off the bat if he is or he isn't."

"I already know he's not."

"Okay, then *we'll* know that. But you'll know when you see the picture, if it's not him, that we'll get back in our car and drive away, leave you and your boy alone for good."

Vic took off his hat and black blazer, started loosening his tie.

"What are you doing?" Russell said.

"I don't want your boy to see a G-man when he looks at me," Vic said. "Just a regular guy. You get customers out here sometimes, right? Just tell him I'm a customer. You can even show me your airboat, or maybe ask him to show me. I'll know in five seconds if he's not who we're looking for."

"Problem is," Russell said, "I'm sure he just heard everything you said. Hears like a bat too. Like his old man." He lowered his shotgun slightly. "Just bring that newspaper over here and let me see it. Let's get this nonsense over with."

Vic walked around the car. Nate handed him the newspaper but still kept his gun aimed at

Russell. Vic walked across the property, then across the dock to Russell's front porch. When he got a few feet away, he held out the paper for Russell to see.

Russell squinted as he looked first at the sketch then at Timmy's picture. "You think that man looks like me?"

"A little," Vic said.

"Maybe. But that definitely ain't my boy. 'Course, I already knew that. Little Russ," he yelled. "C'mon out here a moment, let this nice man take a look at you."

Vic stared at the door. A few moments later, a young boy about five or six walked through it. It wasn't Timmy. It wasn't even close. If the tourist who'd called this in in the first place had a newspaper nearby when they'd taken that airboat tour, they would have known it too. "I'm sorry to have troubled you, sir." Vic turned toward Nate. "It's not him." He reached out his hand. "You and your son have a good day."

Russell hesitated, then shook his hand. "Guess no harm was done."

Vic bent down and smiled. "Just remember, Little Russ . . . we might wear dark suits and black hats, but we're really the good guys." They shook hands, and Vic headed back across the dock.

"Hope you find that little boy soon," Russell said.

45

After dinner that night, the guys, including Colt, went out to the living room to watch Walter Cronkite on the national news. Without a doubt, he'd be sharing more on the world blowing to bits, Gina thought. For once, she was actually glad to be doing the dishes. And tonight she had her sister's help.

The afternoon had crawled by. Still no word from the FBI, and no one had called from the newspapers or local network news. Didn't anybody care about her son? Rose had suggested there probably would have been lots of calls and lots of interest if this Cuban crisis wasn't happening. People were so distracted. Three days had gone by since the president broke the news, and with each day, the possibility of nuclear war seemed to be intensifying.

Gina got that, but it didn't help. It was an odd thing to think, but even if the world was about to be destroyed by a nuclear holocaust, her only concern was to have Timmy right there beside her, holding her hand.

Rose had already started washing the dishes before Gina had finished clearing the table. With each trip back and forth to the sink, Gina looked at the telephone. At dinner, Scott seemed to think the FBI agents would have arrived at their location by now, unless it was in the Florida Keys or at the far end of the panhandle, near Alabama.

She picked up the salt and pepper shakers and the ketchup bottle and looked at the phone again. *Why haven't they called? Shouldn't they have found him by now?*

Just as she brought the last item from the table, a gravy bowl, the telephone rang. Gina almost dropped the bowl. She set it on the counter and hurried to the phone. Scott, Mike, and Colt were already there. Rose walked up behind her, drying her hands on a towel.

Scott lifted the receiver. "Hello? This is Scott Harrison. Oh hello, Vic."

Scott listened a few moments, nodding his head. Then his countenance fell. He looked at everybody, shaking his head no.

They hadn't found Timmy.

Gina didn't know anything else that was said; that was the only thing that mattered. She started breathing again and headed back into the kitchen. A few minutes later, she heard Scott hang up the telephone. He came into the kitchen, followed by the others.

"Vic was sorry to call us with this news. But it wasn't Timmy. They had driven all the way down to the Everglades. Apparently, there's this guy down there who gives airboat tours. Some people who'd ridden with him saw his picture in the paper and remembered he lived in a house down there, just him and a little boy."

Rose put her hand on Gina's shoulder. "I'm so sorry. We've been praying all day that this would be it."

Everyone stood there for a moment, then Scott said, "Anything we can do out here?"

He'd never asked that question before. "No, we've got it covered. Why don't you go back and watch the rest of the news?"

"It's already over," Colt said. "You know what that means . . ."

Gina had no idea.

"*Ozzie and Harriet*," Scott said.

"No, Dad. We don't watch that anymore since you moved out. We watch *Mister Ed*."

"*Mister Ed*? No . . . *Ozzie and Harriet*'s much better," Scott said.

Colt looked at her, as if she would side with him. She wanted to. Not that she liked *Mister Ed* so much, but she liked watching "perfect family sitcoms" even less. "Why don't you let Uncle Mike decide? Since he's our guest?"

Scott and Colt looked at Mike. "I've gotta go with *Mister Ed*," Mike said.

Colt smiled, but Gina noticed that Scott smiled just as much. "All right, Colt. You win." He rustled his hand gently through Colt's hair. The three of them turned and headed back toward the living room. Scott stopped and said to Gina,

"You almost done in there? Might do you some good to hear a talking horse for a while."

Gina laughed. It felt almost strange. "We won't be long." She almost said thanks. She managed a smile, then turned to help Rose with the dishes.

Neither of them said anything for a few moments. Gina found herself thinking about how happy her sister's marriage seemed, what a normal family life she had. Almost as nice as Ozzie and Harriet's, and the Cleavers. But nicer, because Mike and Rose's happiness was real. After all these years of watching Mike and Rose, she decided it was time to just ask. "Hey, Rose, I've been meaning to ask you something for some time."

"What is it?"

"Are you happy?" she said quietly. "You and Mike. Are you as happy as you seem?"

"Hmm," Rose said. "I think so. I mean, we're not pretending to be anything. Do we seem happy to you?"

"Yes, you do. I'd have given anything if Scott and I could have been that happy." She was suddenly overcome by an ambush of tears.

"Oh, Gina." Rose handed her a clean dish towel.

"I'm sorry," Gina said. "Sometimes I hate being a woman." She dabbed her eyes.

Rose smiled. "I wish I could tell you that you and Scott could be that happy again. I know it's not as simple as that, because of what . . ."—she whispered the next part—"what he did at that party. But the secret to our happiness is something you can know. Mike and I have had our share of troubles and, really, a few years after our wedding, we weren't doing very well. We started looking for a new church and began attending one in Savannah. The pastor there teaches things from the Bible you and I never heard in the church we grew up in. He talks a lot about God's love and kindness, and about his willingness to help us get through the difficult things we all face."

"That definitely doesn't sound like the church we grew up in." Gina grew up mostly afraid of displeasing God, and she was pretty sure she was failing most of the time.

"I know. And this pastor met with Mike and me after this men's breakfast Mike went to, and took us through a bunch of Scriptures about God's ideas for marriage and how things are supposed to work. It was amazing. Mike really began to change after that, and I guess I did too."

"And this is a Christian church?" Gina said.

"Definitely. The pastor just teaches things that are a lot more practical than I was used to hearing. He even has a sense of humor. We laugh at something he says almost every Sunday."

This *definitely* didn't sound like the church they had grown up in.

"But he gets serious too. The last few Sundays,

he's been teaching about Joseph in the Old Testament. You remember that story?"

Gina nodded. The guy whose brothers sold him into slavery.

"Joseph went through some horrendous things," Rose said. "The kind of things that would make you wonder if God had turned his back on you completely. The pastor said Joseph didn't hate God because of all these things. Instead, he put his trust in God to see him through. And God did. Not right away, but over time. And he used every single horrible thing Joseph went through to his advantage. When the trial was over, Joseph said that God had turned all the evil men had done to him into good."

Gina was pretty surprised at how much Rose had remembered from one sermon. She could hardly remember anything her pastor said by the time she left the parking lot.

"Then," Rose said, her face all lit up, "our pastor said that God is always with us and for us, just like he was with Joseph. And when we put our trust in him in hard times and do what he says, a time will come when we will look back on those hard times and smile, because we'll know that what follows after is not more misery and heartache but God's blessing and peace. And we'll know it was God who worked it all out."

Gina had never heard anything like this before. She wanted to believe it. If it was true. But how could it be? How could anything good follow after what had happened to her marriage?

Or what had happened to Timmy?

Please, God, bring Timmy back to me.

46

That same evening in DeLand, back in her little house, Mamie Lee was trying to relax over a cup of coffee with her friend Etta Mae. Etta Mae was much better company for Mamie than her own thoughts, which never drifted far away from worrying about little Timmy.

Thankfully, Mister Scott was kind enough to call her with the latest news. Even though there wasn't any good news to tell. Mamie made sure he had called his mama first. Mrs. Harrison cared way more than she let on. In some ways, Mamie felt bad for white folk, especially the wealthy ones. Keeping their emotions locked up all the time. Couldn't be good for your health.

"So how'd your day go, Etta Mae?"

"About the same as usual, I guess. Laundry, vacuuming, dusting. But Mrs. Schaeffer dropped a big surprise on me as I was getting ready to head out for the day."

Mamie sipped her coffee. Nice and hot. Warmed her up from the cool breeze that had just started blowing in from her open windows. "A surprise?"

"Uh-huh," she said, as much with her eyebrows as her voice. "When she first started explaining it, I was getting upset. Then she quickly made it worth my while."

Mamie took a bite of some fresh cinnamon-raisin bread Etta Mae had brought over. "Oh my, this is good. Almost good enough to make me forget all my troubles."

"I knew you'd like it," Etta Mae said. "You know what happens when I bring it to church, folks gobble it up in the first fifteen minutes."

"We might just be doing that here." Mamie dunked a corner in her coffee. "So what's this surprise about? And why did it upset you at first?"

"For the next two days, I won't even be working at the Schaeffer house."

"Where will you be?"

"In Lake Helen, of all places."

"Lake Helen? What you gonna do in Lake Helen?"

"Same thing I do here in DeLand every day. Except I'll be doing it at her sister's place."

"Will Mrs. Schaeffer be there? She going there for a visit?"

"No," Etta Mae said. "It'll just be me. Me and Mrs. Schaeffer's sister. I forget her name now. Wrote it down somewhere."

"So who's going to clean the house here in DeLand the next two days?"

"Nobody, I guess. Not Mrs. Schaeffer, anyway.

Been working for her nearly twenty years. Never seen her lift a finger. Don't expect she'll start now. I'll probably just come home to a mess and have to work all the harder the days after that." Etta pulled the plate of cinnamon bread closer. "I'm gonna cut me another slice. You want some?"

"I better not."

"And why not?"

Mamie thought a moment. She didn't know why. Just seemed like the right thing to say. "All right then, cut me one too."

"She told me life hadn't gone so well for her sister, which surprised me. She never tells me anything personal. Said her sister couldn't afford to hire any help with her place in Lake Helen. You believe that?"

"Guess life hasn't gone so well for you and me, neither." Mamie Lee laughed. "I can't afford any help."

"I heard that," Etta Mae said. "She went on to say, her sister twisted her ankle yesterday and can't do anything for herself 'round the house. Guess her ankle all swelled up. Can't even get the clothes down off the line."

"That's painful," Mamie said. "Done the same thing to my ankle when I was younger."

"Here's the thing," Etta Mae continued, "the buses don't go that far back in some of those places in Lake Helen. So I'll be doing a lot more walking over the next few days." She looked

278

down at the plate. "You know what that means, don't you?"

Mamie followed her eyes. "I think I do. You're going to eat some more cinnamon bread."

Etta Mae smiled. "That's right. And I'm gonna use real butter instead of this here margarine. That is, if you got any?"

"I got a little bit. You're welcome to it." Mamie Lee got up and opened the refrigerator.

"I didn't tell you the best part," Etta Mae said. "Mrs. Schaeffer said she's gonna give me an extra twenty dollars this week for my trouble, more if I'll work on Saturday. Guess I can walk a few extra blocks for that."

Mamie closed the fridge, set the butter on the table. "Why, Etta Mae, you're gonna be rich. You keep that up, pretty soon you won't want to hang around me anymore."

It was time for bed. Colt stood in front of the dresser he shared with Timmy. Another reminder Timmy was gone.

He was looking at his hand-painted monster models, remembering the arguments they created when he'd asked for them at Christmas last year. It was all he wanted. The level of detail on these models was amazing. It took forever to paint them, especially the Phantom of the Opera. That was part of the problem. They were so realistic, they scared Timmy to death. His mom had said he needed to ask for something else for Christmas as soon as she saw them in the Sears catalog. "Your brother will never get to sleep with those things in your room."

His dad had intervened, saying it wasn't fair to punish Colt just because he was older. He thought of a compromise that Timmy and Mom would be able to accept. Colt wouldn't build or paint them when Timmy was around, and when they were finished he had to set them on top of the dresser and push them all the way back against the wall. Timmy was too short to see anything up that high.

His mom had given in, and Colt got all three for Christmas. He had so much fun making them over the next few months. Seeing them now reminded him how much he hated all the hassles that came with being stuck in a bedroom with a brother so much younger.

He turned and looked at the bedroom and, for a few moments, imagined what it would be like to have the room all to himself. How much easier and simpler. He'd had a taste of that the last four days. No little brother rules to follow. No little kid toys cluttering up everything. It actually might be kind of nice—

Wait, what was he thinking? How could he be so selfish? Timmy was out there somewhere, all alone. No family. No Mom and Dad. Who knew how that strange man was treating him?

Colt turned and faced the dresser again. He grabbed his Frankenstein model and threw it against the wall. Then rushed over to his bed, sat down, and cried.

47

After Etta Mae had made that long walk the next morning from where the bus dropped her off in Lake Helen to where Mrs. Schaeffer's sister lived, she was starting to think an extra twenty dollars wasn't near enough to make up the difference. Thankfully, since it was October, it was at least pleasant outside.

All the houses she had walked past were of a modest size. She doubted anyone back here could afford to hire help with the housekeeping. That could mean the white folk were a little nicer and a little easier to be around. Of course, she had suffered plenty of verbal abuse from poor rednecks in her day.

She also liked how pretty the lake looked in the morning. Had a nice mist rising from it, big beautiful birds with long necks and long legs walked around in the shallows. She imagined it would be a good lake for fishing, since everything was so quiet. That was something she didn't get to do much anymore. But she sure enjoyed it as a little girl, cane fishing with her daddy.

Well, she was standing by the screen door now. Should she knock or open it and walk through the screened porch and knock on the main door? She stood there a moment, then remembered Mrs. Adams lived alone, and she had a hurt foot. Wouldn't do to make her have to come out here and let Etta Mae in. And Mrs. Schaeffer said she'd be expecting her.

She walked up the two steps, through the porch to the main door. That was when she saw the note:

Etta Mae, the door is unlocked. You can come on in when you get here.

Josephine

"Josephine," Etta Mae read aloud. That must be Mrs. Adams's first name. Josephine Adams. Is that what she expected Etta Mae to call her? She opened the door, stuck her head inside. "Mrs. Adams? You in here? It's me, Etta Mae. Your sister sent me."

"I'm back here, Etta Mae. Back here in the dining room. You can come on back."

Etta Mae walked in the rest of the way, closed the door behind her. Wasn't a big living room, nothing like Mrs. Schaeffer's. Maybe just a tad bigger than her own. She headed back through the doorway on the right, which led right into the dining room. There sat Mrs. Adams in a dining room chair facing the window, a leg propped up on another chair, resting on a pillow, the ankle all wrapped up in Ace bandages.

That wasn't too odd. The odder thing was the big set of binoculars sitting on her lap.

Working the phones. Wasn't exactly the cutting-edge kind of work Vic had imagined after twenty years in the FBI. But they were shorthanded, and a little boy's life could be at stake. The first problem would be resolved soon enough, either by the world ending in a nuclear showdown or . . . this crisis blowing over and guys with a lot less seniority doing this kind of work for him again.

This Friday morning, things with Russia seemed to be heating up. When Vic had gotten into the office, Mr. Foster, the special agent in charge of the Orlando office, wasn't in. Rumor was, he was waiting in a long line at the confessional in his church. The other rumor was that he hadn't been to confession in over ten years.

"Foster might be in that dark little box a good while," Nate had said.

Vic looked over at Nate, who looked like he had a telephone receiver growing out of his left ear. This plan had seemed like a good idea when Nate had suggested it. And it still might provide the break in the case they were looking for. But already Vic was starting to doubt it.

A secretary was feeding them the phone numbers of the major hospitals in Florida's biggest cities. Then she'd go through a list of midsized cities, then work through the small towns. They were looking for the names of little boys around Timmy's age who had died over the last year. Vic had just finished calling all the hospitals in the Miami area. They had only turned up four names.

That was a good thing, in a sense. Only four little boys had died last year in a city as big as that. He didn't know why, but he expected the number to be much higher. Put that together with big cities like Tampa and Jacksonville, add in the midsize and smaller towns, and they might only have about twenty-five to thirty cases to check out. But really, they only needed one of these leads to pan out.

Just one.

He picked up the phone to call the law enforcement officers in Miami nearest to these hospitals to give them the four names and addresses. The first was in Miami Beach.

"Hello, Miami Beach Police Department, how may I direct your call?" It was a man's voice.

"Hi, this is Special Agent Victor Hammond of the FBI calling."

"The FBI? What can we do for you, Agent . . . Hammer did you say?"

"Hammond."

"Right. Why is the FBI calling us this morning? Got some Cuban spies you want us to pick up?"

"Nothing that elaborate. But we could use your help on a kidnapping case we're working on."

"Kidnapping? Okay, what do you need?"

"It's a pretty simple thing, really. Just need someone to drive by a house on Lenox Avenue, verify that there's no little boy living there around five or six years old."

"Did you say check to see if a little boy is *not* living there?"

"Yeah, I know that sounds odd. But we're working on the idea that the kidnapper might have taken the boy to replace a son that died last year."

"I get you. If we find a little boy living there when there's not *supposed* to be one . . ."

"You got it."

"And what do you want us to do if we find one?"

"Call me back right away. You could do a little more, if you can. I know things are really hopping down there with all the military activity."

"You ain't kidding. I've never seen anything like it."

"Back on Monday, I wired you a picture of the little boy we're looking for. His name is Timmy Harrison. If you find a little boy living at this house, maybe you can have an officer ask to see him and compare him to the picture. But make sure they know they need to be extremely careful. We don't know if this guy is armed. If he won't let you see the boy, just keep somebody watching the house while you get a warrant, to be sure the guy doesn't run."

"Okay, I wrote this all down. To be clear, you don't think this is the likely suspect?"

"Not right now. We're still at the needle-in-a-haystack stage. In fact, I still got over a dozen calls to make all over Florida today. I really appreciate your help on this."

"No problem," the police officer said. "I've got a son that age myself."

As Vic hung up the phone, he looked over at Nate, who was just doing the same. Nate made what looked like a check mark on a sheet of paper.

He looked at Vic and shook his head no.

48

"Sorry I'm a little late," Etta Mae said. "Didn't figure the walk right, how long it took to get here from where the bus dropped me off."

"Don't worry about it," Mrs. Adams said. "I'm not the punctual sister. I just appreciate you coming here to give me a hand. Like a fool, I hurt my foot out there in the backyard hanging laundry. Tripped over a big tree root. Not like I didn't know it was there. Lived in this house long enough, and that tree's been here longer than me."

Etta Mae stepped a little closer. "You been to

see a doctor for that?" Looking at the way those bandages were wrapped, she was pretty sure she knew the answer.

"No, no need. Lived long enough to know the difference between a break and a sprain. Just a bad sprain, is all. But my laundry's been out there on the line going on two days." She lifted up that set of binoculars and used it to look out the window.

What in the world? How far away was that clothesline? Etta Mae wondered.

Still looking through those binoculars, Mrs. Adams said, "Guess that's where you better start then."

"The laundry basket nearby, Mrs. Adams?" Etta Mae asked.

"Should be right out there. Might have to brush it off a little. When I fell, I grabbed onto it on my way down. Wound up sitting on it till I got my bearings. But please, do me a favor. Call me Josephine. And may I call you Etta Mae?"

"You certainly may." That was gonna take some getting used to, she thought. Calling this white woman by her first name. Barely three minutes in the door, and she was already beginning to like her. She noticed when Josephine talked about the laundry basket she was looking toward the back-yard, not the side yard where she was aiming those binoculars.

So what was she looking at? "I'll get right on it then," Etta Mae said, heading toward the kitchen and the back door. "Want me to rewash them?"

"Shouldn't have to," Josephine said. "Hasn't rained since I put them on the line. Just shake them out real good before you fold them, in case any leaves or dirt fell on them. Might have to rewash any that the birds pooped on."

Etta Mae smiled. "I will."

"Now my sister's going to pay you for coming over here, right? She told me she would."

Etta Mae stopped walking. "She is. Even a little more than usual."

"I'm glad. Mabel's always tried to look after me. I'm her younger sister. Of course, you wouldn't know it to look at me. She's got more years, but I've got more miles, if you know what I mean."

Etta Mae did, and she had assumed Josephine was the older of the two. She was more surprised to find Mrs. Schaeffer's first name was Mabel. Been working for the woman all these years and never knew that. Fact is, she knew more about Josephine these past five minutes than she'd learned about her big sister, Mabel, all that time.

Mabel. Mrs. Schaeffer sure didn't look like no Mabel. "I'll just get on that laundry then."

Josephine put those binoculars back up to her face. "And I'll just sit here on guard duty."

Etta Mae shook her head in bewilderment as she walked outside. There was the clothesline tied up between two trees, the laundry basket still upside down. She walked over to it then turned, trying to imagine what Josephine was looking at. Seemed like she must be spying on her neighbor across the way. That was the only thing in that direction.

The lake was behind them. The dirt street out in front.

She picked up the overturned basket, then looked again at the neighbor's house. It was just about the same size as Josephine's, painted an ugly shade of green instead of white. There was an old pickup truck parked out front. She didn't see any people or pets. No livestock of any sort. Nothing worth looking at, really. Let alone staring at all day through a pair of binoculars. She'd just have to come out and ask Josephine what she was up to. She'd never think of doing the same with Mrs. Schaeffer, butting into her personal business. But Josephine seemed like she might not even mind.

Etta Mae got the laundry off the line, then carried it back into the house. Since Josephine lived alone, they were obviously all her clothes. "You want me to put these away for you?"

"That would be a great help," Josephine said. "Guess I better explain where they go."

"That's okay. You just do . . . whatever it is you're doing there. I'm sure I can figure it out."

Josephine brought her binoculars down to her lap. "Guess this looks a little strange, doesn't it?"

"Maybe a little," Etta Mae said, smiling. Maybe a lot, she thought.

"I've been feeling like Jimmy Stewart these past couple of days, you know, in that Alfred Hitchcock movie. What was it called, *Rear Window*?"

Etta Mae liked Jimmy Stewart, but she guessed she hadn't seen that one. Must've showed on her face, because Josephine went on to explain.

"Remember, he was a photographer who broke his leg. Lived in an apartment surrounded by a bunch of other apartments, with a courtyard down below. Didn't have anything to do all day but stare out the window at all the other tenants with a set of binoculars, like these. Tried to figure out their life stories. His girlfriend was that beautiful blonde actress Grace Kelly. You know, the one who married a prince. As he looked out the window, Jimmy Stewart was sure he saw a husband murdering his wife and burying her body in that courtyard. Remember?"

Wasn't ringing any bells for Etta Mae. Sounded like a good one, though. She liked murder mysteries. Throw in Jimmy Stewart and she was sure she'd like it. "Too bad I missed that one," she said.

Josephine put the binoculars back up to her face and said, "Well, I feel like him. Only, I don't think I'm watching a murder taking place. Least I hope I'm not. But I got this crazy redneck neighbor lives next door. Meanest, most unfriendly man I ever met. I've been trying to reach out to him for years, just trying to be a good neighbor, see if I can invite him to my church. There's a man who needs to be in church in the worst way."

"So what's he doing, or what do you think he's doing, that makes you want to watch him with binoculars?"

"That's just it," Josephine said. "He might not be doing anything wrong. But he's been acting stranger than usual this past week. And his little boy is back, after being gone for months. Gone where, I have no idea. I thought maybe he had been living with his mother. Tried to ask August about that; that's my neighbor's name. And he about bit my head off. Thought if he had a broom, he'd have liked to smack me with it."

Etta Mae still didn't understand what that had to do with watching him with those binoculars.

Josephine continued. "See, I never got a chance to spend any time with his boy when he lived here before. August always kept him on a short leash. But I saw him out sweeping the front porch the other day, and I could've sworn he wasn't the same little boy."

Etta Mae's ears perked right up.

Josephine continued. "I've been reading the newspaper every day, because of this Cuban missile crisis. Most days I just read 'Dear Abby' and the obituaries. And I saw this story about a little boy been kidnapped on Monday. Had a picture of the boy and a drawing of the man who took him. I'm telling you, the man looked a bit like August. I only saw that little boy sweeping that porch for a minute, but I could've swore he resembled the boy in the newspaper. I've been watching the house ever since, trying to get a glimpse of him up close. But August hasn't let him out of the house again."

"Timmy?" Etta Mae said. "You talking about Timmy?"

"I think that's his name," Josephine said. "How did you know that?"

49

Friday afternoon was nearly over. Mike and Rose had just left for the store to pick up a few needed things for dinner. Colt was across the street at his friend Murph's. Scott and Gina were alone in the house.

Scott was reading the newspaper, sitting where he'd always sat. Gina sat in her spot, finishing the last few sips of her coffee. In between the moments she unconsciously stared at the telephone, wishing it would ring, she wondered what Scott was thinking. A common pastime for her when Scott had lived here. He would sit there not talking, and she would sit there trying to imagine what was on his mind. Back when she used to care a great deal about this, she'd occasionally ask him.

He would typically say nothing. Nothing was on his mind.

She typically found that hard to believe. Was he just stupid? Were all men just stupid? Of course, he couldn't be stupid in one sense; they didn't give out engineering degrees to stupid people. But could he really just sit there and pass the time with absolutely nothing going on in his brain? Could men, in general, really be content dwelling on absolutely nothing?

"What are you thinking about?"

Gina looked up. Now this was different. Scott was asking what was on her mind. But she couldn't tell him. Not really. He'd be too insulted. Maybe that was it, why he'd always said "nothing" when she'd asked him this question. The truth wasn't *nothing*. He was thinking of something he didn't want to tell her.

"Nothing," she said.

"You sure? Your face looks pretty serious."

She didn't know what to say.

"Well, I've got a question," he said. "When did you stop using the milkman?"

Oh my goodness, she thought. Was that the big thing piquing his curiosity right now? The milkman's fate? "When did you notice?"

"Yesterday, I guess. So, when was the last time he came?"

"It's been awhile. A few months after you left. Wasn't really a big deal. I might have felt bad for the man, if we'd ever met. But he always came and went before we woke up. So I just left him a little note with a little extra tip." Scott cared because he had been a milkman for several years, back when he had gone to night school. It was a hard life, mainly because you had to go to bed and wake up so early in order to get the milk and eggs to all your customers before they woke up. And, of course, Gina had to get up with Scott to get his breakfast and lunch ready.

"They're a dying breed, I think." Scott put the newspaper down. "It's kind of sad, when you think about it, like the passing of an era."

Gina wasn't so sentimental. "I hated it when you worked as one. But having a milkman was pretty convenient most of the time. But now that we get fresh dairy in the supermarket, and it's even cheaper, and I go shopping at least a couple times a week, I just didn't see the point."

"I'm not mad," he said. "Probably would have made the same decision if I was here."

She kind of doubted that. Maybe he would have. He certainly seemed to be doing some things differently than she was used to. Like this, sitting here reading the paper instead of being at work. She still couldn't believe he had walked away from that big promotion, right in the middle of this Expo thing. Technically, he didn't really have a job right now. And it didn't seem to bother him. That was different too.

"I really liked being a milkman," he said. "I don't know why exactly. I hated getting up so early."

"You did? You never said that when you were a milkman. When I'd complain about it, you'd try to talk me out of it and tell me what a good job it was, how much we needed the money. One time you said, 'Milkmen provide a vital service in this country.' "

"I really said that?" He was smiling.

She nodded. "You really did."

"What did you say back?"

"What could I say back? I couldn't believe you said it. I was only complaining because I was so tired from having to get up with Timmy at 1:00 a.m. He was just a baby then. I was just letting off a little steam, and you were trying to defend the rights of all milkmen everywhere."

Scott shook his head. "I was such a dope."

Gina laughed. He really was.

He leaned back on the couch. "I can't believe we lived like that for three years."

"I can," she said. She was going to say more but decided not to pile on. He was being so nice right now. "Can I ask you something?"

"Sure."

"Why *did* we do that for three years? And those other jobs you had for four more, while you attended night school?"

"Because we needed the money. I did it so you

could stay home with the boys. I thought that's what you wanted. What we both wanted."

"I did, but me working wasn't our only option. There was another option on the table that you rejected. And it would've meant you could have gone to school during the day full-time instead of at night, and that would have knocked three whole years off our ordeal."

Scott stood up. Gina recognized this move. He was about to clam up. Then he'd walk away, refusing to talk about things further. He used to say he did this for her protection, so she wouldn't have to hear him get angry and say some things he'd later regret.

But that wasn't what happened this time. He sat back in his chair.

"I know it must look that way to you," he said softly, "but at the time I didn't feel like I had any choice."

"Okay," she said. "Could you explain that?"

"I'll try. To me, that option was a closed door. Because my father made the offer with some pretty short strings. He was pressuring me to go into finance and to go to the same college he and my brothers went to. I wanted to be an engineer. But it was more than that. Even if I could have somehow talked him into letting me be an engineer, I didn't want to be dependent on him. Not like that. I'm not like my father, or my brothers." He let out a deep sigh. "Or like my mother, for that matter."

She knew this but wondered what he meant by it. They had never talked about any of these things before. "What do you mean? In what ways?"

"Don't get me wrong, I love them. All of them. But I'm not . . . I don't know. I'm not old South. Not since Korea. I don't buy into the way they think. For one thing, I don't like the way they treat Mamie Lee. Or black people in general. I never liked that. She's been working for them my whole life, and she has nothing. Nothing to show for it. And they're all okay with that. For them, it's just the way it is."

He stood up again but kept talking. "They won't even let me treat her the way I want to. When I do, I get scolded like a child. But I know what's really going on. When I do nice things for her, I'm making them look bad. And they don't like how that feels. I love them, but honestly?" He paused. "They're just racists, Gina. When you get right down to it. Southern white racists who really believe, at a basic level, that whites are better, smarter, and more deserving of the good life. I grew up with that, but that's not who I am. It always bothered me. And after what I experienced in Korea, I can't do it anymore."

Here was something else he barely ever talked about: his time in Korea. While he was there, he'd written letters, but it was all small talk. Nothing that conveyed where he might be struggling or things he was feeling at a heart level. "What did

297

you experience in Korea that has to do with this?"

"I guess I never told you this, but . . . two black guys turned out to be my closest friends over there, and one of them even saved my life."

Gina had never heard any of these things before. She liked what she was hearing. Why had they never talked like this?

"Mamie Lee feels more like my mom than my own mother does. I think I could have told Mamie Lee everything I was going through, while it was happening, and she would've understood, and she could have helped me understand it all, just like she did when I was little. Because of my parents, I could never talk to her that way. I had to keep Mamie in the dark. She still doesn't know half the things I've been through."

"Scott," Gina said softly, "neither do I, and I'm your wife. Does that sound right to you? Why couldn't you have talked to me like that? Told me everything you were feeling—while it was happening? Given me a chance to see if I would've understood?"

He looked at her a few moments, like he didn't know what to say.

"I'm not saying you shouldn't have talked to Mamie Lee, or have been able to talk with her like that. But that's who I wanted to be in your life, who I was supposed to be in your life. But you never let me in. Do you realize we haven't had a conversation like this . . . ever? I'm hearing you share things now that you were feeling years ago, for the first time. And I'm not judging you. Or telling you how wrong you were to feel that way. In fact, I pretty much agree with everything you're saying about Mamie Lee. I would have even been open to us inviting her over, even if we had to do it secretly behind your parents' back. It could've been our secret."

Gina didn't mean to or want to. It was probably just the emotions of everything else going on this week. But she started to cry just then.

Scott didn't get angry with her. He didn't try to defend himself or make any excuses. When she looked up and was able to see his face through her own tears, she saw tears in his eyes.

"I'm sorry, Gina. I shouldn't have treated you that way. You're right, I should have given you a chance."

50

Etta Mae couldn't help it, she felt tingly all over. Had felt like this most of the day. She'd had this feeling before, mostly in church. But sometimes when she prayed, either alone or with her ladies group. She recognized the feeling as the Holy Ghost.

She was pretty sure that was what this was now.

This tingly feeling happened toward the end of the day. She was finishing up in the kitchen after making dinner for Josephine and for her too. Josephine had insisted she bring some home. She said it was silly making all that food for one person. Etta Mae looked up from the dinette table she was cleaning. There was Josephine still sitting in that chair, hurt foot propped up, eyes staring through them binoculars.

Josephine was all stirred up too after her conversation with Etta Mae that morning. "I don't believe in coincidences anymore," she'd said. "Not since I started following the Lord." She was sure God had set this all up. He'd made sure Etta Mae was the one who got picked to help her with housecleaning after her fall. Because she had that connection to Timmy. Josephine had even said she wouldn't be surprised if God had one of his angels stick out his foot and trip her on purpose, just to make her this helpless. Helpless enough that her sister Mabel was forced to take pity on her and offer to let Etta Mae come over like she did.

Josephine could've used help a dozen other times over the years, had even deliberately hinted as much to Mabel. But Mabel had never once offered the services of "her domestic," as she liked to call Etta Mae.

"No," Josephine had said. "This wasn't any coincidence."

Etta Mae didn't think so either. It was all she could do not to stop these chores and march right over there, demand to see the boy the next-door neighbor had hidden away. She had asked Josephine if she could. Josephine didn't say much when she said no, but it was clear to Etta Mae the very idea almost terrified her.

"No sign of him yet?" Etta Mae asked.

"Not yet," Josephine said. "I've seen old August over there a couple of times. Twice through the living room windows, once out on the porch. But no sign of Timmy."

Etta Mae realized that Josephine wasn't even talking like that boy was anyone else but Mamie Lee's Timmy. "You sure we shouldn't just go over there? You seem pretty sure it's him."

Josephine set the binoculars down a moment. "Oh, I am sure. On one level anyway. But you don't know August, what he's like, what he can be like. I have to be absolutely sure before we start making accusations. If somehow we turned out to be wrong and it was his little boy, I'd never hear the end of it. I might even have to move. I think the wisest thing is to just sit here and wait him out. That little boy has to show up sometime, right? And now that we have his picture from the newspaper sitting right here next to me, I can make a positive identification with certainty."

"We can do better than that," Etta Mae said.

"I've seen Timmy myself with my own eyes. If you think you see him, you just yell for me and I'll run right over."

"I'll do that, Etta Mae." Josephine turned to look at the clock on the wall. "You better start getting ready to leave for the day. You got a ways to walk before you get that bus, don't you?"

"You're right. I almost forgot."

"Say, before I forget to ask. Can you take a look around the kitchen, see what ingredients I have to make a pie?"

"A pie?"

"Yes. I'm thinking about tomorrow. Maybe I can take another stab at making August a pie. He might do the same thing he did the last time, but at least it would give us an excuse to go over there. He's not likely to take a shotgun to a woman bringin' a pie."

"He take a shotgun to you last time?"

"No, but he keeps one nearby. Had a feeling if I pressed him too much further, he might have gone for it. 'Course, I think he's all bluff and bluster, but you just can't be too sure with someone so unstable."

"Then what did he do the last time you brought him a pie?"

"He tossed it in the trash can."

"You mean the leftovers?"

"No, the whole pie. It was blueberry, as ripe and juicy as they get too."

· · ·

Mike and Rose had just gotten home from the store. Rose and Gina had decided to get working on dinner. About that time, Colt walked in the door from his visit across the street at Murph's house. Scott noticed he had a look of concern on his face.

"Everything go okay at Murph's?"

Colt closed the door. "Yeah, it was fine. I came home now because Mom asked me to before I left."

"Is anything else bothering you?"

"I'm not sure." Colt walked over to the front window and looked down the street. "Did anything new happen on the news? About this whole Cuba thing?"

"I don't think so," Scott said. "Why?"

"It's Mr. Weldon. He's acting kind of strange."

"What's he doing?"

Mike got up to look too. He had just started reading the newspaper Scott had finished a little while ago.

"He's walking down the sidewalk in front of his house," Colt said, "holding some kind of meter up in the air. I think it's a Geiger counter."

"A Geiger counter," Scott repeated. "I didn't even know you knew what that was."

"Sure I do. I've never seen one, but we've read about them in school. And I've seen them on some of those monster movies you took me to.

303

You know, the ones with the giant bugs and lizards that got so big because of radiation."

Still standing over Colt, Mike said, "That's exactly what it looks like. A Geiger counter."

Scott got up and looked for himself. "Could be what it is, but it looks a little different from the ones I've seen."

"You've seen Geiger counters, Dad?"

Scott didn't realize something like that would be impressive. "I have, both at school and at work. Why don't we just go ask him what he's up to?"

"Could we?" Colt asked.

"Sure. Mom and Aunt Rose have just started dinner. Just let me do the talking. You want to go with us, Mike?"

"No, you two go ahead. I'll just sit here and finish reading the newspaper."

"Come on, Colt. Let's go have a look." They headed toward the front door, but Scott stopped. "Let me tell your mother first where we're going."

Scott walked back to the kitchen. "Hey, Gina, I'm going to take Colt down to see Mr. Weldon for a moment. Check out something odd he's doing on the sidewalk."

"Something odd? Like what?"

"Looks like he's taking some radiation measurements."

"What? Why? Is something going on?"

"Nothing new, not that I know of. Just thought it

would give me something to do with Colt. He's pretty curious about it."

"That's fine," she said. "We'll just be here pulling the strings out of these beans."

"Let's go, Colt."

They headed out the door, but it seemed like they were too late. No sign of Mr. Weldon. "Can we at least walk down to the corner?" Colt said.

"I guess that can't hurt."

So that's what they did. And it paid off. Mr. Weldon was still outside, still walking the edge of his property. He had turned the corner, so they couldn't see him around the hill. "Mr. Weldon," Scott called out.

Weldon turned, started walking in their direction. "Hey, Scott, can't talk right now. Need to pay attention to these readings I'm taking."

"We won't bother you then. Colt and I were just curious what you're doing."

Weldon stopped walking when he got near them. "This is my new Bendix Radiation Kit. Bought it out of a catalog a few months ago. Hoped I'd never have to use it. Now it looks like I have to."

"Why now?" Colt said. The worried look had returned.

"The Russians have called our bluff. They're not stopping their ships. Which means they're not stopping their work on those missiles in Cuba. Which means, we're going to have to invade and make them stop. Which means . . . well, you know what it means. Those missiles will start firing off. Could be this afternoon, maybe tonight. Maybe in the morning. But I don't see any way out of it now."

"So what's this thing do?" Colt asked.

"It measures radiation fallout."

"You think there's radiation out here now?"

"There's always a certain amount of radiation going on," Weldon said. "Most of it's not harmful. So I'm out here measuring the background radiation, the normal kind. That way I'll have an accurate reading once the missiles start going off. The wife and I can't come out of our fallout shelter until the harmful levels come back down to normal."

"Makes sense," Scott said. Of course, the whole thing sounded ridiculous and unreal.

"You and the wife give any more thought to our offer? You know, to join us once it all starts to hit the fan?"

"We did," Scott said. "Gina's just not sure she wants to go that route. She says she doesn't want to live in a world after something like that happened. But thanks for the offer."

"I'd suggest you give it some more thought," Weldon said. "Once things start boiling over, we'll have to close the door on that thing for good."

"Thanks, Mr. Weldon," Colt said. "But even if we wanted to, we could never go down there. Not without Timmy."

51

This idea wasn't panning out.

Vic and Nate had been on the phone all day calling hospitals throughout the state of Florida, looking for the names of little boys Timmy's age who had died over the past year. Then calling law enforcement personnel in the same area, giving them the names and addresses of their fathers. The leads given them by the officers and deputies who'd gotten back to them had all turned out to be dead ends.

"I really thought this might turn up something useful," Nate said.

"It still might," Vic said. "How many more hospitals you have left to call?"

"Four."

"I have five. What do you say we call it a day, finish these in the morning?"

"I say yeah. Let's do that. You want to call the boy's parents, give them an update?"

Vic stared at the telephone. No, he didn't. "Guess I better. Wish I had something positive to say."

"You'll think of something." Nate pushed away from his desk and stood up. "Guess it wouldn't help to point out the world hasn't blown up yet."

Vic forced a smile. "Don't think I'll lead with

that. But you go ahead. After this call, I'll be right behind you." He watched as Nate picked up his hat, put on his coat, then headed for the exit. He reached for the telephone and dialed the Harrisons' number from memory.

"Hello?"

"Hey, Scott, this is Vic with the FBI."

"No, this is Mike. Scott's brother-in-law. But he's right here. Let me get him."

Vic waited a moment.

"Hello, Vic, this is Scott. Any news? Please say yes."

Vic sighed.

"Guess that's my answer," Scott said. "No leads from that new idea?"

"Not yet. But we're not done. I still have to hear back from quite a few law enforcement personnel. And Nate and I still have a number of hospitals to call tomorrow."

"I see."

"Remember, Scott, it's not the quantity of leads we have that matters. We only need one that works. This is the nature of police work. It's not like the movies. Someone comes up with an idea like Nate did, it generates a lot of work, you work it through over several days, hoping to turn up something solid. Lots of times, it does."

"I understand, Vic. Really, I appreciate all you guys are doing. I just wish there was something we could do. We feel so helpless over here.

It's been five days now. Feels like five weeks."

"Have you gotten any calls from the press? Newspapers or the local news?"

"Not a single one."

Vic couldn't believe it. He thought for sure they'd be hounded by the press. A kidnapped little boy? "It's gotta be this Cuba deal. It's got everybody totally preoccupied. Maybe when this whole thing blows over, this case will get the kind of attention it deserves."

"You think that's going to happen?" Scott asked. "That it's all going to blow over soon? Are you hearing something we're not? My neighbor down the street's measuring the air for radiation fallout. Of course, he's definitely the Chicken Little type. But even from what I'm seeing in the newspaper and on the news, it looks pretty bleak."

Vic thought about his boss taking time off that morning to go to confession. And the overall mood in the Orlando office. "No, it looks pretty bleak from where I stand. I think the only thing that will stop the worst-case scenario is the same thing that's stopped it from happening all along."

"M.A.D.," Scott muttered.

"Mutually Assured Destruction," Vic said.

"Nobody wins if everybody blows up," Scott said. "That's how a guy in our office summarized it."

"I like that. That's what I'm counting on, Scott. I don't have any inside FBI information. Seems to me right now, Kennedy and Khrushchev are like two hot-rodders playing chicken. Somebody's gotta pull off to the side. But it's getting close, I'm not gonna lie."

"I wish somebody would pull off to the side pretty quick," Scott said. "So we could get more help finding Timmy."

You and me both, Vic thought. "But we'll get right back on this tomorrow morning, first thing."

"Will you call me when you're done with this thing, this new idea? Even if nothing pans out?"

Vic dreaded the idea. "Of course I will. But let's not give up yet. Only takes one lead that works, right?"

Scott didn't answer for a moment. "Right," he finally said.

52

When Etta Mae arrived at Josephine's house the next morning, Josephine had already positioned herself on the chair facing her next-door neighbor's house. Already had her binoculars sitting on her lap. She'd told Etta Mae as soon as she came through the door that today something big was gonna happen. It had to, after God had gone to all that trouble to bring Etta Mae here. And she was sure that little boy she had seen for that ever-so-brief moment on the porch had to be Timmy.

Sitting right beside her on a little table was that newspaper, folded so that Timmy's picture was right on top.

"You want me to start cleaning or making that pie?" Etta Mae said.

"The cleaning can wait. You already made it nicer in here than I ever get it. Why don't you get to work on that pie? The sooner we get it done, the sooner we can get it next door."

She said *we,* Etta Mae thought. What did she mean by that? Well of course, she couldn't get over there by herself. With her on those crutches, Etta Mae would have to carry the pie.

Etta Mae walked out into the kitchen, then turned toward the dining room. "Miss Josephine, you've got all the ingredients to make a pie here, except what to put in it. Maybe before I get started, we should drive to the store. You could drop me off by the front door with a list, and I'll get it all together for you. You won't even have to get out of the car."

"Can't you just go by yourself, so I can stay here and keep watch?"

"I don't have a car, remember? I came by the bus."

"You can take mine."

"Take yours?"

"Can't you drive?"

"Well, yeah . . . I suppose." Though she hadn't driven a car since she was in her twenties. Besides that, what would some of these white folk around here think, ones who knew Josephine, when they saw a black woman driving her car without Josephine inside? Etta Mae explained all this to Josephine, but she kept her resolve.

"If anyone bothers you about it, you tell them just to call me and I'll straighten them out. But I don't think anyone will give you any trouble. You might have to wade through some ugly looks and I'm sure you'll catch a few people whispering behind your back. But that's about all."

Etta Mae figured she could deal with that well enough, if that was all there was. "Is your car manual or automatic?"

"Automatic. You ever driven one?"

"No."

"Easy as pie," Josephine said, then laughed at the unintended wit. "Get it? I said *pie*."

"I get it. Do you have the keys?"

"In my purse. If you'll bring it over here, I'll get you the keys and some money. And over there on the hutch you'll find a pad of paper and a pen. If you bring those, I'll make you a little map to the store."

Gina spent a few moments at the doorway of the boys' empty bedroom on her way out to the living room. Judging by the light coming in the window, it seemed like midmorning. No one had come to wake her. But sleeping in hadn't been a blessing this time. Not when she'd tossed and turned until 4:00 a.m.

Her little boy was still gone.

Staring at his perfectly made bed was a glaring reminder. Timmy had never made his bed like that. How many times had she tried to teach him the right way? How many times did she have to redo it to get it to look like it did now? How many times had she raised her voice when scolding him about it?

Tears rolled down her cheeks. She'd give anything, everything she owned, to see that bed made in his messy, Timmy way.

"Just made a fresh pot of coffee, hon. Mike and Rose are on their way over. Did you sleep well?"

She didn't turn toward the voice emanating from the living room, though she'd heard it clearly. It was Scott. He had called her "hon" again. She did feel closer to him now, after this horrific week. Especially after their conversation yesterday. She felt closer to him than she had since the day they had married. She had even occasionally caught herself daydreaming about having him back in her life for good.

But was she his "hon"?

"No," she said. "I didn't sleep well."

Vic stood next to Nate's desk, listening in on his conversation. Nate had waved him over. Sounded like he had a live one on the hook.

313

It was Saturday, almost lunchtime. Vic had just finished up with his list of people to call. All dead ends. He knew Nate had to be close to the end of his list too. Suddenly, Nate had gotten all animated about this present call.

"No, I agree," Nate said. "This sounds promising. But can't someone from your office go by the house and talk to this guy in person?" Nate listened a little more, shook his head no. "I see. No, I get it. These aren't normal times. We've got a lot of personnel out sick here today too. But we're a two-hour drive from there. It's what, about twenty minutes up the road for you?" Nate looked up at Vic, shook his head no again.

Whatever it was, Vic hoped Nate didn't push too hard.

"I understand," Nate said. "Really, I do. Thanks for following up on this. This could turn out to be the break in the case we've been waiting for. We'll take it from here."

Nate hung up and sat back in his chair. "This one's from a hospital in Palatka. Little boy died last year. He lived out in a rural area off Highway 20, between Palatka and a little town called Interlachen."

"Interlachen? Never heard of it."

"Me neither," Nate said. "It's about twenty-five minutes west of Palatka. Anyway, a sheriff's deputy drove by there yesterday and recalled seeing a little boy about Timmy's age on the front porch."

"What, he didn't stop?"

"No, he didn't. Sounds like he didn't have the right information. He was only told to drive by and verify if a boy that age lived at that address. Since the boy was right out there in the open, he didn't see any need to stop and chat."

"Well, can't he go back and do that now?"

"That's what you heard me asking about at the end there. They're saying they're really short-handed today. Bunch of people called in sick. The guy I talked to thinks it's this Cuba situation. Each day the news gets worse, and people are starting to think it's really gonna happen. They're getting scared, like maybe they might only have a day or two before nuclear bombs start falling."

Vic wanted to say something, but he had to admit . . . when he'd stood at the door of his own house that morning and kissed his wife good-bye, he'd had serious thoughts about closing that door and calling in sick himself.

Nate leaned forward, rested his elbows on the desk. "Looks like it's up to you and me to check this situation out ourselves."

"That's at least a four-hour round trip, isn't it?"

Nate nodded.

Vic looked at his watch. "Guess we better get started then. I'll go tell Foster. Why don't you get the car ready?"

Vic walked down the hall to Foster's office. He heard him in there on the phone. The secretary's desk just outside his office was empty. Speaking of calling in sick, she had done that this morning. Vic waited a few minutes until he heard Foster stop talking, then waited a few moments more. He opened the door to find Special Agent Foster was, indeed, off the phone. But something was wrong. He was looking down, rubbing his temples with both hands. He didn't seem to notice Vic had come in. Vic made a little extra noise as he approached the desk.

Foster looked up. "Hey, Vic, what's up?" His face looked grave.

"What's wrong?"

Foster took a deep breath. "That was my friend who works at McCoy Air Force Base. They sent out a U-2 spy plane to see if the Russians had halted work on the missile sites. They just confirmed the Russians shot down the U-2 over Cuba. The pilot was killed."

Both men looked at each other, but neither said a word. Vic could only imagine how President Kennedy and the military generals surrounding him would react to this news.

53

After leaving the office, Vic stopped at the curb where Nate had parked the car. "Hold on, Nate. Let me make a quick call to the Harrisons."

"I don't know, Vic. The trip down to the Everglades fizzled out. Maybe you should wait till we get to this place, see what the story is."

Vic thought a moment. Maybe Nate was right. But the Harrisons were desperate for any news about Timmy. Even uncertain news. "I still think I should call them."

"Go ahead. I'll be right here."

"I won't be long." He hurried back inside.

Back at his desk, he dialed the number. "Hello. This is Vic Hammond. Can I please speak with Scott Harrison?"

"Hey, Vic. This is Scott. Any news?"

"It may be nothing. I'll leave it up to you to decide whether you want to brief Gina or not."

"Brief her about what?"

"Nate and I are heading out to a little town west of Palatka to follow up on a lead."

"Does it look good?"

"Could be. We'll have to wait and see. We were toward the end of our list of hospitals to call when Nate ran across this one. A sheriff's deputy went out to this property and noticed a little boy about

Timmy's age out front on the porch. But the little boy was supposed to have died last year."

"You think this could be it?"

"Hope so. We'll call you and Gina as soon as we know something solid."

"Appreciate that, Vic."

"Are you gonna tell her about this?" Vic waited through a pause.

"I'm not sure. She's had a rough morning. Rougher than usual."

"I understand. No pressure. Just want to make sure you know what's going on."

"Thanks, Vic."

It was just a little past lunchtime now. Etta Mae was putting the finishing touches on a fresh apple pie she had just pulled out of the oven. The blueberries were a little too expensive today. She set it carefully on the windowsill to cool. "You should see this, Josephine. It came out perfect. I dare your redneck neighbor to toss this pie in the trash without tasting it."

"I hope you're right."

"You should smell it."

"You kidding? I been smelling it for the last hour or so. It's been driving me crazy. Should've had you make two, one for him and one for you and me."

Etta Mae lifted her little surprise out of the oven and walked it around the corner into the dining room. She held it out for Josephine to see. Her binoculars were already back up on her face. "Miss Josephine?"

Josephine set them aside and looked at the miniature apple pie Etta Mae was now holding. Her face lit up like a child's. "For us?"

Etta Mae nodded. "I'll just set it here on the sill with its big brother." After she put down the pie, she came back into the dining room. "Still no sign of the boy?"

"Afraid not."

"When do you want to bring that pie over? It should be ready before too long."

"You mean," Josephine said, "when are *you* going to bring that pie over?"

"You want me to do it?"

"Well, I can't on these crutches."

Etta Mae wanted to point out that she most certainly could. A person could do anything if they set their mind to it. "I was thinking you'd head over there on your crutches. And I'll be right beside you holding this pie. You're the one he knows, after all, not me."

"That may be true. But we already know he doesn't like me. He might react differently to you."

"That's right, he might just shoot me. What if he's a member of the Klan? They're all over the place in these small towns."

"Oh, I don't think he's a member of the Klan.

319

I've never seen any evidence of that. I'm sure you'll be fine. Worst thing that would probably happen is, he'll toss your pie in the trash can like he did mine."

What a waste if that happened, Etta Mae thought. But she could live with that disappointment.

Josephine pulled the binoculars down with a mischievous smile. "Maybe we should just send him over that little baby pie you made instead."

Thirty minutes later, the pie was cooled off and Etta Mae had helped Josephine get all situated. They had just prayed together for God to protect Etta Mae and give her strength, as she put it, "not to turn and run the minute that ornery ole cuss answers the door."

Etta Mae was just now putting the pie on a tray with handles. They had decided the Christian thing to do was to give August the bigger of the two pies, fearing that if they gave him the smaller one, he wouldn't share it with Timmy.

Suddenly, Josephine began to shout. As loud as one can shout when they're trying to whisper. "There he is, Etta Mae. The boy. Timmy."

Etta Mae left the pie on the table and ran over to the window. "You seen him?" She looked out for herself.

Josephine, still glued to the binoculars, said, "I did, I did. Just a moment ago."

"Where? I don't see him."

"He walked right past the window. The front window. The first one there, on the right side."

Etta Mae didn't see anything but an old green house. "You sure it was Timmy?"

"I think it was him. It was just for that moment. But he's got to come back by. Unless I already missed him."

Etta Mae looked right at that window again, squinted her eyes all up. But it made no difference, not from this distance. "Well, I guess I better get over there then with this pie. If I go there right now, maybe Timmy'll answer the door. If he's still there in the living room."

"You can try," Josephine said. "But I doubt August will let that happen. I don't recall the boy ever answering the door. Not just this time, but when he was here months ago."

"What you mean, months ago? Timmy's only been took a week."

Josephine set the binoculars down. "August definitely had a little boy living with him before. A good long while. Kept him on a short leash. Not as short as the one he's on now. But then he was gone, the boy, I mean. Not sure how long, but a few months, anyway."

"Well," Etta Mae said, "whoever he was, that other little boy, he couldn't have been Timmy. Like I said, Timmy's just missing since Monday. What's that, six days?"

Josephine looked out the window again but left her binoculars on her lap. "If that's true," she said, "then who was that first little boy? And where is he now?"

54

Now who could that be at the door? August walked over and peeked his head in the dining room. Bobby was in there, coloring in a coloring book. "Didn't you hear the door?" Bobby looked up, set his crayon down. He shook his head no, then nodded yes. That same fretting look on his face he wore most of the time.

"Well, then," August said, "you know what to do. Get in that room. And be quick about it."

"You mean . . . the dark place?"

"No, your bedroom. But I'll put you in the dark place if you don't get up this instant." The boy got up and ran down the hall. "Close the door and stay away from the window. And don't you make a sound." August turned and walked toward the front door. "Let's go see who this is," he muttered.

As he neared the front door, he eyed his shotgun leaning in the corner. He peeked through the crack in the curtain in the front door window. Couldn't believe what he saw. "What in the world?" He opened it and looked down at a colored woman standing on his porch, dressed like a maid, holding a pie.

"Morning, sir," she said, smiling, holding the pie up toward him.

"How did you get here?" Far as he knew, no one in this neighborhood had domestic help.

"I came from next door. From your neighbor's house."

From the direction she pointed with her head, she must mean . . . "Josephine? You work for Josephine now?"

The woman nodded. "Just for a few days, though. Maybe a few weeks. Depends on how long it takes for her foot to mend."

"What, she break it?" Why did he ask that? Not like he cared.

"I think it's just a bad sprain. Anyway, I work for her older sister in DeLand. She asked me to come here for a couple of days to help Miss Josephine. And she asked me if I would make this pie for you. Well, for you and your little boy. So here I am."

The maid started looking past August into the living room, like she was hinting at being invited in. That wasn't going to happen. He looked down at that pie in her hands. The last time his neighbor had sent one over, he'd tossed it out. He wasn't thinking of doing that now. This thing looked and smelled pretty good. Problem was, he didn't want to get too friendly with her, or anyone else in this neighborhood. Especially till things settled down with the boy.

"Do you want it?" the maid said. "If you don't, maybe your little boy would. What's his name?"

"His name's Bobby." Wait a minute, why was he telling this colored woman his business? "I suppose if she went to all that trouble to have you make it, guess I can take it off your hands." He reached out through the doorway, and she handed the pie to him. She looked at him some more, then looked past him and around him. At first, he wondered if she was thinking she should get some kind of tip. Then he decided she was just being nosy.

That was easy enough to fix. He nodded at her, stepped back into the living room, and closed the front door. He was carrying the pie toward the kitchen when he heard a knock at the front door again. He set the pie on the dining room table.

What now? He opened the door.

"I'm sorry to bother you again. But could I get that carrying tray back? That's Miss Josephine's. I only used it because the pie pan was still hot."

"I suppose," August said.

"I see it there on the table," she said. "If you like, I'll just go get it and be on my way."

"I don't like. You stay here. I'll go get it." August wasn't about to have no colored maid walking through his house. He walked back to the dining table and gently felt the edges of the pie pan. It was still hot, but not dangerously so. He quickly lifted it out and set it down, then returned the tray to the maid. "Here."

Then he closed the door.

The man didn't say good-bye, didn't say thank you. Just took the pie and closed the door. *Well, I'll be.* Etta Mae stepped off the porch, glad this little assignment was over. But she wished she could have seen Timmy. Wherever he was, he wasn't in the living room.

She started making her way across the mostly dirt side yard between the two properties. As she did, she looked toward the dining room window in Josephine's house. She couldn't see her there, because of the reflection, but she knew Josephine was probably watching her through her binoculars. So she shook her head no to let Josephine know she hadn't seen Timmy.

When she got to the boundary of Josephine's place, she glanced back at the man's house. Some movement caught her eye. A side window. She looked. A curtain moved. A little hand holding the curtain's edge. It was Timmy's window, the window Josephine had been staring at over the last two days. She couldn't see the face behind the curtains, but it was definitely a little hand. Probably Timmy's hand, she thought. She stopped walking and waved toward the window. Instantly, the hand disappeared.

But she was sure it was him. She stood there a few moments more, but the curtain remained closed. She headed back to Josephine's house. Part of her wanted to go the opposite direction. To walk right back to that man's house, bang on the door, and demand to see Timmy. But one look in his eyes had convinced her he was not a man to mess with. Even if she had tried, he wouldn't have produced the boy. He probably would've chased her off with a shotgun.

She walked up the steps of Josephine's back porch and headed inside. Before she even set the tray down, Josephine called to her from the dining room.

"Did you see him?" Josephine asked.

"Not when I was on the porch. But I definitely saw him on the way back. Did you see where I stopped for a moment?"

"I did, and I saw that little hand holding the curtain."

"Could you see his face?"

"I couldn't," Josephine said. "He must have had the bedroom light turned off. Nothing but shadows."

"Well, at least we know he's in there. Are you going to keep watching the place?"

"I certainly am. All day."

55

Two hours had passed. Vic and Nate were almost to their destination. They had driven up from Orlando on State Road 19 through the Ocala National Forest. Then through the little town of Interlachen. Now they were on State Road 20, very close to the address on the little slip of paper Nate held in his left hand. For the most part, the roads were deserted the whole way here.

"Didn't see any military vehicles," Nate said. "Got used to seeing them."

"My guess is they're all in place already. Down south."

"You mean for the invasion?"

Vic nodded. The invasion of Cuba. Seemed inevitable now. He hadn't heard any more news since the story broke about the Russians shooting down the U-2 plane earlier today. But considering how the tension had been building all week, he couldn't see the military generals in Washington settling for anything less than an invasion now. He remembered the excitement and anticipation when General Eisenhower had announced the D-Day invasion back in '44.

This wasn't like that at all.

Mutually Assured Destruction. That's what this invasion meant. We invade Cuba. They launch their nukes. We launch ours. Vic hoped they would at least wait to invade until he got done with this assignment and drove home.

A man should be with his family on the day they all die.

"This place on the right or the left side of the road?" Nate asked.

"I believe it's on the right, judging by the other address numbers I'm seeing. Should be just up ahead." Also, he could see a lake on the right, set back from the road in between the trees. This house was supposed to be on a lake.

"How do you want to work this?" Nate said. "Go in strong or check things out first?"

"I'm thinking we should park on the side of the road. See what we can see through the binoculars. Maybe we'll get lucky like that deputy did and see the little boy outside."

"If we don't, I think we should go in with our guns drawn. If this is the kidnapper, he might be desperate."

"Agreed," Vic said. He counted a few more mailbox addresses. "Here it comes. You can pull off the shoulder right here."

Nate did, and both men got out. They stood on the driver's side, allowing the car to provide blocking between them and the house. Vic took out the binoculars and began scanning the property. It was a ranch-style house with a big front lawn, set back about a football field's length from the road. A fairly new blue Chrysler was parked in the driveway. No one was walking around outside.

Rats. That would've made it nice and easy.

"How long do you want to wait here, Vic? Before we ring the doorbell."

"At least an hour or two. See if we spot the little boy. If it's him, if it's Timmy, we hop in the car and race down the driveway. You drive, and I'll keep my gun out in case the father comes out of the house."

"But what if that scares Timmy off?"

"We'll just have to chance it. My guess is, he's probably scared and wants to be rescued. I'll flash my badge out the window and call his name."

"All right, I'll be ready," Nate said. He stood by the car, leaned up against the fender. "Wish I had some coffee."

The day had dragged on for Gina. Every hour felt like two. The only reason she knew it was a Saturday was because Colt had watched his favorite cartoons that morning. It was comforting to see him smile, even if for a little while.

Nothing on TV made her smile. Nothing on the radio. Nothing in the newspaper.

She glanced at the telephone in the living room. Again. The only thing that would make her smile would be to hear that phone ring. And to hear Special Agent Vic Hammond's voice on the other end, saying they had found her little boy, safe and sound.

"Hey, Gina." She looked up. It was Scott.

"I'm going to take Colt down to the 7-Eleven to buy a soda and a pack of baseball cards. You want anything?"

"No, but thanks for asking." Mike and Rose were at the store buying supplies for their Sunday dinner tomorrow.

"I could buy you a Creamsicle. Might cheer you up."

She doubted it. Though she did love Creamsicles. During the summer, Gina enjoyed hearing the music of the ice cream truck coming down the street almost as much as Colt and Timmy.

She sighed. "Better not. It'll just spoil my dinner."

"Are you sure?"

She nodded. As he walked by, he patted her shoulder gently.

"Come on, Colt."

It was nice to see him working so hard to be nice. As soon as the front door closed, the telephone rang. She rushed to answer it but was disappointed to hear a female voice say, "Is this the Harrison residence?"

"Yes, it is. This is Gina Harrison."

"I'm so glad it's you. Otherwise I'd have to hang up."

What did that mean? she thought. Could this

have something to do with Timmy? "I don't understand."

"Well," the woman said, "it would take too much time to explain. Let's just say, I called to talk to you, not your husband."

"Do I know you? Do *we* . . . know you?"

"You don't know me. Well, we've met, actually. Once."

Gina didn't have the energy for this. But what if it was a reporter? "What can I do for you?"

"Nothing really." The woman sighed heavily. "I'm the one who needs to do something for you. And for your husband, in a way."

Gina wished she would just say what she needed to say so she could get off the phone.

"See," the woman continued, "I went to confession this afternoon. First time in almost two years. It's all this Cuba stuff. It's scaring me to death. If those nuclear bombs start falling, I don't want to have such a huge sin on my conscience. I know something that big would send me straight to hell."

"I don't see what this has to do with me, or my husband." As soon as Gina said it, she instantly did. Was this . . . *that* woman? The young secretary from the Christmas party? If it was, she didn't want to hear anything she had to say. "Is this Marla?"

A long pause. Then, "Yes."

"Look, Marla, I really don't want to hear this

now, whatever it is you want to say. I've had a terrible day. A terrible week. The worst week I ever had. I can't be your—"

"No, listen, Mrs. Harrison. I need to tell you this. The priest said so. He said for something like this, a few Hail Marys and Our Fathers wouldn't cut it. He said I needed to tell you what I told him."

"Marla, I'm not even Catholic. So if you don't mind—"

"It doesn't matter if you're Catholic or not," Marla said. "I think you'll really want to hear what I have to say."

Gina took a deep breath. "Okay, what do you want to tell me?"

Another long pause. "Your husband and I were not having an affair. He was never unfaithful to you. I made the whole thing up."

Gina couldn't believe her ears. "What?"

"I had developed a serious crush on him—lots of the secretaries had—I'm sure you know how handsome he is. And I was trying to get him to feel the same way about me. For months before that Christmas party. But he hardly noticed me. He never responded to any of my attempts to flirt with him. Not even once. I thought maybe at the Christmas party with everybody drinking so much, this time might be different. So I made up a reason to get him back into that office. That's . . . when you walked in."

"But you were kissing," Gina said. "I saw it. It wasn't just you kissing him. He was kissing back."

"It may have looked that way," Marla said. "But he was definitely pushing me away. Then you walked in, and I felt so humiliated by his rejection that I just . . . lied. I was angry that he turned me down again. So I said . . . what I said. I'm not proud of it now. It was the wrong thing to do. To him, but especially to you. I see that now."

"Why have you waited all this time to tell me? Do you have any idea of the trouble you've caused? Scott and I are separated because of you. Because of that, my two little boys have . . ." She couldn't finish.

"I'm so sorry," Marla said. "So very sorry. The reason I haven't said anything until now is because I was still angry at Scott . . . Mr. Harrison. He didn't just reject me that night. After the party, he told my boss what I did, and I was forced to move to a different job in a different building, working with people I hate. But I know that's no excuse. It's just the reason why I didn't say anything before. I have no excuse. And I'm really sorry for all the pain I caused you and your family."

Gina heard her begin to cry.

"Well, I better go." The girl hung up. Just like that.

Gina sat on the edge of the chair nearest to the phone, stunned. This certainly wasn't the news she was hoping to get from the telephone today.

But as she sat there, and as the realization of what this young woman had just confessed began to sink in, Gina couldn't help it.

For the first time since this horrible week had begun, she smiled.

It was a real smile.

Scott had not been unfaithful to her.

She thought about it some more. The smile remained, without effort. But now tears began to fill her eyes and fall down her cheeks.

Different tears. Tears of relief.

56

It had been a total waste of time.

Vic and Nate got back in their car, ready to head home. They'd been waiting just over an hour, staring at the house through the binoculars from the street, when the father had come out with his little boy and gotten into their own car. Vic could tell, even from this distance, it wasn't Timmy. The hair color was wrong. But even if someone had dyed his hair, you couldn't fake a face full of freckles.

It was so disappointing. He dreaded calling the Harrisons back with this news.

"Guess we're back to square one," Nate said as he drove off down the road.

"Guess so," Vic said. "Got any more ideas brewing? Think we've wrung this one dry."

"Not at the moment. Really thought this one would pan out."

Vic had thought so too. Turned out, the freckled-faced little boy was really the son of the man who lived at this address. He was a twin to the little boy who had died last year, which explained why there was another little boy about the same age still living at this house. The father had explained all this to Vic and Nate when he'd reached the end of his driveway and noticed them getting into their car across the street.

He had asked them to explain what they were doing in front of his house. Vic had apologized for causing him any concern and assured him it was a simple case of mistaken identity. They wouldn't be bothering him again.

But who would they be bothering? They had absolutely no leads left to pursue.

"It might not matter anyway."

"What?" Vic asked.

"Where we go with this case," Nate said. "The way this thing's going with Kennedy and Khrushchev, somebody's gonna push that red button any moment now."

Etta Mae heard Josephine making all kinds of commotion in the house. She was out hanging laundry on the line. She ran inside, dodging the tree roots. "What's the matter, Josephine? Are you okay?"

"He's leaving, Etta Mae. See him?" She was still looking through her binoculars. "He's getting in the truck now. And he doesn't have the boy with him."

Etta Mae bent down below the shade and looked through the window. Sure enough, that mean ole redneck just started his pickup truck. Now he was backing it up. A few moments later, he was driving down the driveway toward the road. And he was alone. He was definitely alone. "As soon as he's down the street and out of sight, I'll get right over there and talk to that little boy, make sure it's Timmy."

Josephine lowered the binoculars to her lap. "Wait a few minutes first, just to be safe. What if you got over there and he got halfway down the road, then remembered he forgot something and turned around?"

An awful thing to think about. "Good idea."

They both stood there, alternating their stares between the house and the road. After a few minutes, Josephine said, "I think it's safe now. You go on ahead. Wish we had a pair of walkie-talkies so I could warn you if he comes back."

"Me too. But I'll be quick. I just want to talk to the little boy, make sure it's Timmy. Once I do, I'll hurry back here."

Etta Mae took one quick look at the road before she stepped onto the porch. She looked back toward Josephine's house and waved, knowing Josephine was looking right at her. After knocking on the door, she stepped back and waited. No one came. So she did it again. She waited awhile longer. Still no one came.

Maybe he's not allowed to answer the door, she thought. "Timmy? You in there?" she yelled. "If you are, you can come to the door. It's all right. My name's Etta Mae. I'm a friend of Mamie Lee, the woman who works for your grandmother."

Still no answer.

He had to be in there. She knocked one more time. Waited. Still no answer. She got off the porch and walked around to the side of the house, stopped at the window where she had seen the hand holding the curtain earlier. She tapped on it gently. "Timmy, you in there?" she yelled. "It's me, Etta Mae. I'm a friend of Mamie Lee, the woman who works for your grandmother. I'm here to help you."

She stepped back. No one answered. But a few moments later she heard what sounded like banging coming from the back of the house. What could that be? She waited a moment. There it was again.

She walked toward it; sounded like it was coming from the other side of a wall near the back porch. She banged on that spot three times. To her surprise, whoever it was knocked back three times. So she did it again. And again, three more knocks in reply. "Timmy, is that you?"

She heard some kind of muffled answer, sounded like a little boy's voice. She ran around to the back of the house and realized what this room was. A screened-in back porch ran across the length of the house except for the last five feet or so, which was a solid room. Looked like maybe a storage room. No windows. But there was a door which you could get to from inside the porch. It was padlocked.

She hurried over to the porch door and pulled. It wasn't locked. She almost ran across the porch floor and knocked on the door. "Timmy, you in there? That you knocking on the wall?"

"It's me," a little boy's voice answered. "I'm Timmy. It's so dark in here. Can you get me out?"

"Thank you, Jesus," Etta Mae whispered, tears welling up in her eyes. "We'll get you out, Timmy. And back to your folks, I promise. My name's Etta Mae. I'm real good friends with Mamie Lee. You know her, right?"

"I do. She's always very nice to me, and my brother Colt."

"Well, she's my best friend. And we're going to get you out of there, as soon as we can. But I can't do it myself. This door's padlocked shut. I'm going to have to call the police. That man took you, right? When you were with your brother at that diner?"

"Yes. Is Colt out there with you?"

338

"No, he's not. It's just me. I'm gonna leave you now, so I can go call the police. They're gonna get you out and arrest this man who took you away."

"It's so dark in here."

"I know, sweetie. But don't be afraid. God can see you just fine in there. You know that? Light and dark make no difference to him. He'll take care of you till the police come. It won't be long, I promise."

He didn't answer for a few moments. "Okay," he said.

Etta Mae was just about to leave, but she stopped and walked back to the door. "If that man comes back before the police do, don't say a word about this. Okay?"

"I won't."

57

Etta Mae ran across that yard like she hadn't run since she was a teenager. She knew any moment she could trip and fall flat on her face, but she didn't care. She hurried up the back steps, through the kitchen, and straight into the dining room. "It's him, Josephine. It's Timmy!"

"I knew it. I knew it would be," Josephine replied. "Did you see him?"

"No, he's got him shut up in a storage room on

the back porch. Got no windows, and it's padlocked but good. But it was him. Hard for me to recognize his voice through the door, but he said it was him, and that the man over there took him from his brother Colt. He's awful scared, Josephine. We've got to call the police right now."

"Oh goodness," Josephine muttered. "Then let's do it. Use the telephone over there. There's a little pad right next to it. The Lake Helen police station's number is right there at the top."

Etta Mae walked toward it and reached for the phone, but stopped. "We should really call the FBI. My friend Mamie Lee—she's the one I told you about, she knows this family directly—she said they got the FBI on this case. Because it's a kidnapping."

"Then we should call them," Josephine said. "Only problem is, I don't have their number."

"I bet Mamie Lee does, or knows how to get in touch with them. Can I call her?"

"Of course you can."

"It's long distance, in DeLand."

"That's not far, go ahead and call it. Tell them they better get on over here. I don't know how long August will be gone."

Etta Mae dialed the Harrisons' number from memory. A few moments later, she was talking with Mamie Lee. "Oh Mamie, you're not gonna believe what I just found out. Lord have mercy . . ."

"What are you going on about, Etta Mae?"

"It's Timmy. Mister Scott's little boy. I found him."

"You found him? Where?"

"He's right next door."

"But aren't you working somewhere else? Mrs. Schaeffer's sister or something?"

"I'm over here in Lake Helen, at a little house right by the lake. Josephine, she's the woman I'm helping out, she got suspicious about this man next door suddenly showing up with a little boy. Caught a glimpse of him a few days ago, thought it looked like Timmy from his picture in the paper. Been watching the house ever since through binoculars. Well, just a little while ago, the man left. So I went over there to see if I could talk to the boy. And it was Timmy. Said so himself."

"Thank you, Jesus," Mamie said. "Is he all right? Is he hurt any?"

"I don't think so."

"Didn't you see him?"

"I couldn't. Got him locked up in a storage room on the back porch. No windows. But it's him, I'm sure of it. He told me so himself. I need you to call the FBI, get them over here right away. Didn't you say they're working on this case?"

"They are, but I don't know the number. I'm sure Mister Scott does. I could call him. Why don't you give me the address of where you are? I'll call him right now."

Etta Mae got Josephine to give it to her, and she read it back slowly to Mamie Lee on the phone.

"I'll call him right now, Etta Mae. This is so wonderful, like a miracle from heaven. Thank you, Lord!"

"Amen," Etta Mae said. "Amen."

As soon as she hung up, Josephine held up the newspaper. "The FBI's phone number's printed right here."

Etta Mae ran over, grabbed it and, quick as she could, called Mamie Lee back. She got a busy signal. "Well, no matter. Looks like she's talking to Mister Scott already. He'll call the FBI straightaway."

Scott could hardly believe what he was doing right now. He was standing in his living room, crying, hugging Gina. A few minutes ago, he had come home from the 7-Eleven to find her crying by herself. He thought she must have received some horrible news. He was glad he'd let Colt run across the street to show Murph his new baseball cards.

But these weren't sad tears. Gina was happy. Apparently Marla had called to confess that she had lied about everything. Now Gina knew that Scott had been telling the truth. He had never been unfaithful to her.

She pulled back from the hug. He grabbed both

her hands before she pulled back too far. "So you believe me? You really believe me?"

She nodded, tears running down her face.

"This is such good news," he said. "I'm so relieved. You stay right there. Let me get the tissue box." He saw it sitting on the hutch in the dining room. As he reached for it, the telephone rang. He took a few out for himself then handed the box to Gina. Then picked up the telephone on the third ring.

"Mister Scott? Is that you?"

He instantly recognized the voice. It was Mamie Lee. And she sounded very excited. "It's me, Mamie. What's going on?"

"Praise the Lord. You're not going to believe it. I'm calling to see if you know how to get hold of the FBI."

"I do. But why do you need to call them?"

"It's Timmy." She started to cry. "The Good Shepherd found him for us. We know right where he is."

58

"They've found Timmy?"

Gina couldn't believe it. Scott was nodding his head yes. He was smiling. She wanted to scream out her excitement, but she also saw another look in his eyes. "What's wrong? Is he okay?"

Scott reached for her and drew her into a hug. "This really is great news, Gina. He's alive, and now we know where he is. And it's not that far away."

"But something's wrong, Scott. I can tell. What is it?"

"Mamie Lee said the man who took him lives in Lake Helen, a little house right on the lake. But Timmy's locked up inside a dark storage room with no windows."

"He hates the dark," she said. "It terrifies him."

"I know. I don't think he's been in there all the time. Mamie's friend, the one who found him, said the man is at the store now. She said he keeps Timmy in there when he goes out. But she's seen him in the house through the windows."

"Oh Scott, we've got to get him out."

"I know. I'm going to call Vic and Nate right now." Scott picked up the telephone receiver again.

"Aren't they gone? Following some lead near Palatka?"

"Yeah, but they said if I called the number on this card, they can get through to them on the car radio." Scott picked up the card and began dialing.

He's alive, she thought. My baby's alive.

Nate pulled the car over at a gas station after seeing the telephone booth on the corner. Vic had just taken a call from the Orlando office with the best of news. The call had come in from Scott

344

Harrison, saying they had gotten word confirming the whereabouts of little Timmy.

"So he's in Lake Helen?" Nate asked.

"Sounds like it. At some house right on the lake."

"Never been there."

"Me either, but I know it's a small, rural town. I don't want to be wasting time when we get there, so we'll ask for directions." Vic opened the car door.

"I'm thinking we're about ninety minutes away," Nate said. "You want to contact the locals on this?"

"I don't think so, Nate. Doesn't sound like the boy's in imminent danger. I can't imagine the guys on the local force have much experience with something like this. Let me call Scott back first, get some more details. When I get back in the car, we'll turn the sirens on and we'll haul it down there as fast as we can."

Vic opened the telephone booth and dialed Scott's number. Scott was excited, which was understandable. This was great news. He answered Vic's questions but wasn't able to shed more light on the situation. He did confirm Timmy appeared safe but was locked up in a dark storage shed. The owner of the house was gone, but for how long?

"We're heading right there," Vic said. "As soon as we get off the phone."

"How long will that take?" Scott asked.

"Maybe ninety minutes."

"Ninety minutes?"

"Maybe a little less. But you said it yourself, Scott. It doesn't sound like the kidnapper has hurt him. And he doesn't know we're on to him, right?"

"I don't think so."

"So things should be fine until we get there. Let us handle it. A guy like this is probably pretty unstable. We're trained to handle these situations, and we're gonna get there as soon as humanly possible."

After he hung up with Scott, Vic got back in the car. "Gun it, Nate. Let's go get that boy."

When Colt came back into the house, everything had changed.

Starting with his mom and dad hugging and acting like they had never been apart. His dad had just hung up the telephone, saying the FBI was on its way to Lake Helen to get Timmy back.

"They found Timmy?" Colt said. "Is he okay?"

His father's eyes were filled with tears. His mom looked like she had been crying too. "He's safe. We know that much. A friend of Mamie Lee found him. Her name's Etta Mae. She's working for a few days in Lake Helen, and that's only about a forty-minute drive from here. I guess that's where the guy who took him lives."

"So the FBI's going to get him now?" Colt asked.

"They're on their way, but they won't get there for ninety minutes."

"Ninety minutes?"

"I know, Colt," his mom said. "But there's nothing else we can do. We have to let the FBI handle it."

"There is something we can do," Colt said. "We can go get him ourselves. Does Etta Mae know where he is? What house he's at?"

"She does," his mom said. "But this man could be dangerous. We need to let the authorities get him. They're on their way now."

"Dad could do this," Colt said. "And I could help him. We could drive by Grandpa's house in DeLand. He's got lots of guns."

"We can't do that," she said. "This isn't some TV show, Colt."

Colt noticed his dad hadn't said anything. He couldn't read the look on his face. "Why don't we get him, Dad? You and me? We could go there now."

His dad looked at his mom. "We could, Gina. Well, I could. My dad has a whole closet full of guns."

"Scott, what are you saying? Let the FBI handle it. Vic and Nate know what they're doing. They know how to handle these situations."

"I know," he said. "But Gina, our little boy is

sitting over there right now in the dark, locked up like some dog. And we know where he is, it's not that far away. The guy's not even home."

"But he could come home any minute. He could get home before you even get there."

His father folded his arms. "Okay, that could happen. If it does, we'll stay out of sight. I'll park over at the house next door, where Etta Mae is working. He doesn't know what I look like or what kind of car we drive."

"But he knows what Colt looks like," she said. "I'm sure he'd remember him from the diner in Jacksonville."

"Okay, Colt will stay here."

"Dad . . . c'mon. You have to let me come. He's my little brother. I'm the one who got him lost."

"I'm sorry, Colt. But your mom's right. This guy knows what you look like. We can't take the chance that he'll see you." He looked at Gina. "I'll go get my keys."

"If I can't go," Colt said, "can I at least go back over to Murph's house till you get back?"

"Sure." His father hurried down the hallway.

Colt hugged his mother, then headed out the front door. But he wasn't going to Murph's house. Instead, he slipped around the back of the car and quietly opened the backseat door on the driver's side. He got in, gently closed the door, and scrunched up his body tightly behind the seat.

He wanted to be there when they found Timmy.

He had to be there. It was his fault Timmy had been kidnapped in the first place. A few minutes later, he heard the front door open and close. That must be his dad. But then he heard it open and close again.

"Wait, I'm coming with you." It was his mother's voice.

"Who's going to watch Colt?" his father said.

"I just left a note for Mike and Rose. They should be back from the store any minute. I told them what's happening and asked them to keep an eye on Colt till we get back."

59

On the thirty-minute drive to DeLand, Scott was all keyed up inside. He could tell Gina was too.

On this day, really within one hour, the two biggest obstacles to his happiness had come crashing down. That lying secretary had finally told the truth, and Gina had believed her, believed him. They hadn't talked through the implications, but they were together again. The joy of that first kiss after being apart so long still lingered in his mind.

And his little boy was alive. They were driving to where he was right now.

But Timmy wasn't safe, not yet. And that angered Scott. Now that they knew where Timmy was, Scott no longer felt so helpless. All week long, he'd fought off thoughts and images about Timmy whenever they surfaced. Where was he? Who had him? How was he being treated? The unknown was just too painful. But now he knew. A real man had taken his son, not some phantom. And he'd locked him in a dark storage room all by himself whenever he left the house.

Nobody treated his little boy that way.

He looked over at Gina; her eyes were staring out the side window, full of fear and dread over what might happen next. The things this man had put her through this past week, had put them all through. No one deserved that. And no one should get away with that.

It was time to end this. Time to take back what this man had stolen from them.

He pulled into his parents' driveway on Clara Avenue and opened the car door but left it running. Without looking at Gina, he said, "I won't be long. I know exactly where the guns are."

So far, Colt's plan was working. No one had seen him in the backseat. He got real nervous when they had stopped at his grandparents' house and his dad opened the car door. He knew his dad was there to pick up one of Grandpa's guns to bring with him to get Timmy. His father must have picked out a handgun. Colt was sure if he'd grabbed a rifle, he'd have put it in the backseat or the trunk. Either way, he would have likely spotted Colt and forced him to stay in DeLand with his grandmother.

It felt like fifteen minutes had gone by. Colt thought they must be getting close to Lake Helen now, because the car was driving slower. For most of the drive from DeLand to here, his parents hadn't talked very much. Colt felt the car turn left.

"Scott," his mother said, "I want to say something before we get there. Really, two things."

"What are they?"

"First, I want to apologize for not believing you all this time about the secretary. It just looked so much like you were kissing her, and then when she said the two of you were in love, I just knew it was true. Well, I believed it was true. But she was lying all this time. I'm sorry I didn't believe you."

Colt's dad didn't say anything for a moment. But now he understood why his parents had separated. She thought he loved someone else.

"Gina, I'm so glad you believe me now. But I need to apologize too. For why it was so easy for you to believe something like that, even after I told you over and over again it wasn't true. I had a long talk with Mike about it. It's because I neglected you for so long, you and the boys. All I cared about was my career. But things are going to be completely different from now on. I'm not just saying it. I've already told Mr. Finch I'm giving up the promotion."

"I know. I heard you tell him."

"You did? Well, I meant it. You mean more to me than any job. From now on, I'm just going to be a desk grunt. I'll work hard when I'm at the office, but I'll be strictly eight to five, no more climbing the corporate ladder. I'm going to be home for dinner every night. Saturdays too, unless they force me to do overtime. I'm going to be there for you, Gina. You and the boys. Throw the ball with them. Go fishing if they want. We'll take family trips together, and not just once in a blue moon. I mean it."

"I believe you."

"You do?" The car slowed, then turned right.

Colt loved hearing what his father just said. He didn't hear what his mom said back, but it must've been something his father liked because the next thing he knew his father stopped the car, and they were both kissing. And not a little bit. A long, mushy kiss like they did in the movies. The kind he and Timmy would always look away from and act disgusted by. Colt never let Timmy know, but lately he was starting to peek at the end of those kiss scenes. He wanted to peek at his parents right now.

"Scott, we should get going, we're at a stop sign."

Were they going to kiss some more?

"You know," his father said, "after today, Timmy's going to need his bed back."

"I know."

"That means I've got no place to sleep. Well, there's that place I've been renting."

"I've got a better idea," she said. "I've got a room down the end of the hall."

"You do?"

"But it's much more expensive than that place you've been renting."

"I don't care what it costs, Gina. I'll pay any price." He kissed her once more, a fast one. "Let's go get our little boy."

"Oh, that reminds me," his mom said, "of the second thing I wanted to say." A car horn blared behind them.

"Sorry," his father yelled and poured on the gas. The car lurched forward.

"Ow," Colt said as the jolt banged him hard against the backseat.

"What the . . . ?" his dad said.

"Colt, is that you?" His mother was leaning over the front seat.

Colt sat up. No sense hiding anymore. "It's me. I had to come. I'm the reason we're here trying to steal Timmy back from that man. It's all my fault."

"Look at me, Colt."

Colt looked up at his father's eyes in the rear-view mirror.

"It is not your fault, what happened here. If anything, it's mine. If I had been treating you guys and your mom the way I was supposed to, none of this would have happened. Now, listen, this is Lake Helen, where we're driving through now. We're going to be at the house in a few minutes. I need you to stay out of sight. I have no idea what we're going to face once we get there."

"Okay."

"And Gina?"

"What?"

"A minute ago you said you had a second thing to say."

"Oh, right. Promise me you won't do anything stupid when we get there. By stupid, I mean brave. Vic and Nate should be here soon. Please let them handle this."

60

Now look at what they made him do.

The groceries had spilled all over the front seat of his truck. Some items fell out of the bags and rolled onto the floor. And look, August thought, they weren't even teenagers. Old enough to have a kid in the backseat. He had just pulled up to the stop sign on his way home, to find a car all but parked there with a couple making out in the front seat. He had to blow his horn to get them to break it up.

What was the world coming to? Maybe it needed blowing up.

August drove through the intersection and pulled off to the side of the road to clean up the mess. That was when he noticed something. He had forgotten to buy milk. Dang, now he'd have to go back to the store just for that. Wasn't only for the boy's cereal; he needed it for his coffee too. A few months ago, the milkman had stopped coming out to the houses by the lake. He still wasn't in the habit of buying his dairy at the supermarket.

After getting things sorted out, he turned the truck around and headed back the way he came.

Colt's father had followed the directions Etta Mae had given him through Lake Helen and out to the property by the lake. He'd driven extra slow. Didn't want to take a chance of getting a speeding ticket. Colt had never seen such a small town before. Barely even seemed big enough to be called a town.

As they pulled into the dirt driveway, his mom said she agreed with Mamie Lee that a full-fledged miracle was underway. If God hadn't set things up to bring Etta Mae out here the way he did, no one would've ever thought to look here. They'd have lost Timmy for good.

"Is that the house?" Colt asked, pointing to the house next door. "The green one?"

"I think it is," his father said. "And that room in the back there, that must be where Timmy is right now."

"I don't see the man's truck anywhere," his mom said.

"Me either." They stopped the car, turned off the ignition, and got out.

It was eerie and strange for Colt. The whole thing was, but especially seeing a pistol in his father's hand.

"I've got to do something," his father said. "I can't just leave Timmy sitting in that dark room like this. He's been in there over two hours already."

"What are you going to do?" his mom said.

"I don't know. But I want to talk to him at least, let him know we're here to get him out, so he won't be so afraid."

"But what if the guy comes back?" Colt said.

"Maybe he will. But he'll be driving in from the front if he does get home. And I'll be way in the back where Timmy is. He won't see me. I'll wait till I hear him go in the front door, then I'll run back here and wait for the FBI to arrive. You guys go inside, meet with Etta Mae and the owner of this house, tell them what I'm doing."

"But what if you don't hear his pickup truck when he comes home?" Colt's mom said.

"I'm sure I'll hear it. Most trucks are pretty noisy. But even if I don't, I've got a gun. It's been awhile, but I'm pretty good with it. Now you two go inside. I won't be long."

Maybe it was adrenaline, maybe it was the grace of God, but Scott didn't feel an ounce of fear as he approached the house. If anything, he felt bold as a lion. He walked straight to the back porch and noticed that the right side had been enclosed to form a storage room.

His little boy was in there. "Thank you, Lord, for bringing me here," he whispered. "For helping us find Timmy."

He climbed the steps and went inside the porch, noticed right off the padlock and chain around the door. Putting his ear to the door, he listened a few moments. He didn't hear a sound. "Timmy, are you in there? It's Dad." Still no reply. Scott knocked on the door a few times and repeated the same words.

Finally, that wonderful voice.

"Dad? Is that really you?"

Scott's eyes filled with tears. "I'm here, son. We're here to get you out."

"It's so dark in here. I can't see anything."

"I know, Timmy. But you're going to be okay. I'm not leaving here without you."

"Can't you get me out now?"

Scott thought about it. The only thing he could

do was shoot the lock. They did that all the time in the movies. In the movies, it always worked. But he had no idea where the bullet would go in real life. He couldn't take a chance of it hurting Timmy. "I can't right now, Timmy. I can't break the lock. But the FBI will be here any minute. I'm sure they'll know how we can get this door open."

Then Scott remembered something. On his way over here, he'd run past a pile of cut logs and an axe leaning up against a tree. "I'm going to try something, Timmy. I'm going to go but just for a moment. To get an axe. I'll be right back."

"Okay. Is that man who took me here now?"

"No, he's still gone. Do you know where he went?"

"He said he was going to a few stores and he'd be gone awhile. He's very mean, Daddy. He pulls me around and hurts my arm. And he calls me Bobby, even though I told him my name. And he keeps putting me in this place." Timmy began to cry. "Please get me out."

"I will, son. Let me see if getting that axe will help."

Colt had to do something. Right now. The man was coming back.

He and his mom, along with Etta Mae and a woman with binoculars who said her name was Josephine, had all been looking out the dining room windows at the house next door. Colt had watched his dad run to the back porch and go inside. Then he came back out and headed this way. He picked up an axe and had just now gone back into the porch with it.

"He's probably gonna use it to bust that lock," Etta Mae said.

Just then, the man who lived there drove up in his pickup truck.

"Oh my," Josephine said. "It's August."

He got out of his truck and walked to the front door.

"Get out of there, Scott," Colt's mom said.

Everyone looked toward the back porch, but he still hadn't come out.

"Why isn't he getting out of there?" Josephine said.

"He must not have heard the truck drive up."

"August is inside the house," Josephine said. "If he sees your husband back there, I think he might kill him."

That was all Colt needed. He ran outside, down the back steps, then as fast as he could, across the yard toward the room where Timmy was. Just as he came around the corner, he saw his father through the screen lifting the axe, his eyes fixed on that padlock. "Dad, Dad," he whispered. "The man's home. Didn't you hear him drive up?"

"No, I didn't."

"He's already in the living room."

"Then we better get out of here." He leaned up

close to the door. "Timmy, we'll be back in a few minutes when the FBI gets here."

"Okay."

"It won't be long, I promise."

Colt and his father began running down the stairs and into the backyard. The screen door slapped shut behind them. They'd forgotten not to let it slam. Even though his dad carried the axe, he ran faster than Colt. Suddenly, Colt tripped on an oak root and fell flat on his face. He looked up, saw his dad stop about fifteen feet ahead. He turned around and immediately pointed his pistol.

Colt heard a voice behind him, very close. "I wouldn't do that." Then, "Get up, boy." Colt turned around and looked up into a double-barreled shotgun pointed right at his head.

61

"What are you doing on my property?"

Colt didn't know what to say; he waited for his dad to answer. His legs began to shake.

"I asked you a question. What are you two doing on my property?" The man stepped closer, still aiming the gun at Colt.

"Lower that shotgun right now," his father said, "or I'll put a bullet in your forehead."

Colt turned and saw his father pointing his pistol

at the man's head. The axe lay at his feet. Colt could see in his father's eyes, he meant every word.

"I don't think you're going to do that," the man said. "You do, and the last thing I'll do is squeeze this trigger with this shotgun pointed right at your son. Assuming he is your boy."

"He is. And so is that other little boy you've got locked in that room over there. The one you stole from my wife and me on Monday."

"That ain't your boy in there. That's Bobby. My boy."

"His name's not Bobby, you old fool. I don't know what happened to your Bobby, but you and I both know that little boy you took is not him."

Gina felt her heart beating in her head. She couldn't believe the scene unfolding behind the house next door. A man was holding a shotgun on Colt, and Scott was pointing a pistol at the man.

"I can't look," Josephine said, lowering the binoculars.

Gina heard Etta Mae praying softly. Something black caught her eye out by the road.

"The FBI. They're here," Etta Mae said.

Gina ran out the front door. She continued running toward the car as it pulled into the long driveway next door, waving her hands frantically, pointing toward the back of the house. "It's happening right now, outside, behind the house."

"What is?" Vic said through the window. Nate stopped the car, and they got out.

"The kidnapper's got a shotgun pointed at Colt. And Scott's got a pistol pointed at him."

Vic and Nate instantly drew their weapons and hurried toward the back of the house. "I'll take this side," Nate said, pointing to the right side of the house.

Vic was running toward the left side, the side closest to Josephine's.

"Come here, young man."

Colt looked at the man's eyes and at the shotgun pointing at his head. Fear moved him to obey.

"Colt," his father said, "don't—"

But it was too late. As soon as Colt got close enough, the man grabbed his collar and dragged him closer.

"Now, you put down your pistol, unless you want to see your boy die."

Everything that happened in the next few moments happened so fast.

"Put down that shotgun. Now!" A different voice. Colt recognized it. Vic's voice, spoken from the back corner of the house. "This is the FBI. My partner has another gun trained at your head from the other corner of the house. Put the gun down now."

Colt watched his father lower his pistol. He must've thought the FBI agents were talking to

362

him. He also felt the man holding him move his arms, but it was clear he wasn't lowering the shotgun. He was raising it, pointing it right at Colt's father. Colt could tell he was just about to pull the trigger. Colt shoved the barrel of the gun upward with both hands, just as an explosion of fire and smoke erupted in front of his face.

It was quickly followed by a second, lesser gunshot. He could feel the bullet hitting the man with the shotgun, hear the sound of it tearing into his body. He was leaning into his side.

Colt's father yelled out in pain.

The man did too and fell backward, dragging Colt to the ground with him. The shotgun fell out of his hands, and he loosened his grip on Colt. Colt jumped to his feet and ran toward his dad lying on the ground, just as the two FBI agents ran toward the kidnapper. "Dad!" he screamed. His dad's right shoulder was covered in blood. Colt bent down beside him.

"I'm okay, Colt. I'm okay. It's just my shoulder."

"Scott, Scott!" his mom yelled as she came running from the side of the house. "You're shot, you're bleeding!"

"It's just my shoulder," he said, sitting up. "I think that's all."

Now that his mother was there, Colt's mind went straight for his little brother. He picked up the axe lying beside his father. Vic and Nate were pulling the kidnapper to his feet. He had blood all over his other shoulder.

"You're lucky that boy pushed you," Nate said to him. "Or you wouldn't be standing up right now. We'd be waiting on the coroner. That shot in your shoulder was meant for your head."

The man didn't respond. He winced as Nate put on the handcuffs. "This may hurt a little," Nate said. "But I'm okay with that."

Colt wondered how Timmy was doing. He hadn't made a sound since all this commotion had begun. Colt headed toward the back porch, carrying the axe.

"Where you going, Colt?" Vic asked.

"To get my little brother."

"Wait a minute. I'll go with you, but we won't need that axe. Let me show you how the FBI does it."

Just then, Etta Mae came running out from the house next door. "Ambulance is on its way," she yelled. "I just called them."

"Better make that two," Nate yelled back.

Colt followed Vic up the back porch steps and through the screen door. He banged on the door leading to the storage room. "We got the bad guy, Timmy. The FBI's here. We're going to get you out."

"Better step back, Colt." Vic got close to the door. "Timmy, if you can hear me, get as close to the back wall as you can. When I count to three,

I'm going to shoot off this lock. But that's all I'm doing. You won't get hurt if you just stay back against the wall. Okay?"

Colt didn't hear Timmy's reply. But he knew Timmy could hear him.

"Listen up, everyone." Vic now directed his words to those in the backyard. "You're going to hear another gunshot. I'm just shooting off the padlock."

Colt covered his ears as Vic pointed the gun at the lock. He heard a muffled "one, two, three," then *boom*. The lock fell apart, then it and the chain fell to the floor. Vic opened the door. Colt looked inside. It was black as night. "Can I go get him?"

"You can just call him," Vic said.

"No, I can't. He won't come out. He's too scared. Can I go in and get him?"

"Sure."

Colt stepped inside. It felt colder in here too. "Timmy?" he whispered. "It's me, Colt. You're safe now. It's all over. That man can't hurt you anymore. I'm here to take you home."

He looked toward the darkness. Seemed to go on forever, like a black tunnel burrowing into a deep cave. His poor little brother. He hated the dark way more than Colt did. "It's me, Timmy."

"I'm back here," Timmy whispered.

"You're safe now. You don't have to whisper." Colt reached out his hand. It was so dark he couldn't even see the end of it. But a few steps more, and he felt Timmy's arm.

He was shaking. Not just his arm, but all over.

Colt hurried toward him, grabbed him with both arms, and pulled him close. "I've got you now." He began to cry. "I'm so sorry I left you all alone back at that restaurant. And I'm so sorry that man took you. But everything's okay now. Mom and Dad are even back together again. I don't know what happened. But Dad is moving back home. They're even kissing again." He held him a few moments more until Timmy stopped shaking. "I won't ever leave you alone again, Timmy."

Etta Mae had come over now, bringing some towels. She was pressing one against the wound in Scott's shoulder. She had handed the other to Nate, saying he could do the same to the kidnapper if he wanted. She called the man "August."

Gina had jumped when she heard the gunshot on the back porch, even though Vic had warned them all to expect it. But now that she knew Scott was safe and the ambulance was on its way, she wanted to see her little boy.

She squeezed Scott's hand. "I'm going to be with Timmy now, okay?"

Scott winced in pain. "Definitely. Give him a hug for me. But maybe he shouldn't see me like this, after all he's been through. All this blood."

"All right. I'll keep him on the porch until the ambulance arrives."

"After they put him on the gurney," Etta Mae said, "they'll probably cover your husband with a blanket. You can probably bring your boy out to see his daddy before they drive away."

"I'll do that, Etta Mae. I don't know how we can ever thank you . . . or Josephine."

"No need to thank me, Miss Gina. God made all this happen. Only thing that could explain it. I'm just so happy he let me be a part. I can't wait to tell Mamie Lee the news. She been worried something awful this past week. And not about the world blowing up, either. Just about you all and your little boy. She was hurtin' like it was her own kin."

"It was her kin," Scott said. "Will you tell her I said that?"

"I will, Mister Scott," Etta Mae said, tears welling up in her eyes.

"Please, Etta Mae. Just call me Scott. After today, as far as I'm concerned, you're kin too."

Gina leaned over and kissed Scott on the lips. Then she got up and walked toward the back porch. She opened the screen door but didn't see Colt or Timmy. Just Vic near the open door leading to the storage room. It looked like he was blinking back tears.

"That's one special young man you've got there, Mrs. Harrison."

She stood at the halfway point between the screen door and the open doorway. A moment later she heard footsteps. Then her two little boys appeared from out of the shadows.

Timmy was leaning tightly against Colt, Colt's left arm around his shoulder. Timmy's eyes were closed. "Look, Timmy, Mommy's here."

His eyes opened, and he turned and looked at Gina's face. Colt let him go. She bent down and held out her arms. Timmy ran right to her and squeezed her with all his might. She wrapped her arms around him, buried her head in his little shoulder, and cried.

"Mommy," she heard him say through his own muffled tears.

"I'm here, Timmy. Mommy's here."

Many years later, Colt's mother would tell both Colt and Timmy that she had known a depth of happiness in that moment greater than all the happiness from all the happy moments she had ever known . . . combined.

62

The Present

I was standing now on that same back porch, on the very spot where my mom had hugged my little brother Timmy that day in 1962.

Three days had passed since I had come to this lake house to consider whether or not I could put the past behind me, treat this place as just a nice getaway spot for Elaine and me. I had made my decision. It was time to call Elaine.

I had called her each of the last three days, sometimes more than once, to let her know how things were going or just to hear her voice. Besides, I didn't view this as just my decision. She convinced me it was. I was the one carrying all the baggage. She'd be just as happy to sell the place as use it, so she insisted I make the call for both of us.

Of course, August was the man who'd sent that registered letter to me, informing me that this house was now mine, free and clear. He'd left it for me in his will. He'd died recently in prison after receiving a life sentence for kidnapping, and a host of other charges the FBI had brought against him stemming from his conduct that week in '62. There was also the matter of how his little boy, Bobby, had really died. His body had been found buried under an oak tree on the property. August had insisted he had drowned in the lake, said he'd decided not to report it since it wouldn't change anything and it might make a world of trouble for him. The autopsy proved inconclusive, and after that, Bobby was buried in a proper cemetery in Lake Helen.

Not sure why exactly August had left the property to me. I guess it was because I had come to feel some sympathy for him during the trial, which my father allowed me to attend. He was one sorry, messed-up individual, to be sure. But I also knew he wasn't intending to harm my little brother, although he clearly did. He was just grieving and trying to find some kind of way to fill the hole in his heart left by his son Bobby's death. A few months into his prison sentence, he actually sent a letter of apology to my family.

So every now and then over the years, usually when the Cuban missile crisis would come up for some reason, I'd send August a little note in prison.

Speaking of the Cuban missile crisis . . . you probably already guessed. The world didn't blow up.

The day after our tearful family reunion at the lake house, Khrushchev agreed to turn his ships around and remove all the nuclear missiles from Cuba. World War III was averted. The whole world breathed a collective sigh of relief. Of course, it was hard to know if that included Mr. Weldon. I could never decide if he was relieved or disappointed. I also wondered how long he waited before opening up that shelter food.

Anyway, the world not blowing up was the headline in the Sunday paper. On page three, a little story ran about a kidnapped boy being rescued by the FBI. We barely paid attention to either story.

For our family, that Sunday dinner was a celebration for the ages. Better than any we had at Christmas or Easter, before or since. Timmy was home safe. Dad and Mom were back together again. Mom announced she had decided to quit her job. Though after she sat down, I'd heard her tell my dad he would never see her cleaning the house wearing pearls. I don't think he got the June Cleaver connection. Our favorite aunt and uncle, Mike and Rose, were there too.

And we had two special guests at that Sunday dinner, and at many other dinners and picnics and cookouts over the years that followed. Mamie Lee and Etta Mae.

For the rest of Mamie's life, my father visited her and his own mom on Mother's Day. Gave them both flowers, a box of candy, and a hand-written card. And after that day, Mamie Lee's fortunes also changed in the Harrison house on Clara Avenue. My grandfather showed his gratitude for Mamie Lee's role in rescuing Timmy by setting up a pension fund for her, which allowed her to retire in some comfort when she turned sixty-two.

And he and my grandmother did something nice for both Etta Mae and Josephine. He'd said he was just about to put up a sizable reward for any information that led to his grandson's rescue and the arrest of the man who'd taken him. So he gave that sum of money to Etta Mae and Josephine to split between them. Not sure how much it was, but my dad was there when Etta Mae received her reward. He said he'd never seen her smile so much as the day she opened that envelope.

There's probably one other thing I should mention. My father made good on his pledge to my mom that day in the car, as they neared this house in Lake Helen. The pledge I heard him make as I hid in the backseat. About putting her and us boys ahead of his career from now on. For the balance of their years together—and they made it all the way to their fifty-first anniversary before Dad passed—they behaved like a couple still very much in love. And he took us fishing, coached our Little League games, and planned at least one decent family vacation every year for the rest of our childhood.

I smiled as I recalled this to mind, then walked over to the edge of the porch and looked out toward the lake. It really was a beautiful sight. As calm and peaceful as you could want to find in any getaway cottage. But even then, seeing that same beautiful view I had been enjoying the last few days . . . I knew.

We couldn't keep this place. I could never fully relax here.

The emotions stirred by the events of that week still felt too close to the surface. I'd trip over them every time I came out here, like any one of the dozens of oak tree roots spread out across the property. Even if I could get past those memories, I wouldn't feel right being here because of Tim. That's what we all called him since high school.

He and I had remained close all these years, even though his family lived in Virginia. We always took one week's vacation every year to bring our families together, usually somewhere in Florida. I could never ask him to come here to this place. If being here three days troubled me, what would it do to him?

The last couple of years Elaine and I'd had to pay for him and his wife to join us. Things have been pretty slow in his construction business. Almost lost his house last year. In our last phone call about a month ago, he said there were signs things were starting to pick back up, but money was still very tight.

No, it was time to call Elaine. I pulled my cell

phone out of my pocket and called her. She answered almost right away.

"You make a decision?" she said.

"I have. You sure you still want me to make this call without you?"

"I'm sure. I'll be happy with you anywhere."

She always said things like that. She was the easygoing one between the two of us. "Well, I've decided we should sell it. It's a weird thing, though. What followed after the things that took place here in '62 actually changed our lives for the better. In some pretty big ways. I was just thinking about some of them. Made me remember the last conversation me and my dad had about it. He quoted that verse he loved in Genesis 50."

"What men meant for evil, God meant for good," Elaine said.

"Sorry, guess I've told that story a few too many times."

"No need to apologize, Colt. About that or about selling the place. I don't have any sentimental attachment to it. I'm just grateful God gave us such a gift. Think about it. We're going to be able to buy a great little getaway somewhere. A dream we thought impossible till you got that letter. I've been looking on the internet. There's lots of cute little places on lakes all over Florida."

"It's just, I want someplace that Tim can feel comfortable visiting too."

"I know. We'll find something. We can price

that place to sell and buy something else pretty quick. Speaking of Tim, I've got some exciting news to tell you about that comic book you found."

I had told Elaine about that Spiderman comic book the first day. Tim wound up getting rid of all his comic books after what had happened. "What did you find out?"

"Are you sitting down?"

"Why, should I be?"

"Maybe. I did some checking on it. That one's the first issue of Spiderman. With all the movies that have come out about him and the other comic book heroes, vintage comic books have become a big business."

"How much is it worth?"

"Anywhere from twenty thousand dollars to over a million, depending on the condition it's in."

"You're kidding."

"I'm not. Thought that might bring a smile to your face."

It certainly did. "I'm not sure how they judge these things, but this one looks like it's in great condition. I can't wait to tell him about it. Maybe I should drop it off at a safe deposit box on the way home."

"Maybe you should. Wouldn't that be great if he got a million dollars?"

I told Elaine, nice and slow and in a few different ways, how much I loved her and that I'd be heading home soon. I was already packed up, even had my luggage in the car. But I decided to repack that comic book, make sure it wouldn't wrinkle or fold on the ride home.

As I walked through the backyard toward the driveway, over that same area where the shoot-out had happened, I stopped to take one last look. Not just at the house but the entire property. It's crazy how life goes sometimes. How God can take something so awful and turn it into something that becomes a great blessing in your life.

Even now, so many years later.

What my father said just before he died was true: "No one fixes broken things better than God."

Author's Note

I was born in 1957, which would make me one year younger than little Timmy in *What Follows After*. Some of the things in the book (though not most) were drawn from things that happened in my life. But the memory of a five-year-old is often fuzzy. Because of that, and because most of what happens in this story did not actually happen to me, I relied heavily on research to get the details right about life in 1962. Thankfully, there was an abundance of material to draw from.

And I might add, I really enjoyed the research. It stirred some wonderful memories from my childhood. In many ways, my memories of those early years are rather idyllic. Not unlike the stories you'd see depicted in shows like *Leave It to Beaver* or *The Dick Van Dyke Show*. But I must confess, my research wound up tarnishing some of my memories. Life wasn't always as rosy as I remembered . . . for a lot of Americans.

Many things about the "Camelot years" of Jackie and JFK were not what they seemed. Certainly, some things were better back then. Even statistics that measure certain aspects of society, such as the economy, the education system, levels of violent crime, divorce rates, suicide rates, etc., all indicate life back then was simpler and, it would seem, safer (the world blowing up by nuclear annihilation notwithstanding).

But even with these positive things—things that many who lived back then may long to see restored—serious problems were simmering beneath the surface. For example, consider the way many white people treated black people. The way men treated women. The way bosses treated their employees. The way the government treated its citizens. The way all of us viewed money and materialism. Even the way people viewed church in general, and how little of what Jesus actually taught found its way into people's daily lives.

We were thought of as a "Christian country" back then, and the overwhelming majority of Americans did attend one church or another. But those who cherish those days and wish they would return must face this hard reality: Could all of the societal problems that blew up like a volcano during the cultural revolution of the sixties have happened in a truly Christian country? Could they have happened . . . if all the people dressing up on Sunday, going off to church, and enjoying Sunday dinners together genuinely loved God and sought to love their neighbors as themselves?

I think a more honest assessment would suggest that many Americans' church experiences in the fifties and sixties had more to do with the religion of Christianity than a clear understanding of the gospel.

Part of the reason I decided to set *What Follows After* in the early sixties was to explore how the timeless truths of the gospel could have applied in an average American family during the *Leave It to Beaver* years. The things that cause relationships to succeed or fail are not dependent on the society or culture we live in.

They are just as relevant today in this "post-Christian" era.

And because of who Jesus is and the power he has to still change lives and make them better, no one should feel hopeless, no matter how challenging their circumstances. God can unravel any ball of twine we hand him, no matter how snarled and knotted it may be. We may not like the methods he chooses, for he often works through the trials of life and even our own failures.

But what follows after any life that is surrendered to him will one day be a life well worth living and lead to an eternity of everlasting joy.

Acknowledgments

For starters, I want to thank my wife, Cindi. As always, I cherish her input and advice, reflected throughout these pages. Her memories of the years depicted in this story were a little sharper than mine and very helpful.

I also want to thank my editor and friend, Andrea Doering, for her valuable input. It's a rare privilege in this business to be able to work with the same editor for so many books, especially an editor as talented as Andrea. I'm grateful for the entire staff at Revell, who make all the behind-the-scenes things happen. Folks like Twila Bennett, Michele Misiak, Robin Barnett, Claudia Marsh, Kristin Kornoelje, and so many others.

I want to thank my friend John Wills, for his expertise and help in all the scenes involving the FBI. John is also a fine author who's won multiple awards for his novels, short stories, articles, and poetry. His forty-one years in law enforcement as a Chicago police officer, FBI agent, and use-of-force instructor have enabled him to use his experience to bring realism to his writing, and to help fellow writers like me get things right. John's latest novel, *The Year Without Christmas*, released last October. Visit him at www.johnmwills.com.

On a local level, I want to thank Vince Clarida and several of the members down at the Halifax Historical Museum in Daytona Beach—people who lived and worked in the areas shown in *What Follows After* during the time of the story. Their memories and recollections were invaluable. I'd also like to thank my Word Weavers critique group in Port Orange, Florida, for their input on several chapters.

Lastly, to my fabulous agent and friend, Karen Solem, who takes such great care of me and helps me navigate through the ever-shifting maze of the publishing world. Her work sets me free to just write, which is what I love doing the most. I'm especially happy that she's moved her agency, Spencerhill Associates, down here to Florida, just a few short hours from where I live.